A Country of Paper

A Country of Paper

Laura Benedetti

THESPRING

Washington, DC

Library of Congress Control Number: 2022939982
ISBN 979-8-9852214-5-9 paperback (alk. paper)

THESPRING is an imprint of New Academia Publishing

New Academia Publishing
4401-A Connecticut Ave. NW #236, Washington DC 20008
info@newacademia.com - www.newacademia.com

Contents

What you read and what you experience in life are not two separate worlds, but one single cosmos. Every life experience, in order to be interpreted properly, evokes your readings and blends into them. That books always derive from other books is a truth which is only apparently in contradiction with the other truth, that books always derive from practical experience and from our relations with other people.

—Italo Calvino

L'AQUILA, ITALY
JANUARY 20, 2011

Sara tossed and turned in bed, listening to the noises in the apartment, straining to hear if Concetta was still at home or had already left. She had no time for small talk; her flight back to the United States was only a few days away, and she still had so many things to do, including the task that had brought her to L'Aquila in the first place. She put on her plaid slippers and sneaked into the living area with her laptop under her arm. The room was empty, but she could hear Concetta's voice from the hallway, mixed with the chatter of the other tenants. Sara caught bits and pieces of their conversation—more cold weather in the forecast, cars parked illegally in front of the building, water and electric bills undelivered for months and then, as if by magic, finally arriving all together, and astronomical at that. She brewed herself some coffee and turned on her phone, although she dreaded getting a call from the States—her mother had the uncanny ability to sense when she could be reached. She did need to be reachable, though. The Professor might call at any minute to set up their last meeting. The moment had finally arrived.

She threw the window open, and the fresh air greeted her. The night's snowfall had transformed the barren landscape into a wonderland. Even the abandoned field between the four massive apartment buildings seemed inviting, and the footprints—from a man's weighty boots alongside the lighter tracks of a dog—indicated that at least a few tenants had already ventured outside to explore its delights. More than anything else, the snow softened the contrast between the soulless buildings and the majestic, impassive mountains beyond them. Sara greeted them all: Pizzo Intermesoli, Pizzo Cefalone, and, farther away, the most striking of them all, Corno Grande—at 9,000 feet, the highest peak of the Apennines. Alessandro had taught her to recognize the mountains from nearly any point in the city. She realized that she would miss that sight, and Alessandro. For a moment, she contemplated the idea of staying. She could change direction and bring her life back to L'Aquila, where everything had started. The possibility flashed through her mind, but it felt like the plot of a novel rather than a real option. The moment had arrived; she could feel it. She rushed back to her room and pulled a backpack from beneath her bed. As she reached in, all she could see was the silver plaque.

Alice Arienti
L'Aquila, May 23, 1930 – Bethesda, October 9, 2010

"Don't worry, Nonna Ali" she whispered, "we're almost there. We're going home."

Holding the urn tightly against her chest, she thought she felt a jolt. Impossible. Her heart must have skipped a beat.

"Time to go home. For both of us."

MOAB, UTAH
JUNE—AUGUST, 2010

"Why did you start?"

Julia hated her accusatory tone, but she needed more than the few tidbits that Jane, Sara's mother, had offered when asking that she host Sara "out west" for the summer.

"Because I liked it..."

As for Sara, she desperately wanted out of the conversation, out of Julia's house, out of the desert. Talking to Julia was even worse than going to her therapist; at least there she didn't have to speak if she didn't want to—a nice loophole she had taken full advantage of. She remembered her mother's best friend differently, less blunt, less determined, but it had been years since she'd last seen her. Julia pushed on.

"You liked heavy liquor? It didn't make you sick?"

"At first, no, but then I liked how I felt, I was... looser."

"Looser?"

Sara would have gladly avoided the topic of her alcohol-induced looseness, which had been immortalized in the restroom of one of the most expensive private schools in Maryland. Captured by a single cell phone, her performance had ended up on Facebook. She had the impression that all her friends and even some teachers, though they pretended otherwise, had seen those pictures.

Sara had never seen her mother so distraught.

"How did this get on the Internet?" Jane asked as soon as Sara came home from school.

The question belied Jane's scarce familiarity with social media. Sara for a moment hadn't understood what her mother meant.

"Who was that boy? And who took those photos?" Jane insisted, as if contemplating old-fashioned family dynamics that included arranged marriages and shotgun weddings.

Sara didn't remember enough of that day to be able to answer those questions. She was surprised anyone could identify her as the girl in the pictures, she could barely recognize herself. She tried to reconstruct the events through her mother's incoherent monologue, and little by little realized that Jane hadn't learned of the events from the school but from a stranger, a man so vile that Jane shuddered at the thought of his calling their house to ask not just if, but *when* Sara Westbridge—yes, he knew her daughter's first and last name!—would be available to have a drink with him, and perhaps afterwards visit the restroom in the photos, with the Kohler toilets and the imported tiles. Jane had hung up, as she knew one is supposed to do in such situations, but the man's words had aroused her suspicions. He seemed to be referring to something very specific, a scene he couldn't have invented. She tried to call him back, but his number was blocked. She didn't have to wait long, though, before he called again. This time Jane was more prepared, maybe thanks to the shot of Southern Comfort that she neglected to mention when relating the story. With the information she gathered in the second phone conversation, it didn't take long for her to find those awful images online. At this point, Jane interrupted her tirade and pointed dramatically at the laptop on the kitchen table which, however, at that moment only displayed her screen saver—an elephant and her calf, a particularly fond memory of her safari in the Serengeti. A cell phone ringing in the living room revealed Jeff's presence, and Sara realized that her mother's awkward boyfriend must have played an important role in the Internet search, since Jane by herself was barely able to check the weather.

Jane was taken aback by the sudden changes in her life. From one day to the next, her daughter had grown up and her mother had gotten very ill. Both phenomena struck her as the result of obscure, dizzying, uncontrollable proliferations of cells that left her helpless and confused. Her natural re-action was to fall back on the principle that she stubbornly believed could bring order to human chaos: the law, or rath-er, the Law, and its representative on earth, Jeff. And Jeff, of course, had not missed his cue. His first, crucial suggestion, was that Jane should not call the police unless she wanted to give the story more publicity and the pictures greater circula-tion. Threatening to call the police was much more effective than actually calling them, he stated, as if repeating a prov-erb. Then he sprang into action. His baritone— "This is Jeff Ross of Ross, Justin & Westbridge" —brought everyone at the school to heel, from the principal to Sara's classmates, with the specter of lawsuits, public shame, and long-lasting reper-cussions on everybody's reputation. In less than three hours, the Facebook post had been deleted and the possible culprits suspended. How to deal with Sara was a little less clear, but everyone agreed that an open and honest family discussion should precede any disciplinary intervention. So this is where we are, Sara thought, this ambush must be Jane's idea of an open and honest family discussion. She wasn't the only one feeling uneasy. As Jane harped on the importance of commu-nication, Jeff grew more and more restless in his armchair, until, at a lull in Jane's monologue, he got up and prepared to leave, making a face-to-face confrontation between mother and daughter inevitable.

If Sara was apprehensive about that conversation, Jane, as she accompanied Jeff to his car, was absolutely terrified. She wished she could pinpoint the moment when Sara had started to harbor all of that resentment toward her, stop everything right there, rewind. Sara's childhood had been, all things considered, serene, mostly thanks to Alice, her ever-present and caring grandmother. Maybe, in hindsight, Jane's divorce from Sara's father, Xavier, however amicable—as amicable as a divorce can be, really—had upset her more than they all realized. Xavier had been away for so long for his inconclusive missions with dubious NGOs that he was little more than a stranger to Sara. And yet, their divorce and his decision to relocate to East Timor—where, Jane suspected, another woman was waiting for him—had thrown the entire family dynamics off balance. With her other children already grown and far away, perhaps Jane had relied too much on Sara, she had pushed her into the adult world too quickly. She recalled with a certain embarrassment how she had bared her soul to her, sharing doubts and fears that, as the therapist later explained, Sara was not mature enough to understand and process. But even so, what about her, Jane? How come she was always the one saddled with understanding everything and everybody? When did she ever sign up for that role? How come nobody ever seemed to realize that she also needed help? In the space of just a few months, her marriage to Xavier was over—a sham of a marriage, sure, and yet convenient and reassuring, a shield against the brutal dating scene out there—and Alice had started to get sick, withdrawing into herself, unreachable. Sara was the only one left. It felt natural for Jane to treat her daughter as a grown-up, to have some woman-to-woman talk with her. Big mistake! She had overestimated Sara. Despite her mature attitude and all those foreign language books she liked to read, her inability to deal with her mother's revelations proved she was still a child. Take the issue of her birth, for instance. It was true that Jane had gone back and forth between whether or not to carry her third pregnancy to term. After all, she was just beginning to establish herself professionally after sacrificing so much for her family, and she knew she couldn't count much on Xavier's moral or practical support. Eventually, it was Alice's intervention and her promise to help that had convinced her to let nature decide, and Sara was born. Alice had kept her word, and spent every free moment with the child. The bond between the two had grown so strong that they seemed at times to have their own private code, also because Sara's first language was the Italian she learned from her grandmother, Nonna Alice or, as she called her, Nonna Ali.

If in the end everything had worked out so well, what was all the fuss about? Jane felt her initial hesitation had been human, logical, understandable. And yet, that wavering had become the central pillar of her daughter's identity. For Sara, it explained everything—her loneliness, her need to be loved unconditionally, her rivalry with her siblings, especially with Richard, the first child, the boy, the one who, unlike her, had been desired, cherished, cared-for. It wasn't true that Jane didn't love Sara. Yes, maybe she'd neglected her at times, there was always so much to think about, so many distractions. Yet... ah hell, you can certainly love someone even without paying attention to them all the time. Can't you love someone without paying attention to them all the time? In Jane's darkest moments, the statement turned into a question.

The previous Thanksgiving had been a total disaster. Alice must have seen that coming because, at the last minute, she called to say that turkey didn't agree with her anymore, so she would only stop by for ten minutes to say hello. What a brief, peaceful truce, those ten minutes had been. As soon as Alice left, Sara started again with her provocations. Richard tried everything in his power to play the patient and understanding older brother, but Sara still ended up running to her room. When Jane finally managed to convince her to open the door, Sara immediately brought up their past conversations to punish her mother. It was awful when Sara accused Jane of seeing her only as a failed abortion... If motherhood is more than a biological event, Sara blurted out, then her real mother was her grandmother, Nonna Ali. She was completely beside herself yet articulate as ever, almost technical, really.

She had obviously mulled over those accusations for a while. Jane sought out a therapist, who sat for a few hours in the same room with Sara never managing to extract a single word from her. When the situation seemed to be heading downhill, they all got a welcome and unexpected reprieve. Alice recovered from a second round of chemotherapy. She resumed her routine of baking, walks by the river, and reading. Sara fell back into her grandmother's orbit, and all that drama receded into the background. Jane had stifled her jealousy. It was her turn to feel unloved, excluded, superfluous. The respite only lasted a few months. Jane barely had time to catch her breath when Alice fell ill again, and Sara started visiting her mother's liquor cabinet. Sara's distress seemed to follow the same pattern of remission and relapse as Alice's disease.

Jane reviewed the events of the past year with Jeff, who knew them only too well and was eager to regain the tranquility of his bachelor's condo, though he didn't dare cut her short and nodded politely now and then, shifting his weight from one foot to the other. When he finally managed to drive off, Jane had no choice but go back and resume that painful conversation with her daughter. The living room was empty, though. Sara must have grown tired of waiting, or had just decided to sneak off somewhere else in the house. An arpeggio on the piano coming from her bedroom reassured Jane. She took advantage of the lull in the hostilities to put her plan into action. While she was dragging out her long goodbye to Jeff, she had suddenly remembered her best friend from childhood. Julia, yes, Julia was the only one who could help her get out of this mess. Without a second thought, she dialed the number of *Etcetera*, Bed and Breakfast-Café-Restaurant-Art Gallery in Moab, Utah.

She got straight to the point as soon as she recognized her friend's voice on the other end of the line.

"Listen, Julia, you have to do me this favor."

Jane heard the sound of a door opening and lowered her

voice. Sara, protected by the darkness of the stairway, tried to guess who was on the line with her mother.

"No, Sara is not ready, you know how close she is to her grandmother, she's not taking it well at all."

Jane's sobs startled her as if they came from somebody else in the room.

"No one is taking it well," she continued, "How can anyone take this crap well? No, at this point there is nothing else they can do, the oncologist was clear about that. It's only a matter of time."

Sara held her breath, hoping her mother wouldn't realize she was listening to the conversation. Barefoot at the top of the stairs, she was shivering because the air conditioning was on full blast, just the way Jane liked it.

Dealing with Alice's illness was exhausting. It was proving tough for everybody, certainly, but especially for the youngest in the family. Sara thought she could hide the fact that she was drinking, but her mother was no fool. Julia must have managed to make some kind of objection, because Jane fell silent for a moment before protesting indignantly.

"But at least I'd remember it, right?"

She then mentioned a detail that dispelled Julia's suspicions that it was Jane, and not her daughter, who was visiting the well-stocked home bar. The liquid in the bottles was not going down but was becoming clearer, weaker. Sara was filling up the bottles with water to keep them at the same level, to try and trick her mother! And how exactly had Jane found out about this ruse? Well, one evening, she had poured herself a shot of Jack Daniels and realized right away that it had been watered down. She'd checked the other bottles only to find that they had all been tampered with the same way.

Julia couldn't help smiling. She gently petted her oldest cat, who had jumped onto the shelf next to the phone, with her tattered garden glove. Maybe her childhood friend wouldn't remember drinking the night before, but watering down Jack

Daniels? No way! That would run against her principles. Sara mustn't know her mother very well if she hoped to get away with such an inelegant subterfuge. Julia kept a snide comment to herself.

"You're right," she agreed.

"Can you believe it?" Jane started up again, enjoying the unexpected concession. "An alcoholic at eighteen? Have you ever heard of such a thing?"

Julia did some quick math and concluded that it was some thirty-five years earlier when she and Jane had taken a memorable trip to the emergency room to have their stomachs pumped. They must have been about sixteen at the time. So yes, she had heard of such a thing before, but she also knew Jane could get quite frustrated when specific details threatened her interpretation of events. She decided it was not the right time for nitpicking.

"Never," she confirmed.

"Listen," Jane continued, "I know I'm asking a lot of you. You have your life, your way of thinking, your habits. You had the courage to review your priorities and quit the rat race. You don't know how much I admire your decision, your determination. I know so many people who have been talking about doing something like that for years, but you are the only one who up and did it. I would not be asking you if I weren't desperate."

The sobs resumed and were so loud this time that Jane jumped and looked around, as if surprised by the noise. Pierced by her mother's stare, Sara tried her best to act natural as she walked down the stairs, towards the fridge.

"Are you hungry, dear?" Jane asked, placing her hand on the receiver and instinctively adopting the solicitous tone of a TV ad.

Sara mumbled something as a reply, drank a glass of milk, and quickly retreated back upstairs.

"You see, she just came down, I bet she wanted to go to the

wet bar... Yes, sure, I will lock the cabinet doors, but can you please do me this favor?"

Julia couldn't remember for sure if she'd said yes, but she couldn't recall openly rejecting Jane's plan either. She blamed herself for being so naïve and missing the crucial turning points in the conversation where she could have slowed her friend down. As agitated as she seemed, Jane still remained lucid enough to discuss all sorts of practical details, from the weather to airfare. Julia realized she had basically agreed to host Sara only after hanging up.

What bothered Julia the most was not the fear of having her routine disrupted, the inconvenience of sharing her home with someone, or even the responsibility of taking care of a young stranger, as present and legitimate as these concerns were in her mind. Deep down, what frightened her was the prospect of getting enmeshed again in the neuroses she had decided to leave behind by moving to Moab. She saw the family portrait all too clearly before her eyes: Jane who took the progression of her mother's disease as a reminder of her own mortality; Jeff who surveyed the territory eager to prove useful, or rather, indispensable; Alice who, after keeping everybody together for years, was fading away and needed help herself; and finally, Sara, the most vulnerable of them all. Julia's memory of Sara was vague. It was hard for her to piece together an image from the token answers Jane had provided through the years to her perfunctory inquiries. Sara was fine; she spent most of her time with her grandma; didn't get along much with her siblings, though; Sara did very well in school; she was doing great, actually. Until she wasn't.

In the few weeks that had gone by between Jane's phone call and Sara's arrival, Julia had ample time to mull over her fears. Her first pointless conversation with Sara confirmed all her concerns. She watched the girl in front of her run her fingers along the rim of her coffee mug. She seemed younger than eighteen, with her dimples, her long eyelashes, a sort of shabby beauty, the exact opposite of the compulsive control that Jane had exercised over her appearance, even as a young woman. Julia repressed a stirring of affection. The more helpless they look, the more dangerous they are, she said to herself. It was imperative that she lay down a few house rules right away if she wanted to avoid trouble.

"Jane must have thought that Utah would be a good place to avoid alcohol, but you can actually find it quite easily around here. I am not one for strict rules, and I won't ask you to stop drinking altogether. However, if I catch you drunk or if you try to pull the same stunts as you did in school, you'll go straight back home."

That had come out a little harsher than she'd intended. Julia looked for a way to soften her words.

"But if instead you adapt to our ways and learn to enjoy nature, hiking, kayaking, the great outdoors..."

She was annoyed at finding herself capable of such banality.

"... if you adopt a healthy lifestyle... Well, I think you'll find plenty of interesting things to do around here."

She stopped abruptly, afraid of sounding like the Utah state brochure: Life Elevated.

Sara felt it was her turn to say something.

"If you're concerned about my creating trouble and possibly tarnishing the reputation of your Bed and Breakfast you needn't. I really don't like alcohol, and it's never been a problem, or at least, it's never been my main problem."

Julia knew that line of reasoning from having heard it many times from Jane. Maybe mother and daughter were really alike deep down, in spite of their physical differences. Julia told Sara something that she had never had the courage to tell her friend.

"All alcoholics say the same thing. So, believe me, the first thing to do is to get rid of the alcohol and see what lies underneath. Who knows, perhaps you'll get lucky and find there's nothing there."

Sara was somewhat surprised but not offended by Julia's bluntness. A strange serenity had settled over her as soon as she set foot in Moab. She was relieved at the idea of skipping the final weeks of school, graduation, and more useless appointments with her therapist. From a strictly educational point of view, there was no reason for her to go back to school. Her self-destructive bent hadn't prevented her from doing well, so much so that she had already been accepted at Princeton, a springboard, according to Jane, for one of the most prestigious law schools in the country—here's where Jane's imagination and ambition ran wild: Chicago? Columbia? Maybe even... Harvard? The years spent with Alice had helped refine Sara's body and mind, and her recent confusion had not quite managed to destroy everything she had built over the years. Not yet, at least. However, something had changed. Though the show proceeded according to the script, Sara realized she was no longer interested in the lead role, or any role at all, for that matter. Something had cracked within her and she had started to harm herself. She realized that for quite some time her only desire had been to drop out of the performance and enjoy her place in the audience, commenting on the play while pondering if, when and how she would get back on the stage. Unexpectedly, it had been her school principal who'd come up with a solution, during a meeting that she'd done everything in her power to avoid and that had instead turned out to be rather informative.

"I would suggest a gap year."

"A gap year?"

"Yes, a gap year," the principal repeated. Sara listened carefully. She could tell that Jane had suddenly grown very alert too.

"It's a time between your senior year of high school and your first year of college" the principal went on to explain.

"It's a relatively new concept, but it's becoming more and more popular. Many young people are ready academically for college but are not quite there yet in terms of maturity. It may be just a bit too early for them to live alone and take on real responsibilities and obligations. In Europe, students actually spend an extra year in high school compared to the U.S., which makes a lot of sense. A year is a long time at their age."

Jane got instinctively suspicious every time someone brought up Europe as an example. The slight accent—German, perhaps?—that she detected in the principal's speech increased her wariness.

"But… What about the end of the school year and graduation? What about Princeton?"

Jane was already dreaming about the moment Sara would join Ross, Justin & Westbridge. She'd be firm with her associates, the name needed to be changed—Ross, Justin, Westbridge and Daughter. And daughter! She proudly looked at Sara's elegant profile.

The principal had anticipated all those objections.

"Sara's academic record is stellar, I am sure none of her teachers would object if I recommend that she take her final exams earlier and skip the last few weeks. She could still come back for graduation if she wanted to, of course. And as far as Princeton is concerned, you can ask them to defer Sara's freshman year, I think they would accept. Universities, especially prestigious ones, actually regard the idea of a gap year quite favorably because it allows them to build a more mature first-year class and reduce the percentage of students dropping out, along with other more worrisome scenarios such as depression, suicides…"

He stopped abruptly, afraid he'd gone too far. Sara wondered if all that flexibility was a result of his eagerness to get her—and Jane, and that bully of a lawyer who acted on their behalf—out of his school.

Gap, that is: interruption, break. But also, a hole, and worse—a breach, a laceration. This was Jane's fear: if Sara's trajectory went off-course, she could very well fall into a world of indistinct dreams and aspirations without being able to regain a direction. But nobody seemed to share her concern.

"A tour of the real world can only do her some good," Jeff chimed in with his best fatherly tone, relieved at the prospect of a calmer and more productive year ahead for everyone. Between drama and disease, Jane's family had kept him on his toes. Jane's older kids, Richard and Kate, agreed, responsible adults that they were. Even Alice, for completely different reasons, approved of the idea of some time off that she felt would help Sara regain her passion for reading. That last year had been a disaster on that front, between the obsession with perfect grades and the time spent on college applications. Alice had even managed to compile a list of authors missing from Sara's curriculum: Cervantes, Akhmatova, Kundera... Sara listened patiently and respectfully, but for the first time she felt inclined to share Jane's fear that the disease had ended up discombobulating the brains of the venerable matriarch, as she was known in the family.

Once the decision had been made, everything followed very quickly. It turned out that the principal's proposal fit well within Jane's plan to send her daughter away some place for a while. Sara didn't have the energy or the motivation to put up a fight, and once she arrived in Moab she realized how much she'd needed a change in pace and scenery, a break. Naked under the covers, in the bedroom that Julia had set up for her in the attic, she looked over the body that had grown so hastily, snatching her from an enchanted childhood and tossing her into the midst of a stormy adolescence. A difficult body to deal with, whose desires she wasn't yet able to divine. She felt like a snake that had just shed its old scales and lay admiring its new skin, stunned and vulnerable on a heated rock. Time to uncoil.

Moab's main street was lined with stores, cafés, and restaurants. Sara learned from Julia and from her work at the café about the city's strategic position as the gateway to two of the country's most famous national parks, Arches and Canyonlands. Mountain bike enthusiasts, lovers of the outdoors, and photography buffs all flocked to the area. When Julia had decided to take her early retirement there, she calculated that between the sale of her home in Northern Virginia and decades of savvy investments in the stock market she could buy one fifth of the town. Another option was to settle for a reasonably-sized home and have enough left to live for about seven hundred years. She opted for the nice home and the seven hundred years, and started taking hikes, watching sunsets and sunrises, and trying to find the best afternoon light to capture the sheen of the apple skin with her paints and brushes, now that she could finally devote herself to art. It took her only a few months of that routine to start dreading the prospect of having to spend seven centuries that way. She then came up with the idea of converting her ground floor into a café, open only until three in the afternoon because she liked to go to bed early. Gradually, she started to showcase Navajo necklaces and rings, then paintings by local artists, and the coffee shop became something between an art gallery and a craft store. In the summer months, some occasional tourist would ask her about room rentals, which gave her the idea of turning a section in the back into a bed and breakfast. She quickly forgot that she had moved to Moab specifically to avoid appointments, commitments, and bookkeeping. The contemplative life did not suit her, as much as she hated to admit that. She had to restrain herself from starting to organize guided tours to the parks, photography trips, and white river rafting. Jane was astonished by her friend's knack of turning everything she came across into a money-making venture.

"You can take Julia out of the business, but not the business out of Julia," she would tease, but she meant no harm, and there was actually a certain degree of admiration in her words. Who knows, she thought, maybe Julia's attitude would provide a healthy example for Sara.

The first couple of weeks in Moab went by smoothly. Sara, contrary to Julia's worries, didn't seem to be in any rush to strike up new friendships, and adapted nicely to the routine of the bed and breakfast. A large part of the clientele was French because Julia, for some reason, had ended up in one of the most popular guidebooks in France. They were people who preferred a frugal place rich in personality like *Etcetera* over one of the many comfortable but drab hotels along the highway. They were thrilled that Sara spoke some French and occasionally invited her to join them for a night out. The morning after, Julia carefully observed Sara's behavior, but she didn't detect anything suspicious. Every so often, Sara struck up a conversation with the few Italian tourists in the area, and marveled at the difference between the language she had learned at home and this new contemporary version. At first, her interlocutors seemed full of admiration for her mastery of the language, but after a few exchanges they became rather amused at hearing her talking like a book, as one of them said, which she wasn't sure was a compliment. She intended to write to Alice about that, but in the last few months their conversations had become strained, preoccupied as they both were with overwhelming issues they weren't comfortable discussing. A generic letter didn't feel right, but dealing with her grandmother's illness in writing was even more difficult than doing it in person. Even a generic "how are you?" was problematic—indeed, just thinking of that question, and of the only possible answer, made Sara anxious. And then there was the incident at school that had caused her abrupt departure. Sara didn't know how much her grandmother knew about that, she could only hope that Jane had spared her the details. Not to mention the fact that writing meant, well, writing, because Nonna Ali had only made some concessions to email when her job forced her to do so, but had reverted to ink and paper as soon as she retired. So, Sara would have had to find paper, an envelope, and a stamp, and then probably type her letter on the computer and copy it in the shaky handwriting of her generation. This was all doable, of course, but also a bit time-consuming, unnecessarily cumbersome, a curious way to spend your time, like hand washing your clothes when you have a washing machine in the basement. And so, after postponing the letter day after day, Sara eventually just forgot about it altogether.

When Sara finally decided to accept Julia's offer and borrow one of her bikes to explore the town, she regretted having waited so long. Some of the restaurants served unusual dishes that made her mouth water, like ginger pancakes with apples and butter. She wanted to try them someday, but for the time being her priority was to gain some independence. She would take advantage of the tiny kitchen in her bedroom—Julia's first move toward a studio for weekly rentals—and get organized so that she wouldn't be stepping on Julia's toes more than necessary. She had been so eager to leave home that she hadn't given much thought to her mother's tendency to dismiss other people's wishes as frivolous. In this particular case, Jane had basically ignored Julia's legitimate desire to shield herself from everything she generically labelled as East Coast Syndrome, from ambition to addiction—in short, everything she had left behind, and that Sara seemed to embody. Sara didn't know how long she would stay in Moab—she doubted she could last the summer there, let alone a whole year—but Julia's welcome speech had been a clear indication that it was important to set boundaries. In retrospect, Sara wondered why she hadn't started to go out on her own earlier rather than spending days in her bedroom—her lair, rather—licking her wounds and trying to put some order to her thoughts.

She quickly found the organic grocery store at the corner of main street. She loaded her shopping cart with hummus, pita bread, milk, cereal, chicken breasts, and peanut butter. The price of fruits and vegetables was discouraging. She was determined not to accept money from her mother, but it was not clear how much Julia would pay her for her work at the café, since she was already giving her free room and board. She grabbed two tomatoes, looked at the price per pound, and put them back on the shelves. Carrots were a cheaper and more versatile alternative, she decided, good on their own as a snack and great with hummus. She put a package in the cart and proceeded to the dairy section, trying to ignore her grandmother's voice in her head warning her to buy canned goods first and milk last. I am almost done anyway, she said, as if Alice were right next to her. It wasn't unusual for her to talk to her far away grandma like that.

"Excuse me!" someone called from behind her. Sara turned around.

"Sorry, I think that's my cart."

Sara looked into the cart. Hummus, pita bread, milk…

"I think you must be mistaken; these are all my things."

The other woman seemed perplexed.

"That's strange, I could have sworn…"

Sara pointed at another cart in the middle of the aisle.

"Is that yours by any chance?"

The woman looked in that direction.

"Ah, yes, that must be it."

She started walking towards the cart, then turned with a smile.

"Ah, you're right, sorry about that."

"No worries, it happens to me all the time," Sara lied, just to be nice.

She turned back to finish her shopping. She had her hand on a can of tomatoes when the woman with the other cart came up to her.

"I am sorry to bother you again, but I'm almost positive that you did in fact take my cart."

Sara looked into the woman's shopping cart: hummus, pita bread, milk, peanut butter…

"The peanut butter is the culprit! I'm allergic," she said, almost apologetically.

Sara looked at the peanut butter jar and then again at the woman. She had thick jet-black hair that looked still wet from a shower, and a triangular face with sharp, high cheekbones. Her tan made her skin, which must have already been naturally dark, appear even darker in contrast to her small teeth that showed through her slight smile. The unbuttoned top of her linen shirt showed a glimpse of a small, turquoise stone necklace.

Anyway, back to the peanut butter.

"I'm sorry, you're definitely right," admitted Sara, switching to the other cart.

"No problem, it happens a lot, as you said," the woman replied. She then showed her the tub of hummus.

"There's a sale going on, two for the price of one, if you're interested."

The embarrassment prevented Sara from thanking her. She grabbed more hummus before going to the check-out lines, tightly gripping her cart to avoid making any additional mistakes.

That really is a very common mishap in supermarkets. There was no reason to blush.

"This is how we make quesadillas," Julia said while cutting thin slices from a block of cheese. She had finally decided to offer her customers a wider selection of food items, after trying to resist the idea for a long time. It was true that, besides the guests from the Bed and Breakfast, people mainly visited *Etcetera* to browse around and kill the time between one hike and the next, but those who did sit down for a bite sometimes wondered out loud if the menu was missing a page. Julia eventually realized she couldn't just rely on her coffee, though the beans that came straight from Seattle and her Italian coffee machine had earned her the reputation of best barista in Moab.

"After Starbucks, we Americans no longer have any excuses for making bad coffee," she liked to repeat to Sara, who would nod politely.

Julia had initially been vague about Sara's tasks, reluctant as she was to entrust too many responsibilities to a person she barely knew, but she'd warmed up to the idea of sharing the daily operation of *Etcetera*. And Sara, in spite of the strange circumstances that brought her to Moab, had proven reliable, and on a couple of occasions had shown a surprising assertiveness when minor issues came up in the running of the café. Julia suspected that her presence had even inspired her decision to offer a proper lunch menu. Things just look less daunting when you are not alone.

"So, I'm going to put my clothes in the dryer, while you clean up a little here and keep an eye on the desserts, sounds good?"

"Sure, no worries," Sara responded.

It was a dead hour of a beautiful day, everyone seemed to be out hiking. Sara went to the backroom and turned on the oven light. Divided into twelve equal molds, Julia's famous cranberry orange bread, the house specialty, was taking on a lovely, golden color. She put away the sugar and the flour and wiped down the countertop. The doorbell chime alerted her that someone had entered the café. She returned to the main dining room, picked up a notepad to look more professional, and walked toward the only occupied table.

"Oh hey!"

The woman from the grocery store looked at her with surprise.

"Hi…"

Sara felt strangely happy to see her again. She tried to be funny.

"Good morning, what would you say to a plate of hummus and pita?"

The woman laughed.

"For Heaven's sake, no! That's all I have been eating since the beginning of that sale… Julia's not here by any chance, is she?"

"She's upstairs."

Sara felt she needed to explain her presence in the café.

"I… work for her. Can I get you something?"

"Yes, if you don't mind. I'll have a cappuccino, but…"

"But?"

"…the way Julia makes it."

"And how's that?"

"Well, I don't know exactly, I've never asked. Not much foam, that's for sure…"

"No foam, cream instead of milk, and a splash of vanilla," Julia interjected walking towards them.

"Is this how you guys make cappuccinos around here?" Sara asked.

"Only for very special customers," Julia replied. "Have you already met Una?"

Una, Sara thought, her name is Una.

"Yes, well, no…" she mumbled.

"We met at the grocery store," Una explained.

"We had a little mishap with the carts," Sara added.

Julia stared at Una, who looked away, then took the notepad from Sara's hands.

"You can keep chatting, I'll go make two Una Specials. How does that sound?"

Sara would have preferred skimmed milk for her cappuccino, but she didn't dare give Julia more work. She took a seat in front of Una, still feeling like she had to justify her presence in Moab.

"My name's Sara, I'm here to help Julia for the season."

Una remembered Julia talking about her niece, or rather, a good friend's daughter who had some issues and had unceremoniously been dumped on her. She had imagined a completely different person, though. There was something peculiar about Sara, she had already sensed it during their short meeting at the store.

"Are you from around here?" Sara asked to break the silence.

"Yes, can't you tell?"

"How could I tell?"

"Well, from the color of my skin, for example. No, I'm not Mexican, I'm Ute."

"Ute?"

"Yes, we were here long before the white settlers arrived. The name Utah comes from us, the Ute people."

Sara looked at her with curiosity and a little embarrassment.

"Sorry... I only arrived here a couple of weeks ago and I don't know much about this place."

Una gave her an encouraging look.

"That's a nice condition to be in, and much better in any case than getting here with all these preconceived notions about Native Americans and the Wild West that so many people have."

"Here they are: two Una Specials, as well as two slices of cranberry orange bread straight from the oven!" Julia exclaimed. She put everything on the table, grabbed a chair and sat down with them.

"What are you doing here, don't you work today?" Julia asked Una.

"I just came back from work, if you can call that work. I chased the moon up and down across Canyonlands... with little success."

"I actually work as a park ranger," she continued, looking at Sara, "but about a year ago I decided to become part-time, as long as I can afford it. They want me to spend way too

much time at the office, which is not what I think a park ranger should be doing. So, when I am not working there, I take
tourists out on foot or by bike, mostly people who stay here
at Julia's. I also try to take photos for my postcards. I hope
to publish a whole photography book on our parks someday."

"Which reminds me, I sold a few of your postcards last
week," Julia said.

"I saw them!" Sara exclaimed. "I sold a few of them too, I
didn't know they were from a local photographer. The night
shots are my favorite. Do you visit the parks at night?"

"That too."

"May I just say how much I disapprove of these night excursions of yours?" Julia chimed in.

"Oh, come on! I know these mountains like the back of my
hand."

"I am not questioning your expertise. I am more worried
about humans than nature. I am afraid you might find somebody on your path who's eager to teach you a lesson, especially now, with all these people just passing through town."

"Teach me a lesson?! What for? I don't bother anyone! And
I don't ask anybody for anything."

"Exactly. I am afraid you may run into someone who objects to your being young, being a woman, and not asking
anybody for anything."

"Come on, Julia, don't exaggerate. This is the city-dwell-
er in you speaking now. Besides, the season is almost over,
you'll soon have fewer reasons to worry about me."

"By the way, if you ever need company, count me in," Sara
said instinctively.

"Listen to her! You just started to work, and you are already asking for time off?" Julia chimed in.

"Well, I thought we were talking about night excursions,
and the café does close at three p.m...."

"I bet you'd work really well after a night spent chasing
the moon, to quote your friend here."

"You know that you're being a real grouch, right? Come on, you won't go bankrupt if you give your employees half a day off, stop playing the boss!" Una said, laughing. She turned back to Sara.

"Agreed, then. Full moon is in a week. I'll pick you up after dinner."

Mulling over that conversation during the week that followed, Sara thought there was a good chance that Una knew the real reason for her presence in Moab. Nobody in their right mind could believe that Julia all of a sudden needed full-time help with her café or that Sara was such an outdoor enthusiast that she had even skipped her last weeks in school, and her graduation ceremony, to rush to Moab. Julia seemed to be on very good terms with Una. Sara thought she'd even detected some complicity between them, especially when she described the scene at the organic food market. It was very likely that Julia had shared the real reason why the daughter of her childhood friend had just turned up in town. But if that was the case, Sara concluded, it was better to give Una her own version of the story, though that meant being asked the same old questions she found hard to answer. In the silence of the starry night, among the dense shadows cast by the rocks, she seemed to have even fewer answers than usual, almost as if she'd been requested to explain a stranger's behavior and not her own.

"And so, what happened after that... episode, the one in high school? I mean, are you still drinking? How are you doing now?"

Una was whispering, as if afraid of disturbing the silence of the night. She placed the camera on the tripod so that she'd be ready to take a shot of the moon rising under Delicate Arch, and then sat down on a rock.

"Well, after that incident my mother started guarding the wet bar like a watchdog. And here, Julia basically has me go through an X-ray machine every time I come home..."

Her words and light-hearted tone sounded forced and hollow. It was the first time she found herself out in the middle
of nature at night and she really wanted to say she liked it. Instead she was almost frightened and somewhat lightheaded,
and she wondered whether she had made the right decision
by joining Una on that excursion. The noises were particularly unnerving—the rustling, the swishing, the crackling. Each
conjured a different danger, from rattlesnakes to men lurk-
ing in the dark. Now that they were no longer walking, they
sounded even more ominous. Sara tried to ignore them as
she lay down as best as she could on a flat rock that was still
warm from the daytime sun. They had stopped at the margins
of the vast sandstone amphitheater. At the edge of the cliff,
the outline of Delicate Arch, clearly visible in the full moon
night, framed the La Sal Mountains, far off in the distance.

"And there, when you were home, I mean, why did you
start?"

Always the same questions, Sara thought. She felt though
that the attention that Una was devoting to her deserved a little more, maybe even the truth. Had she known the truth, she
would have been delighted to share it with Una, and with that
striking landscape that seemed to be listening too.

"I'd like to know that myself."

And that was the truth, after all. None of the explanations
proposed by the therapist, or by Jane when she tried to play
therapist, fully convinced her. Now she just wanted to forget
about that other version of herself that everybody seemed to
be interested in but that she found a bit boring, somewhat
predictable. Lying on the rock, with her arm bent under her
head, Sara had finally found a comfortable position for her
body. Harmony, fragility. Una forced herself to look else-
where.

"I don't think it's a good night for taking photos," Sara
said after a while. "Just look at that cloud."

Una looked up at the clear sky.

"What cloud?"

"That one."

Sara pointed at the light strip that veiled Sagittarius.

Una moved closer to her.

"That's not a cloud, that's the Milky Way."

Sara feared she had shown herself to be a hopeless city girl. The Milky Way, of course. She must have read about it somewhere. But she had never seen it like this. Perhaps she had never seen it at all, now that she thought about it.

"It's normal to mistake the Milky Way for a cloud, you know," Una consoled her. "There aren't too many places left where you can see the full night sky of stars. You should come hear my presentation one of these evenings, when I am working at the office. That's precisely what I talk about—light pollution, light that hides instead of revealing."

The paradox struck Sara, who looked intently at Una's profile. Everything invited Sara to get even closer to Una—their stillness after the night walk, the darkness all around, the heat of the day slowly escaping from the ground, and the rocks shaped by ancient geological phenomena that seemed to be silently waiting. She closed her eyes, tried to gather her courage. They remained quiet for a few minutes, then Sara was startled by a noise close to her. She opened her eyes and saw Una near the tripod.

"No!"

"What's wrong?" Sara asked, getting up herself.

"I got distracted, or perhaps I made a mistake in setting the tripod, but it's gone."

She pointed to the full moon.

"What do you mean... What's gone where?"

"The moon. It kept rising while we were talking, and now it's impossible to frame it the way I wanted, right under the arch."

She looked up unhappily at the moon.

"I am not giving up, though, I'll see you in a month!"

Sara looked up at the full disc that seemed to be sailing away through the night sky.

"But you are trying to do something really difficult! Why do you have this passion for the full moon? Maybe you should try following its various phases, from when it's barely visible... Follow its path, getting to know it, something like that, I don't know. Then maybe even this appointment with the full moon would be a little easier to schedule, don't you think? It would feel a little less like an ambush."

Una stared at her.

"Do you really believe that?"

"Yes... Well, I mean, it's not like I've thought about it much, but it seems more logical to me. You want to capture the moon, trap it under the arch. Instead, what you should do is follow it with more patience, let it grow. I'm sure it would make for some interesting photos, with or without the full moon."

Una raised her eyes towards the starry sky, then lowered them to the ground.

"I'll think about it... Thanks."

They descended the hill in silence. Una could have walked the path with her eyes closed, but not Sara. When the moon disappeared behind the slope, the night became darker, wrapping them in its sticky embrace.

"Go this way, be careful, you have to jump a little, maybe a foot, a foot and a half even..."

Una went first, then stretched out her hand to guide Sara, who held it as she leapt into the dark, landing on fine pebbles that carried her down several inches.

"Careful!" Una exclaimed, squeezing Sara's hand harder. Sara held on longer than she needed to and even when she regained her balance, she didn't let Una go. For safety, she said to herself. They continued their descent side by side in silence, almost holding their breath. They only spoke a few, awkward words when Una dropped Sara off in front of *Etcetera*.

"Well, goodnight, I'm sorry I didn't bring you much luck," Sara said.

"No, that's not true, you gave me a lot to think about. See you around. Goodnight."

"Goodnight."

BETHESDA, MARYLAND
OCTOBER 8, 2010

Alice was proud that she managed to stay sitting up in bed for more than a few minutes without her head spinning. Encouraged by her success, she ventured toward the bathroom on her own, but once she got halfway there, that is to say after a few feet, she had to lean on the wall. Her daughter rushed over to help. Now she was laying down again and looking at the textured ceiling that, she recently discovered, formed various patterns at different times of the day. It was getting dark, but Alice hadn't turned on the light yet. The warm glow from the window announced that autumn was just around the corner, the Japanese maple saturated the garden in reddish hues.

Attracted by the colors, Jane approached the window. She basked in the twilight, trying to free her mind of the concerns of the day. Her iPhone vibrated, signalling the arrival of a text.

"It's Sara, all is well in Moab, she asks how we are doing and she sends her love," Jane summarized, translating for her mother "Moab ok, what's up, ILY."

"That's all? Do they charge you more for longer messages?" Alice asked, still unsatisfied. The telegrams are back, she thought, but she wasn't sure that Jane, let alone Sara, would know what a telegram was, and an explanation would have required too much effort. The idea that her cherished granddaughter was now using some generic and incomprehensible code instead of actually writing intensified Alice's many discomforts and caused her a raw, sharp pain. "She sends her love." What a joke.

Jane decided to ignore her mother's sarcasm. Alice didn't seem to realize how hard it had become to communicate with Sara. In the last few weeks, since her illness had taken a turn for the worst, Alice had become more intolerant than ever. She had also completely reverted to Italian, her mother tongue, as if she hadn't spent half a century in the U.S. It was the language that she had passed on to both Jane and Sara, their special code, but there had been long periods when Jane had resisted that imposition, as she had resisted everything that made her feel different. Now she didn't dare object, or answer in English as she used to when she was a teenager or whenever she felt lazy or annoyed, but she resented having to make that additional effort. Her mother's voice, and her mother's language, seemed more and more to reach her from a foreign land.

Between the language issue and her mother's tantrums, as Jeff referred to them, Jane had to admit that those daily visits had become a bit of a chore, and she tried to keep them short and efficient. That evening, however, she couldn't make up her mind to leave. For one thing, Alice seemed both tired and restless.

"Mom..."

Alice opened her eyes.

"What is it?"

"Aren't you tired? Don't you want to go to sleep?"

"I can't, it's not the right time. I need to stay vigilant, vigilant... It only takes a moment of distraction, at this point... just a moment, and it slips away."

"What slips away?"

Alice looked up from her bed. The irregular bumps on the ceiling now seemed to form a continent, a mix between Africa and South America, in her own personal atlas.

"What slips away?" Jane repeated.

Alice tried to move her neck just enough to be able to look at her daughter.

"Everything… The little that is left."

Usually a short incoherent answer like that would prompt Jane to mention something mundane, as if she feared the conversation might otherwise veer off into some dangerous territory. But now instead she seemed to be waiting.

"When I left Italy," Alice said, "my mother told me to write all my essential information on a slip of paper: my name, date of birth, the names of my parents, what I cared about most in the world. That way, if something happened, if I became disoriented, I could always recover my bearings, and I wouldn't be completely lost."

"And what did you write?"

"Alice Arienti, daughter of Cesira and Raffaele; born in L'Aquila on May 23, 1930; loves poetry. I am not sure that constitutes much of a foundation at this point. Cesira and Raffaele are dead and L'Aquila… forget it. You do the math, tell me what's left… me and poetry. And soon, just poetry."

They never spoke of death, the guest at the door. A myriad of little everyday tasks—eating, bathing, taking the right medicine at the right time—absorbed all their attention. In the ballroom of the Titanic, the orchestra kept on playing as the water level rose.

"I'll miss being by your side when you die," Alice continued," I am happy to be going before you, the opposite is just inconceivable, but I'll miss being there to encourage you, to share how it felt for me, to spread my arms wide to welcome you. You know, like when you took your first step."

"How can you know for sure what happens in those moments? Maybe you will still be there, in some form."

Alice smiled.

"You know how I feel about these strange philosophies of yours, and about metaphysical consolations of any kind.

Actually, since we are talking about it, in case you have any doubts, no last-minute tricks… no priests."

"No priests, sure."

"Promise."

"I promise. Even if I wanted to, I wouldn't even know where to find a priest!"

"Good, that way you won't be tempted. And mind you, when I say 'priest' I mean a religious figure in general. Please spare me whatever spiritual guru is trending in the neighborhood these days."

"Ok, ok, I won't bring anyone, I swear!" Jane huffed.

Alice gathered her strength before continuing.

"But maybe you're right, I should be more humble, there's no reason to be sure about anything. Maybe a mother does come back to pick up her child, who knows? Where I come from, whenever anyone was about to die the door was left open, so that the women could come and take them. Maybe mothers do come back."

"The women? Who are 'the women'?"

"I don't know. That's what they called them, and it never occurred to me to ask."

Alice had felt a presence stirring in the room earlier on, but she was not sure she wanted to share that discovery with Jane. Too challenging, for her little strength, for the short time still left for the two of them together.

The silence was so thick that Alice's heavy breathing was clearly audible. Exhausted by the conversation, she let her head fall onto the pillow and closed her eyes. Yet she felt there was something more she needed to say.

"Jane…?"

"Yes, I'm here."

"I know it's late, but stay a little longer, will you? Do you mind if we go over some Italian verb conjugations? It would help me fall asleep. How about some *passato remoto*? The historical past tense?"

"The historical past tense?!" Jane protested. "But nobody uses it anymore, apart from you and Corleone!"

"I wish you'd stop getting information about Italy from mafia movies. It's embarrassing, especially for someone who is half Italian like you."

"But what's the point? Let's be serious..."

"The point," Alice tried to explain, "is to prevent everything that happened, yesterday or a century ago, from becoming one single meaningless blur."

She wished she could come up with a better argument. It was way too easy for Jane to spot the weakness in her reasoning.

"If it were up to you, we would need a different verb tense for every century, your grammar rules would fill volumes!"

"Not really, but sometimes I do feel that we're missing some categories. I wish I had a specific tense to convey what happened during the war, for instance. Yes, I'd want a tense for the war, to indicate disasters, deprivation... What we lost in the war, no economic miracle could bring it back."

Why had she never told Jane about everything the war had taken away? Her peace, and that of so many others, that's what the war had stolen, and not just for the few years it had lasted. But how could she explain that to Jane, or to Sara, who had only seen wars in movies? She should have at least tried, though, instead of hoping that her silence would make the past disappear. No matter how thoroughly you erase, there is always a mark, an imprint left on the page. Sooner or later, you find yourself looking for verb tenses that don't exist in any grammar.

"Yes, there should be a tense to indicate things that are lost, a bit like the verbal equivalent for the abessive, you know, the case they use in Turkish to indicate that something is missing."

"Turkish...?!" Jane cried, "Now Turkish?! And to think that I complained about your obsolete Italian! Are you by any chance suggesting that we review some Turkish grammar, just to pass the time, to relax after a long day at work..."

Alice smiled. In the last few weeks, Jane had treated her like a poor sick old lady who deserved pity and compassion. She brought her books without complaining, she listened to her stories with a suspicious amount of interest. All bad signs. Alice was glad to welcome back the impatient daughter she used to know.

"Alright, alright, let's not complicate things, I think that the present circumstances call instead for a simplification. But at least two..."

Here Alice made a gesture that Jane would remember forever, because gesticulating required an energy that her mother no longer had. But from under the sheets a scrawny hand emerged and made something close to a peace sign. It took Jane a moment to realize that Alice simply wanted to indicate the number two.

"Especially if you think that there are two tenses for the future, now that's an exaggeration... can't we please preserve at least two layers of our past, or is that asking too much?"

"Okay, okay, two layers, it's a deal. Let's keep them, at least here in Bethesda, okay?" Jane joked, trying to shake off the anxiety descending upon her. "It's your house and you can preserve as many shades of the past as you want."

Here we are, in the trenches, she thought, keeping death at bay with jabs of historical past.

"Let's start then, it's really getting dark out there."

"That's because you refuse to trim that Japanese maple."

"How could I?! You should see the glow on your hair right now... No, don't move, and don't change the subject. We were going to review the *passato remoto*. Let's start with an easy one, *parlare*, to talk. You go first."

Jane opened her mouth but realized she didn't even know how to begin.

"What is this? Are we back in school all of a sudden? You go ahead and I'll follow."

"Alright, but then I get to choose where to start, no matter how challenging these verbs may seem to you. And I want to start from the beginning, it kind of makes sense. *Nascere*, to be born. *Nacqui, nascesti, nacque, nascemmo, nasceste, nacquero.*"

Jane had trouble reciting along. She hoped to redeem herself with the next verb.

"*Crescere*, to grow. *Crebbi, crescesti, crebbe, crescemmo, cresceste, crebbero.*

Not a chance.

"Let's try a regular one," Alice suggested. "*Amare*, to love. *Amai, amasti, amò, amammo, amaste, amarono.*"

Not even a regular conjugation could help, there is no point in being regular in an unpredictable universe. Jane continued the game trying to guess, almost lip-syncing. It had been a long time since her mother managed to stay lucid for such an extended period. That made her happy, although the surreal conversation rekindled her fear that the illness had spread to Alice's brain. But dammit, no two of those verbs were the same. She ended up producing the weirdest combinations, and stuttered when trying to pronounce them: *particqui, forserono.* After a while Jane realized that her mother's voice was fading, and she thought that their litany resembled the prayers she heard rise from the church benches during her only trip to Italy, many years before, when she had given in to the temptation of looking for her roots, only to come away disappointed. The little old ladies in the first row repeated their devotions until they were almost asleep, hypnotized by mnemonic repetition, finding comfort in that ritual formalized by the many frightened women who had preceded them, squeezed tightly together in the belly of a church threatened by dark and incomprehensible forces. They let themselves be cradled and comforted by arcane words, magical formulas. *Nunc et in hora.* She approached the bed. Alice's eyes were closed but her voice was still audible.

Morire, to die.
Morii.
Moristi.
Morì.
Morimmo.
Moriste.
Morirono.

BETHESDA, MARYLAND
OCTOBER 9, 2010

"Liliana, what do you mean you can't? Hello?"

Only confused sounds came from the other end as the train left the station and entered another tunnel. Jane put down the phone and began to nervously measure the distance between the fridge and the sink. She went to the dining room, without sitting down she looked up the website of the *Washington Post* on her phone. The latest update of the local news spoke of delays on the metro's red line, between Shady Grove and Bethesda. There had been an accident earlier on. The problem had been solved but it would take some time for things to get back to normal, trains were still single-tracking. Single-tracking. For goodness sake, what kind of language was that?

The phone rang again, but it wasn't Liliana. Jeff's booming voice skipped the pleasantries.

"Don't forget to bring the letter from the owners, where they commit to resuming their mortgage payments in January."

"Already printed out," Jane lied, moving swiftly toward her mother's home office and hoping there would be enough ink left in the cartridge.

"And leave on time. With the delays on the metro everybody must be driving today, you can bet the beltway is jammed up. Try to be punctual."

"Okay."

"At nine o'clock sharp."

"Okay, bye."

"Bye."

Jane looked anxiously at the clock while she waited for the letter to print. In order to be at Hyattsville at nine o'clock she would have to leave in five minutes at the latest. Impossible for Liliana to show up before then, who knows what metro tunnel she was stuck in. Being at Hyattsville on time meant leaving her mother there, alone, there was no way around it. But it would not be for long, Liliana would arrive soon, maybe even before Alice woke up from the hypnotic slumber that the opioids induced in her. Cancelling another appointment was a big deal. She had done it a few times already, when she thought the moment had arrived. But who can know for sure that the moment has arrived? Her friends who had gone through similar experiences had received a call from the clinic for the terminally ill. Quick and clean. Instead she had allowed that house, her childhood home, to be invaded by illness, by death. Her mother had refused to go to a nursing home, and to have full time assistance, and hospice care. She could prove incredibly stubborn, in that regard Jeff was right. Luckily Liliana, aside from cleaning the house, had also accepted to provide a bit of company and care. But Jane knew how these things go, you must always keep the situation under control. That is why she stopped by to see her mother every day, before and after work. It was important to have a little chat with Liliana every time, organize the schedule for the hours ahead or review the day that had just ended, and make sure everything went as planned. Her house in Kenwood was not very far from her mother's in downtown Bethesda, but those visits added another complication to Jane's busy schedule, especially since she was always forced to drive during rush hour. For a while things had worked out pretty well, overall. The problem was Alice's rapid decline during the past few weeks. The doctors seemed not only incapable of explaining it, but also reluctant to acknowledge it. According to them, at Alice's age, you could continue to fade for four, six months, even a year. Jane, however, had become apprehensive. She cancelled work appointments, found a thousand excuses to show up at her mother's place at all hours of the day. After the last false alarm, which forced her to postpone an eviction that had been scheduled for months, Jeff got really upset. He couldn't wait to express his condolences and move on, file away. All those complications seemed incomprehensible to him. Jane was under the impression that he took Alice's illness as a personal affront. Just a few days before, they had had lunch at a restaurant below their office and Jeff had taken advantage of the wait for the special 350-calorie meal—chicken breast with julienned carrots—to send some messages on his iPhone. Jane, on the other hand, had instinctively called Alice but then she realized she had nothing to say. She reminded her mother to take her medication, urged her not to argue with Liliana, and advised against her going to the bathroom on her own. Exactly the kind of phone calls that Alice could not stand. The result was a choppy, unnatural exchange that left Jane uneasy and slightly resentful. Whatever she did, no matter how hard she tried, she always displeased everyone, herself included.

"It's not a great time for us professionally, and that's an understatement" Jeff reminded her as soon as she hung up. "We can still get through it, but we have to stay focused, ready to snatch up the few opportunities around."

While she nervously paced between the kitchen and the living room, Jane recalled Jeff's harsh stare and clenched jaw as he gave her that little speech. From his long-lost family, he had inherited a military demeanor that both reassured and frightened her. Pushing back that eviction was unthinkable. She made one last vain attempt to reach Liliana, then checked the contents of her purse—car keys, sunglasses, cell phone. She walked briskly to the bathroom to glance at her reflection. Not bad, the anxious look suited her, maybe she had even managed to lose a few pounds. She gave up the idea of weighing herself right there and then, fully dressed, she knew she wouldn't be happy with the scale's verdict. She walked up the stairs and tip-toed to the edge of her mother's bed. A groan.

"Mom…"

Alice opened her eyes. They were clear, a sign that the effect of the sleep medication had worn off. Jane handed her an orange pill.

Here, it will do you good.

Alice tried to pull herself up to sit but slipped. Jane arranged the pillows, put her hands under her mother's armpits to help her. The fragility of that body that resembled hers so closely always managed to disconcert her.

Alice took the pill between her fingers. Water.

"Water?" Jane repeated, wondering if she heard correctly. Since when did her mother need water to swallow her pills? She remembered what the doctor had told her and what she had noticed herself many times in the past few months. Terminally ill patients are different from the people they used to be, you need to get to know them all over again, with their habits and their idiosyncrasies. *Know*, the doctor had said, not *love*. Jane loved Alice to death, but at times she wasn't too sure about her feelings toward the person who now occupied her bed and needed water to swallow a pill. She hurried downstairs to the kitchen, she had two minutes left if she wanted to get to the appointment on time. Instead of a cup she chose a bowl, it would be more difficult to spill the water, and now her mother only drank a sip at a time, a half inch at the bottom was enough. When she returned to the room, she found Alice completely awake and eager to collaborate, her lips closed, the pill evidently already in her mouth. She had even taken her favorite book from the bedside table, with pen in hand she seemed to be taking notes. She closed it when Jane walked into the room and tried to put it back, but it was a complicated maneuver that required her daughter's intervention. Alice grabbed the bowl as tightly as she could with both hands, rested her lips on the rim, diligently tilted her head back. When the water touched her mouth, she felt herself drowning. The eyes that looked back at her from the bottom of the bowl were those of a little girl. The water had a sickly, sweet taste that slid over her tongue and down her throat.

Love the bread, heart of the home, smell of the table, joy of the hearth.

Thus read her schoolbook. But Fascist bread, baked with little or no flour, was difficult to love. It was dry, grainy, made of bran, rye, and buckwheat. War bread. Luckily the bees knew nothing about the war and continued to make their honey, which had never seemed as clear and fragrant as in the summer of 1942. It filled the craters of that inedible bread, it made it smooth and soft, delicious when soaked in milk. It left a dense, sweet streak that Alice loved to chase until the last drop, when her eyes, greedy and satisfied, looked back at her from the bottom of the bowl. Like they did now.

"Is everything alright?" Jane asked, trying not to make her hurry apparent.

From the bottom of the bowl, the little girl winked at Alice. She stopped pretending to drink, put the bowl down and looked at her daughter.

Jane's youthful splendor was not completely gone, and neither was the attitude that accompanied it—the awareness of being the object of admiration, the benevolent tolerance towards the less fortunate. She had been, indeed, a beautiful young woman, with a delicate profile, bright eyes, a slightly stiff, aristocratic demeanor. Earlier on, she had been a sensitive little girl. The night the neighbors had warned them that they had a flat tire, she had snuck outside to put Band-Aids on the injured wheel. She suffered for every little mishap in ways that Alice found distressing, out of proportion. A drawing that came out poorly, her old hamster's death, the distracted indifference with which her childhood friend said goodbye to her, could cause her to be inconsolable for days. At school, history terrified her, with its intolerable litany of rapes and murders. It did not take much to understand the mechanism, and studying its infinite variations struck her like a mighty waste of time. She liked medicine in theory, but in practice she couldn't stand being near blood and suffering. Maybe she should have devoted herself to something abstract, immutable—mathematics, numbers—but she had shied away from that glacial perfection, a rejection that back then seemed just natural for a girl. She had suffered a great deal before she learned how to protect herself—foundation, mascara, lipstick, and a few drinks when cosmetics were not enough to hide the cracks. One day she realized that she was no longer suffering. Only Alice was able to see, just like a series of Russian dolls hidden one inside the other, the girl her daughter used to be, and that helpless creature that had emerged from her womb and then, diving even deeper, the time when it was impossible to even tell the two of them apart. Looking at Jane, Alice entered the pre-history of her own self. It was an odd sensation. She shook it off, dazed. Jane stood by her smiling, unaware and unscathed.

"I think you're doing better today."

Alice nodded. Whatever, she thought.

"Listen, do you mind if I go? Liliana is already on the metro but trains are single... Never mind, there's a delay but she should be here at any moment, and I have that eviction to take care of. I'll call later and then stop by at the end of the day as usual, okay?"

Alice waved goodbye.

"Are you sure? Do you need anything?" Jane asked.

"No."

"I'll go then."

She kissed her forehead, her hair. Alice watched her daughter walk away towards the door in her smoky gray suit.

Bambina.

"What?

Already at the door, Jane turned around to meet Alice's stare.

"Did you call me?"

"Yes, I..."

Alice couldn't remember what she wanted to say.

"You look good like that. You know what would go well with that color? My necklace."

"What necklace?"

How strange that her mother should start offering advice on accessories, Jane thought, frugal as she was. Driven more by curiosity than anything else, Jane turned back and followed Alice's directions till she found a little box on the shelf.

"This one?"

It was a round silver pendant. From an inner ring of eight loops sprang a ray of small pillars that supported twelve arches, the tops of which rested on a middle ring. The pattern repeated itself, doubling, in the space between the middle and the largest ring. The result was stunning, slightly hypnotic.

"Beautiful," said Jane with hurried sincerity, trying to open the clasp. "Where did you find it, in one of your antique stores?"

When she turned around, the rose window of Santa Maria di Collemaggio sparkled on her neck. Collemaggio! There were summer days when the rays of the setting sun filtered through the rose glass, painting a perfect pattern around the tall arched window on the back wall of the church. It looked like a woman dressed in light. The reflection blinded Alice, forcing her eyes to close.

Jane hesitated a little longer, there seemed to be something left to do, to say.

"I'll go then, okay? I'll call you."

"Okay, have a good day."

***

Alice listened to Jane's fast descent down the stairs, the front door shutting behind her. Holding her breath, she could hear the engine starting, the car driving away. She put her hand under the pillow, removed the orange pill from its hiding place so that it would not stain the sheets, and carefully placed it on the bedside table. Taking it would mean falling into her usual daze, while she needed to stay alert.

We have come to take you away.

Incredible that they found their way to her, her mother Cesira and Aunt Rachele, two sisters who had only ever taken a few buses in their whole life. The farthest they had travelled, as they repeated over and over, arguing more and more about the details as they grew older, was to Rome, when they went looking for Alberto. Cesira somehow believed that the Germans had brought her son to the Regina Coeli prison, after capturing him along with his reckless friends who had taken to the mountains to liberate Italy, in the twilight of that summer of '43.

Regina Coeli, the Germans, the summer of 1943?

Stories from a different planet.

Their journey to Rome had been epic. When the cart driver had quoted the price for taking them to Regina Coeli, Cesira told him right to his face that she only wanted a ride, not the horse.

"But not as a joke, no! She really thought he'd misunderstood, she really thought he wanted to sell us the horse!"

Aunt Rachele laughed herself to tears every time she told that story, but Cesira would sulk, anything that brought up Alberto reopened old wounds. Besides, it wasn't fair, she was always the one who had to take all the risks, ask for directions, buy the tickets, while her little sister sat back and took notes for the duly embellished stories that she would tell at each family gathering, stories that invariably made everybody laugh and Cesira look like a fool. In any case, if it hadn't been for her, they'd still be in Rome, in Piazza Esedra, standing back to back while scanning the square, purses tightly pressed under their sweaty armpits to ward off pickpockets.

Not the shrewdest of travelers, those two, and frankly, how could one blame them for that?

And yet, they had found her.

Alice couldn't be mistaken, she had heard their light footsteps, she had sensed their dark silent presence by the bed. At some point, she had even had the impression that her mother was wiping away her sweat with an enormous handkerchief, blindingly white and cool to the touch. She could not swear to that, though.

She was sure of one thing, however. She had no intention of being numbed by the opioids and spending another day in a chemical daze. She had lingered too long already, taking advantage of her condition to relive her childhood and youth, to organize her thoughts, and to finally finish that book. Yes, that book... what a shame she'd never had the chance to discuss it with Fulvio. She couldn't remember why she hadn't, but it was too late now.

It was all her fault. She had given in to the temptation of letting others take care of her for a change. But it was not fair, especially to Jane. Alice could sense her daughter was worried about work, the long-term repercussions of the global financial crisis, or something like that. Jane's refusal to tell Sara how ill her grandmother really was gave Alice the exact measure of how inconvenient, even obscene, her condition was, just as her death would soon be. She was inhabiting a different plane of existence, and perhaps that's why Rachele and Cesira had managed to find her. Maybe she'd been the one to reach out to them, and not the opposite.

Following these thoughts, she approached the bathroom with an ease that surprised her but she did not trust. She knew from experience that a wave of pain could arrive suddenly, force her to double over, break her before receding. When it subsided, after attacks that seemed to become increasingly stronger and longer, it left her drained, almost like the contractions of labor. She cautiously combed her gray hair, splashed some cold water on her cheeks. Better not to linger. Liliana could arrive at any minute and resume her litany of *pobrecita,* sometimes Alice pretended to be asleep just to avoid being treated like a two-year old. From the living room a door led to the garage, but the car was missing. She remembered the muffled sound of the engine earlier on. Of course, Jane had taken the car. So, what now?

She got closer to the wall and caressed her bike. Maybe. She climbed on the seat, tested a pedal, wavered dangerously, and put a foot down. She tried again. The garage walls forced her to follow an unnatural trajectory, a continuous curve. She would definitely have done better on a straight path. The faint smell of humidity and gas lingering in the air was strong enough to give her nausea. She saw the garage door in front of her and abruptly turned the handlebars. She hadn't realized she was moving so slowly. The rotation was enough to make the bicycle stall, stay balanced for a moment and then start to veer to the left. She put her foot down just in time to avoid falling. Whoever said that you never forget how to ride a bike was obviously misguided. She needed to find another solution.

She let the bike fall with a bang and pressed a button, the garage door rose slowly, a thick fog drowning out the colors of her neighborhood. It was colder than she thought. She put on Jane's old oversized jacket that was hanging on the wall, she breathed in deeply and stepped out of the house.

It isn't easy to tear yourself away from the indefinite and perfect your strictly individual version of reality—your very own birth certificate, name, signature, favorite mug, college degree, personalized keychain. And then you realize that it's all an illusion, or rather it's all on loan, and that bit by bit you have to give everything back. Cancer had taken from her, in quick succession, her bicycle, walks, sleep, control over her bowels, independence. She had rebelled at the beginning, she had cried and shrieked. She had even blamed Jane, as if for some mysterious reason she enjoyed treating her like a cripple, coming to see her twice a day, and relying so much on Liliana. Poor Jane, she was only doing what she thought she was supposed to do. Didn't Alice recite Edgar Lee Masters's verse for her over and over again? *Act your part well, there all the honor lies*. It wasn't Edgar Lee Masters, it was that other one, whatever his name was. Enough with the quotes, what an awful habit. She recalled with embarrassment the scene of the night before, how she had gone over conjugations as if they held the key to her life, exploiting Jane's uneasy compassion. Now her clinging to grammar struck her as inadequate, pathetic. No verb tense can make sense of the fog that engulfs you. Or rather, you would need to invent a new one—the indefinite. Different, less presumptuous than the infinitive, which does not truly befit mortals. The indefinite, the only way to avoid subcategories, tenses. No present perfect, historical past, pluperfect, imperfect. Infinite indefinite, indefinitely infinite. There, she had fallen for it again, she always gave in to her passion for cataloguing, to her faith that language could bridge any chasm. The less she managed to speak, the more it seemed important to her to understand the reasons behind words and silence.

The fog was not dense enough to shield Alice from her neighbor. She was certainly coming back from a trip somewhere, she got out of a taxi and the driver unloaded her suitcase. Alice crossed to the other side of the road acting indifferent, she did not want to give the impression that she was avoiding her, but she most certainly did not want to waste time talking about the weather or the latest addition to downtown Bethesda's dining options. She pretended to focus on the road and make herself invisible. She could feel the eyes of the woman on her back and looked down at her legs, worried. The purple flannel leggings comforted her. It was one of her fears, when she had started getting old, that she would one day go out of the house naked, or wearing something inappropriate for a respectable lady. It's easy to let yourself go, drool while eating, avoid cooking, wear the same undershirt for days on end, bask in your own sour smell. Nest, shelter, den, and the sense of unreality of those never-ending days when you don't say a word to another living being.

The thought of Sara, her beloved and distant granddaughter, took her by surprise. In a memorable fight with Jane, less than a year before, Sara had yelled that her real mother was Alice, because she owed her life to her. It was a crude interpretation of their family history, presumably put forth only to hurt Jane, who in fact looked quite offended when she related the exchange, word for word, to Alice. True though, that if there had ever been a time when Alice had managed to have an influence on her daughter, it had been precisely at the beginning of Jane's third—and last, thank God—pregnancy. The consequences of that victory had been more relevant and long-lasting than she had anticipated. When she'd convinced Jane to accept yet one more child, when she'd assured her that she'd be there to help, she'd been thinking of a few outings during the weekend, perhaps some sleep-overs, pancakes with blueberries in the morning. She certainly hadn't intended to suggest that she would become the child's primary caregiver. Jane, however, had interpreted the offer differently, and when Alice realized there had been a misunderstanding it was too late to revise the terms of the deal. She had faltered at the beginning, under the weight of the sleepless nights, her messed up schedule. But it had been a matter of a few weeks. Sara had soon overcome all resistance, she had wrapped her in the vortex of that new maternity, so strong and untimely. And to keep up with Sara's pace that got steadier and more demanding every day, Alice—she understood it well now—

had stopped aging. She started taking care of herself and her appearance like she hadn't done in ages, perhaps like she'd never really done, because for little Sara every dinner was a party, and she was disappointed if Alice did not prepare herself meticulously in front of the mirror before sitting down. And Alice, who after a day of work would have happily changed straight into her pajamas, resorted to buying fancy dresses just for the pleasure of wearing them for those elaborate dinners in honor of her princess. She insisted that Sara finish getting ready on her own, wash her hands, maybe read a bit if there was time, and in the meantime she set the table, gave the last touches to the dinner, lit the candles, arranged the flowers in the vase. Sometimes she even managed to print the menu, which she carefully arranged on the plate, on top of the napkin. The menu in question often consisted of grilled cheese sandwiches with a side of baby carrots, but neither she nor Sara felt this detail detracted from the grandeur of the experience.

She was the one who owed her existence to Sara, not the opposite. Her granddaughter had extended her life by at least ten years. Maybe it wasn't a coincidence that she'd fallen ill when Sara had dived into that incomprehensible adolescence and she had been left with nobody to look after. Now she was sorry to leave like that, without a chance to say goodbye. Oh Sara, Sara, what are you doing so far away, you should have seen me in these last few months, when everything required so much energy, you should have seen me eating reheated foods straight from the pan to save myself the effort of washing a dish, drinking from the same cup for days, and once even swallowing spoonfuls of cold chickpeas directly from the can. Why can't we have just one last fancy dress dinner, what am I doing in these awful flannel leggings? What are you doing out West, and why don't you ever write?

That's what other people are for, after all. They ensure that we don't lose sight of ourselves. Remembering the basic rules of sociability cannot do anything but good. That train of thought brought Alice's attention back to the clothes she was wearing. No need to be picky, she concluded, it was already an accomplishment that she had succeeded in getting dressed, in a bit of a haphazard manner, yes, but luckily she was in the United States. To leave Italy had been the right decision for her, it would have been hard to put up with the old country's obsession with fashion, all its unwritten rules about what you can and cannot do, eat, say, the blind allegiance to protocol and appearance. Leaving had been easy after all, she was a young woman in love back then, eager to put an ocean between her and her painful memories. Deciding to stay had been much harder, especially after receiving that letter from Fulvio. Lately there had been days when she thought she was waking up in her bedroom in L'Aquila, the sliver of light under the door was just the same, strange she hadn't noticed that before. And now that the fog was dissipating, the autumn crispness evoked walks in the woods, her father bent down to collect yellow mushrooms with elaborate tops that Alice thought belonged to marine creatures, like corals or anemones.

She realized she was out of breath despite having covered only a short distance. She sat on a bench, one of those little benches decorated with floral motifs and poems that were scattered around downtown Bethesda. She had always loved them, she liked to walk past them, read the verses and imagine a story. Fulvio would certainly laugh if he glanced at those awkward lines, and mock her for calling them "verses." Or maybe he would get angry instead, because poetry is a serious thing, because Esenin used his own blood as ink? Give me a break, Fulvio, you're as grouchy as ever, poetry changes with the latitude and the passing of time. Poetry does not need to be tragedy. Poetry can be a colorful bench that invites passersby to rest, and an old lady to imagine a story.

The back of that particular bench—she did not have to

turn around to know it—bore the phrase "Clouds caught in the treetops." She silently went over the line a few times, until she realized it contained an invitation, and that all she wanted to do was visit the clouds trapped in the treetops along the Capital Crescent Trail. Walking all the way there was out of the question, but she somehow remembered that the benches marked the stops of the trolley, the little tram-looking bus that made its way around Bethesda. And even before the thought had completely formed in her mind, she saw the trolley approaching, red and noisy, with its wooden seats and little balcony at the back. Since her illness had started taking hold of her, the trolley had become particularly important. She knew the route well, just like she knew the drivers with their lunches hidden under the dashboard and a cup of coffee on hand at all hours of the day. When they got halfway, near the metro stop, they would say "crossover" into a bulky Walkie Talkie. With only two trolleys going around in a loop, a driver had once explained, it was important to time their passage right.

The door opened in front of her.

"Good morning, it's so nice to see you again!" the man at the steering wheel exclaimed cheerfully, but his voice quickly faded, because the woman who got on the trolley was very different from the friendly librarian he used to know.

Very nice indeed, said Alice, or so she thought. Two boys respectfully got up from the wooden seats in the front row. She motioned to decline their offer, but then gave in, how polite of you, thanks. Cradled by the noise and bouncing of the trolley, she rested her head against the window.

"Have a nice day ma'am," said the driver while she carefully climbed down the steps. "It was a pleasure seeing you."

"Same here," Alice thought of replying, but she didn't trust the sound that would come out of her mouth. She limited herself to turn around once she landed on the sidewalk, and slowly waved her hand. The man looked puzzled, unsure whether or not to close the door, add something, perhaps offer his help. But Alice turned around again and began walking, one step cautiously after the other, towards the beginning of the Capital Crescent Trail. The cars behind were waiting, a horn honked. The trolley returned to creaking along its route.

The Capital Crescent Trail, a bike path built over an old railroad, was crowded as usual, at that time of day. Dogs—purebreds, naturally—trotted along, tethered by their leashes to their proud owners. Young women unwilling to surrender to motherhood chased the dream of a perfect body, pushing their babies in jogging strollers. Commuters sped by on racing bicycles, sporting yellow windbreakers and streamlined helmets. The most determined among them carried large saddlebags packed with important documents, a change of clothes, a couple of energy bars. Now and then, they glanced at their watches to make sure they were making good time. "On your left!" they called out as they approached, but they shouted without animosity, out of habit. The most polite even found time to utter a distracted "thank you" as they passed pedestrians and slower bikers and rushed toward their offices on Massachusetts Avenue, in Georgetown, even on Capitol Hill.

There were also old ladies who walked in pairs, because the doctor recommended 30 minutes of daily exercise to lower blood pressure and cholesterol, a chore that is not quite so boring if you do it with a friend while talking about the time when Bethesda was little more than a village, or about the last summer that was even hotter than back in 1988, or of the kids coming home for Thanksgiving. These women went only as far as Kenwood, where they commented on the luxury homes and cherry trees that in the springtime grew blossoms that were even more spectacular than the ones around the Tidal Basin, didn't you see that article in the *Post*.

Alice was familiar enough with the Capital Crescent Trail to know that it was rare to spot a couple holding hands, as if displays of affection were prohibited. Everybody, from the moms to the commuters to the old ladies, seemed to be on a mission—to get in shape, to break the previous personal record for the fastest commute, to reach the right level of cholesterol and blood sugar. Suddenly, Alice found something obscene about taking her disease, her death, out on the trail for a walk. A bit like that old movie, *Death Takes a Holiday*. She wrapped her oversized jacket more tightly around her skinny body and tried to look presentable.

"Watch out... on your left!" somebody shouted, startling her. Perhaps without realizing it, she had veered into the center of the path. She decided to leave the pavement altogether and move to the gravel that ran alongside it. Better, that was better, she could go straight just by walking alongside the paved surface, and she could follow her own pace, with no fear of disrupting the bike traffic. That way, she could even try to go as far as the aqueduct tunnel and beyond. She didn't care what she would do next, or how she would get back. Whatever happened, she thought, that excursion was an unexpected gift, given the season.

A bicycle bell made her jump. A little girl went by on her bike, training wheels and all. A little girl without a helmet, that was strange. What was her mother thinking? Alice, who was trying to make herself inconspicuous, wasn't pleased when the girl turned to her, smiling, and waved hello. It lasted only a split second, but it was enough to make Alice stop, her heart racing. The pink bows in the girl's braids looked a bit too tight. They created a part on the back of her head that revealed a glimpse of fair skin under a veil of fine hair.

"Celestina!" Alice exclaimed, but soon felt ashamed. It must be a mistake. What could Celestina possibly be doing on the Capital Crescent Trail? And yet, the little girl turned around again, her crystalline laughter seeming to shatter as it struck the pavement. I was right, then, it is you, Celestina! Of course you are riding without a helmet, then, nobody wore helmets in those days. You still make mischief, though, don't you, frightening old ladies with your magic bicycle bell?

Alice tried to walk faster but soon realized she'd never be able to catch up; the girl was already disappearing from view. It had always been that way, with Alice huffing and puffing and Celestina coming out of nowhere at the last turn of the road, passing her effortlessly to win yet another race. How could things go any differently now, when Alice had grown so old and frail and Celestina was still a little girl? The age difference puzzled Alice, who grew pensive. She forgot her pursuit and resumed her careful walk, her eyes fixed on the ground. At first she didn't notice the tall dark figure walking beside her.

Ne reminiscaris, Domine, delicta nostra vel parentum nostrorum, neque vindictam sumas de peccatis nostris.

The voice was little more than a whisper, yet unmistakable.

"Sister Arcangela!"

The figure kept talking as she walked, barely glancing at the book in her hands.

Domine, ne in furore tuo arguas me, neque in ira tua corripias me. Miserere mei, Domine, quoniam infirmus sum: sana me, Domine, quoniam conturbata sunt ossa mea. Et anima mea turbata est valde: sed tu, Domine, usquequo?

"Sister Arcangela!" Alice called again.

Yes, it was her, with her threatening Latin phrases that she recited with such devout stubbornness, as if her salvation depended on their perfect articulation. It occurred to Alice that if she wanted to attract her attention, she needed to try something different, perhaps speak her same language. The words of the penitential psalm rose to her lips. She repeated the antiphony.

Ne reminiscaris, Domine, delicta nostra vel parentum nostrorum, neque vindictam sumas de peccatis nostris.

Sister Arcangela did not seem to notice Alice's presence but waited until she finished before resuming her lines.

Discedite a me, omnes, qui operamini iniquitatem: quoniam exaudivit Dominus vocem fletus mei.

Exaudivit Dominus deprecationem meam, Dominus orationem meam suscepit.

She was walking faster and faster. Alice tried to keep up but soon fell behind. She screamed, as if trying to shake off her weakness.

Ne reminiscaris, Domine, delicta nostra vel parentum nostrorum, neque vindictam sumas de peccatis nostris.

But Sister Arcangela's dark silhouette was already merging with the trees along the trail. Alice's words were scattered to the wind.

Words scattered to the wind? Wasn't that a line from a poem?

"Yes, but not one of *my* poems" said an animated voice at her side. "You always mix things up, silly... But no, it's that other guy who wrote it. Shoot, I can't remember his name... Why are you looking at me like that? You're mad because I called you silly, aren't you? But it's not your fault, you're still a child! You actually know a lot of poems for a little girl..."

Alberto?! Why are you running so fast, and what are you doing with Daddy's hunting rifle?

"Did you really believe I was going to shut up and obey the Germans, march wherever they told me to go? Eins, Zwei, Eins, Zwei... Is that what you thought of me? You heard about the armistice, didn't you? What are they still doing here? Why don't they pack up their bags and go home? What are they waiting for?"

You're right, Alberto. What are they doing here? But wait a minute, I'm coming with you.

"Come on now, you're being silly again. How can you possibly come with me, when you are so little!? I am seventeen, and they're even saying that *I* am too young! Speaking of which, just in case somebody asks you, you tell them I just turned eighteen, okay?"

He suddenly seemed uncomfortable. He loosened the scarf around his neck, opened his jacket, and took out a big stack of papers held together by a purple ribbon.

"Listen, Alice, you gave me an idea... My poems... Why don't you keep them? They'll only weigh me down."

He put the packet in Alice's hands and ran away, light on his feet. She tried to chase him but quickly fell behind. Perhaps he was right, she would never be able to keep up. She was so weak that she couldn't even take care of his papers. One after another, they escaped from the ribbon and flew along the path like fallen leaves. Was it autumn already?

The pointless pursuit had taken Alice close to the entrance of the tunnel. The traffic of pedestrians and occasional cyclists had thinned out, and the path was empty except for a few late commuter bikers. To enter the tunnel Alice would have to abandon the gravel and walk on the pavement, in the dark. She wished she had brought a flashlight, not only to see where she was going, but also to signal her presence to those entering the tunnel behind her. She looked back. Perhaps if she hurried, she would get to the other side before another cyclist approached the tunnel. She took a deep breath before diving into the darkness. She knew she could not rely on her eyes, and that the only way to walk in a straight line was to use the wall as a handrail. She stretched out her fingers to brush the side of the tunnel, felt dirt and dampness under her nails, focused on her breathing and kept marching toward the light.

At the end of the tunnel, a familiar presence sends shivers down her spine. It's Eric with his torn jeans and indigo t-shirt, smiling his ironic smile, his blond head leaning slightly to one side. He is stretching out his thumb, asking for a ride. How can Alice say no? She slows down. Eric's smile is now triumphant; he turns around and heads toward the river, as if forgetting about her. But she is tired of elusive encounters and fleeting ghosts, and without a second thought runs after him. The ground around the path is not landscaped. It is slippery, rugged, full of creepers, smooth moss, fallen trees. Alice realizes she is barefoot, though she can't tell whether she just lost her slippers or left them by her bed earlier on. Her flannel leggings are torn and muddy. She scrapes her hands as she reaches for branches, bushes, anything that might slow her descent toward the river. When she finally stops on the banks of the Potomac, Eric has once again disappeared. Exhausted and frustrated, she tries to catch her breath as she looks around.

The Potomac is still recovering from a rainy season. For weeks its impetuous currents have carried and deposited the debris left behind by the summer storms. Finally, in this mild beginning of fall, the river is returning to its regular majestic course. Alice is mesmerized by the sun's reflection on the ripples.

"Hi there..."

Unlike Alice, Eric does not look tired at all. He smiles at her as he sits on the grass with his usual casual air, the expression of a man who is not yet home and is already planning his next journey.

"Long time no see," he reproaches her with a smile. "I was beginning to think you'd never make it."

She moves closer. I'm sorry I'm late, she thinks of telling him. I got distracted, half a century goes by in the blink of an eye.

"Why don't you sit down?"

Alice bends over with great caution, as she learned in physical therapy. First one knee, then the other. She tries to move closer to Eric, but the sloping ground is tricky, and she ends up flat on her back. The shape of the few clouds above reminds her of the ceiling above her bed. She is not uncomfortable, but how can she possibly get back on her feet now?

"They were wrong, all of them! You did great... How is our little girl doing?"

She is fine, very well actually. She is so beautiful, our Jane, so confident, so grown up. We are grandparents, you know? We have three grandchildren, and our eldest granddaughter is pregnant. We will be great-grandparents soon!

She is not sure whether she has actually told him all of that, or these are just her thoughts, and she searches for clues in his reaction. Parenting, grand-parenting, great-grand-parenting... These are strange notions for a guy in his twenties, she wouldn't want to upset him.

But if Eric has heard her, he doesn't seem to mind being almost a great-grandfather. He smiles as he slowly combs the grass with his fingers. Once in a while he lifts his eyes and looks at the river shimmering, just a few yards away. The fog has dissipated completely; it's going to be a glorious autumn day.

Alice is beaming with delight and trembling with fear. Now he will realize I am old, she thinks. She is suddenly concerned about her looks and her age. She leans on her elbow and lies on one side, surreptitiously checking the condition of her flannel pants. She cannot believe her eyes. Her legs emerge from under a miniskirt, and they are firm and tanned, the legs of a person who has never set foot in a gym but has walked all over, out of desire and curiosity. She has not seen those legs in a while and bends her knee just to watch the muscle flex under the tight, smooth skin. When she overcomes her surprise, she realizes that Eric has gotten very close, so close he is practically leaning on her. Alice recognizes that unforgettable smell of wet underbrush and salty mist and follows his lips as they move toward hers until they are so close they become blurry, and then invisible.

Kissing her with my soul upon my lips
It suddenly took flight.

***

Jane hesitantly looked at her cellphone.

"Why don't you just go ahead and call her?" Jeff suggested.

"And what if the medication has already worked and she's asleep?"

He didn't answer. They had finally arrived at their destination. He pulled in front of a modest two-story house, with bars on the windows of the first floor and a "foreclosure" sign standing in the neglected front yard.

"Dear God, how much did they pay for this shack?"

"Too much, I'm sure," responded Jeff dryly, as he flipped through the documents in a folder labelled "Hyattsville."

"Here they are," he said. "The house's estimated value is $300,000 and they owe $400,000 to the bank. How the hell can you be so stupid?"

Jane looked for Liliana's number in her recently called log.

"They bought it at the end of 2005, when the housing bubble was about to burst," Jeff scoffed, continuing to leaf through. "Here is the sales contract. $450,000 for this shed in the middle of nowhere. They tried to sell it for $350,000 but no one wanted it. Nobody wants this thing right now, especially when they don't know whether prices will fall even lower. He's unemployed, she's a housewife. The bank has waited on them way too long, if you ask me."

"Shh... Liliana, is that you?" Jane had barely followed Jeff's reasoning while trying to reach Liliana on the phone. "Oh, thank goodness you've arrived. Okay, I have to turn off my phone right now, but leave me a message if I need to stop at the store, I'll call you back as soon as I'm done. Bye."

Liliana's "I am here" was a bit of an approximation. She was just coming into view of Alice's house when she received the call. Jane, on her part, cut her off as soon as she heard exactly what she wanted to hear, and hung up reassured.

"Liliana just got to mom's place, everything is fine," she reported to Jeff.

"Good."

They walked a few steps along the driveway. Jane tried to concentrate on their task.

"Who did you say lives here?"

She hadn't listened to a word he said, as usual. Jeff tried not to show his irritation.

"A couple, young, he's back from Afghanistan, she's a housewife. Jane, please let's not start again. We're not social workers, and they should've thought twice before biting off quite a bit more than they could chew."

"It's not like they bought a mansion with a pool," Jane said, looking around.

"It doesn't matter, everything is relative. They could've done what I did and rented a place until they were sure they could afford a home."

"Yes, but what about the idea that each generation must have a higher standard of living than the one before... What did they use to call that? Oh yes, the American Dream, remember that? What a dream that was, and what an awakening we're living through right now!"

Jane looked at her reflection in the glass door and adjusted the necklace around her neck. Her mother was right, it looked good on her.

"Anyway, you're right, we're not social workers," she conceded, hoping to dodge an argument."

Jeff rang the bell. A cry startled Jane.

"Now what?" asked Jeff.

"Did you hear that? It sounded like a baby crying."

"Yes, of course, the picture wouldn't be complete without a baby. Please Jane, if you keep reacting this way, sooner or later we'll end up just like them."

Jeff rang again.

"Are they pretending not to hear us?" Jeff asked, nervously. "If this doesn't work, we'll have to come back with the police."

He was about to ring a third time, when the door opened. Dressed in a Marine's uniform, a stout, bald man filled the door frame, towering a good six inches over Jeff. His arm held a child who looked tiny with his head bent in the hollow of his father's neck. The man ignored their outstretched hands. Without a single word, he turned around to lead the way inside the house.

They were already sitting at the table and Jeff had already started off with his legal rituals and formulas when a young woman came up from the basement, holding a suitcase. She took the child from his father's arms, spread a blanket near the window, and proceeded to change his diaper. Jane instinctively got up and followed her.

"Do you need any help?"

The woman shook her head. She was very young, Jane thought, maybe just a little older than Sara, probably a high-school drop-out.

"My name is Jane."

"I'm Olga," the other woman said, shaking Jane's hand and looking already more relaxed.

"It's a pleasure to meet you, Olga. Listen, if you'd like to go sit with your husband and go over the… transaction, please go ahead, and I'll look after the baby. You know, I have three kids and a lot of diaper experience."

Jane smiled, feeling almost apologetic for using motherhood as a tool to impart solidarity.

"How old?" Olga asked.

"What?"

"How old are the kids?"

"Oh, well, they're not really kids anymore. Richard, the oldest, is 28, Kate is 24, and Sara, the baby, is 18."

"That's wonderful! I always thought I'd like to have many children myself, but now I'm not so sure…"

She looked around the bare living room.

"Oh, don't say that, you guys are young…" Jane said unconvincingly.

Young and in trouble. Jane heard Jeff's patronizing voice inside of her, and she struggled to silence it.

"And then," she continued, "even if you don't have any other children, it's not the end of the world. I'm an only child, and a very happy one."

"Really?" Olga asked incredulously.

It was true, thought Jane. An only child, and a very happy one. She made a mental note to tell Alice that evening. Deep down, she didn't even regret not having known her father, Eric, the hitchhiker in the indigo shirt, who must have been a bit of a troublemaker.

Look at those two, brooded Jeff, still stuck at the table with the man. He couldn't hear their conversation, but he could easily guess what it was about. All those stories of equal opportunity and pay, but then women can always fall back on gossiping about milk and children while men are doomed to take care of business. To make matters worse, the business in question proceeded at an excruciatingly slow speed, since the brute in camouflage insisted on reading every single line in the pile of documents he had to sign. Had he read the mortgage contract with the same scrutiny, Jeff thought, he would have spared himself a lot of trouble.

Every now and then, the man asked a question. Jeff answered the best he could without resorting to technical terms—the legalese that Alice used to tease him about, not always kindly—that might sound mysterious to his interlocutor and even provoke his anger. Jeff didn't feel comfortable. He thought he knew that absent gaze, that calmness that could in a matter of seconds turn to blind fury. He had learned to recognize it in his father. Jeff couldn't shake off the feeling of danger that had settled over him when the door snapped open and the man had appeared. It wasn't just his height; he was truly imposing in every way. And why had he donned his uniform to welcome them? Where did he think he was? If Jeff hadn't been afraid of looking ridiculous, he would have asked Jane to switch places, changing diapers all of a sudden seemed a desirable task.

Finally, the last form was filled out, and Jeff began to feel safe. Too safe.

"Remember," he said, as soon as he had collected all the documents, "that you'll have to be out of here in two hours. There's no need to leave your keys, we'll have all the locks changed by the end of the day anyway."

"Thanks for reminding me, dickhead, otherwise I might have just spent the rest of the day napping on the bare floor," the man hissed, rolling his mad eyes before pointing them at Jeff.

"No, that's got nothing to do with it, I was just saying that so you don't get scare..."

Jeff didn't have the courage to finish his sentence.

"Jane!" he called, in a slightly sharper pitch than he intended.

The women turned around. From their viewpoint at the window, they could see a camouflaged back and Jeff's tense expression facing them.

"Jane, we're done, we should go..."

The other man took advantage of the fact that the women could not see his face to throw Jeff a dirty look.

"Jane!" he whispered mockingly, imitating Jeff's voice. "Jane, mommy dear, come, quick, this ogre here scares me!"

The man realized that Olga and Jane had noticed something was wrong, he felt their eyes on his back. And he could also sense it from Jeff, who was staring in their direction, trying hard to avoid the angry glare focused on him at close range. The man quivered with rage. All those hours of training to end up like putty in the hands of lawyers and real estate agents, without being allowed to fire a single shot. What a waste.

"Men like you are not even worth getting my hands dirty."

That signaled the end of their conversation. The man stood up and walked towards his wife at the window. Both she and Jane had already gotten up.

"Everything done?" Olga asked.

"Yes, everything is done," the man responded, taking the baby from her arms. His gaze moved from his wife to Jane, who instinctively touched her bare neck.

"Please, if you'll let me, I would very much like to offer this necklace to your wife," she said, pushing aside all her convictions about female autonomy. She had followed her instinct when she had taken off her necklace to give it to Olga, but she didn't want to create more tension for the couple. Who knows what would happen to these two, between these two, after she and Jeff left. The man looked at the luminous circle resting on his wife's neck.

"That's beautiful," he said. "It really suits you."

Back in the car, Jeff slumped into his seat with a sigh of relief.

"So, let me recap… First, you leave me alone while I deal with that giant, and then you give your mother's precious necklace to his wife! Look, foreclosures are our silver lining these days, I bet we'll end up doing many of them. Do you intend to present every loser we come across with a piece of jewelry?"

Jane looked pensive.

"But there was something about those two, wasn't there? And there was also something about my necklace. As soon as I thought of giving it to Olga, I felt like it was the right thing to do. I'm sure my mother will agree."

"Look, we need to talk, it's not fair that I should have to take care of everything…"

But the thought of her mother reminded Jane to turn her phone on. She found seven messages. Most of them were from Liliana, each more anxious and incomprehensible than the one before. Another was from her neighbor who had just gotten back from a business trip. Then, the one from the police.

MOAB, UTAH
OCTOBER 15, 2010

This time her mother had crossed the line, Sara thought. Jane had a tendency to make all decisions on her own, even when they had repercussions on other people's lives, but this was too much. How could she possibly deprive her children of the chance to even attend the ceremony...

"What ceremony?" Jane interjected. There had been no ceremony. Everything went very fast. After all, Nonna Ali herself had explicitly reiterated, the evening before she died, that she didn't want priests around her deathbed. Jane's usage of Alice's nickname struck Sara as a cheap trick to placate her, and it had instead the opposite effect.

"She told you this the evening before? So, you knew she was about to die, and you didn't tell me anything?"

Now, Jane began talking to her like a small child, or rather, Sara thought, an idiot.

"There's always an evening before, isn't there? But how can you possibly know?"

This was in fact one of her regrets, but she didn't know how to explain it to her resentful daughter.

"You only really find that out later, in hindsight."

The conundrum further annoyed Sara.

"Had I known," Jane continued, oblivious to her daughter's growing irritation, "I would have done everything differently. Not only would I have called you, but I would also have stayed by her side myself, don't you think?"

Fine, fine. Dying is inevitable, yet unpredictable, and it's only after the fact that we realize that the evening before was, in fact, the last evening—would her mother ever stop with her platitudes?! They could safely agree on that. But the funeral? Wasn't it a bit inconsiderate to tell Sara about it all when everything was already said and done?

"But I just told you!" Jane protested. "The body was in bad shape, we had to hurry. We went to the closest funeral home. It's not like we could postpone it, so what was the point of having you all rush here?"

"But you could have let me decide, right? You know how much Nonna Ali did for me, how close we were, how much I owe her…"

Jane nobly decided to ignore the reproach hidden in those words. All she needed was for Sara to pull out the failed abortion story again.

"Come on, we'll talk about it at Thanksgiving… It's coming up, and we'll all be here together."

Sara shivered at the thought of the whole family around the table, siblings and significant others, with her mother's efforts to avoid all possible arguments resulting in no meaningful talk at all, for an entire interminable day. Jane's unfailingly dry turkey would sit at the center of the table. It would be impossible to survive another Thanksgiving without Nonna Ali, who could always sense when the small talk was becoming unbearable and would get up, announce that the doctor had recommended a digestive walk, and ask Sara to join her.

"Tell me about you instead. How do you like Utah?"

The mere name of the state conjured dinosaurs and Mormons in Jane's mind. Sara cut her off.

"Fine, thanks. Anyway, I need to go, there's people here, bye."

She returned to the dining area. It was about 11:00 a.m. and the café was almost empty. The only customers were a couple of very committed hikers who had left at dawn and were already back, ready for Moab's best cappuccino and a slice of Julia's famous cranberry orange bread. Sara brought them their order and disappeared behind the counter.

Her mother had shown once more how shallow she was. She had acted as if mourning Nonna Ali among strangers in Moab was the same as mourning her among those who knew and loved her. She was sure that many people, from colleagues at the library to fellow volunteers at the homeless shelter, would have wanted to get together to commemorate her. Jane had taken advantage of the situation to assert her power over Nonna Ali, to reclaim her, it was as simple as that.

And yet it wasn't. Remorse crept in, carried by a nagging feeling that she hadn't behaved much better than her mother. She wasn't even sure she had mentioned Nonna Ali to Julia or Una. She was too busy navigating her stormy present to think about her. And what was the point in talking about her now, in reconstructing a figure that was already fading away, a person that had already reverted to ash? All she needed to do was change verb tenses. It was enough to say "Nonna Ali *was* a librarian," and "Nonna Ali *loved* poetry," instead of "Nonna Ali *is* a librarian, she *loves* poetry." Nobody would even notice. She *was* your Italian grandmother, right? Once it swallows you, the past blunts all differences. Nonna Ali was dead, just like Eric, the mysterious hitchhiker-lover-wanderer who had perhaps passed on to Jane, and from Jane to Sara, his restlessness, his anxiety. In the only photo of the two of them together, Alice and Eric were smiling, next to one another, on a dusty road somewhere. Then he stopped, while she kept walking further and further away, increasingly distancing herself from that moment frozen in time. But now she was back in the frame, her fifty-year journey reduced to its right proportions, a ripple on the surface of the ocean. Imperceptible, insignificant. And Nonna Ali, once passed the ford, was back with Eric, and far away from them all, the noisy living.

Now, when speaking of her, everyone would instinctively correct the syntax, as they did when referring to Eric, the few times he still came up in conversation. Death relies on verb tenses, Sara concluded while carefully slicing the warm cranberry orange bread, afraid it would crumble under her knife. Death relishes the imperfect or, even more, that strange tense they have in Italian, the historical past.

"Sara..."

Julia's voice was a whisper. From the look on her face, Sara realized she had heard the news.

"There is another call for you. Come here, I'll take over."

"Hello!" rang Una's voice from the other side of the line. Her tone, on the contrary, seemed to suggest she didn't know anything.

Finally, Sara thought. All summer long, Una had replaced colleagues on vacation and that had forced her to travel to various parks, further and further away from Moab. Their excursions had become less frequent. Sara realized she had spent the last few months waiting for her rare visits.

"Hi. You're back from Bryce."

"Yes, finally! How is it going?"

Sara feared she wouldn't be able to control herself if she told Una the truth.

"I... I'm okay, I guess."

"Look, why don't you come see me this afternoon? We can take a walk and grab a bite to eat. You down?"

"I have to ask Julia and make sure she doesn't need me."

"Sure, perfect, ask her," Una said, trying to hide her disappointment at Sara's scarce enthusiasm. What could there be to do, on an October evening, in a café that closes at three in the afternoon even in the height of the tourist season?

"Yes, of course you can go," Julia responded immediately, peering deeply into Sara's reddened eyes.

Una had thought of everything.

"I'm leaving the office as soon as possible. You can borrow one of Julia's bikes, head over to my place and if I am not there yet just go in anyway, ask Julia for my house keys. Should we say around five?"

"Sure. See you later."

Una's place consisted of one large room with separate areas for a basic kitchen, a couch, and a futon on the floor. The drawn curtains kept the daylight at bay and allowed the shadows to wrap the interior in an embrace that softened its corners and contrasts. Sara took off her shoes, enjoying the cool brick floor under her feet. She walked over to the window and pulled back the curtain. Tomato plants, heads of lettuce, and aromatic herbs graced a vegetable garden. Two mountain bikes were parked in a little shed. Sara was tempted to step out, the outdoors seemed to be a natural extension of the house. She thought of the mess in her room, back in Bethesda. Clean and dirty clothes strewn everywhere, Victoria's Secrets catalogs resting on a neglected skateboard. That clutter reflected her confusion. She had turned the corner running and lost sight of the child she had been, without forming the faintest idea of the woman she wanted to be. In this no man's land, she had fallen prey to the strangest fears. Maybe it all started when she'd abandoned Nonna Ali. Or maybe it was just a curious coincidence, that her grandmother's illness and her own confusion overlapped so closely? Nonna Ali had reacted to surgeries and therapies like a cat, withdrawing into herself and avoiding the compassionate and mildly disgusted looks of others. And Sara, strangely enough, had chosen to listen to her mother's lies about the slow progression of the disease in old people, the great medical strides of the 21st century, and so on. Hard to tell if Jane really believed everything she said herself. But the end result was that Sara had lost sight of Nonna Ali, even as she became more and more convinced of her importance in her life. Nonna Ali had raised her with books, songs and walks, leading her in the exploration of all the trails around the Potomac. Their names seemed to come straight out of a fairy tale, and still conjured wondrous landscapes in Sara's mind—Billy Goat, Cabin John, Capital Crescent. And when a bad car accident forced Sara to skip school and face a grueling physical therapy regimen, Nonna Ali had become even more protective. She had taken her granddaughter to work with her, at the library, day after day, first in a wheelchair, then on crutches, and finally—finally!—standing.

"Look, Nonna Ali!"

Sara had just discovered that she could walk again, but waited until there was no one at the reference desk to surprise her grandmother. She clung to one of the shelves of dictionaries and pulled herself up.

"Look at me!"

Her legs were tingling but felt strong, despite her lack of exercise and overwhelming excitement. Sara waited until her grandmother's eyes rested on her before moving a tiny step, from the "A" of "Astonishment" to the "B" of "Birth." And Nonna Ali, usually so restrained in her reactions, burst into tears and came closer to her, torn between the desire to hug her and the fear of upsetting her delicate, newfound balance.

Then disease, distance, and death—Nonna Ali's lonely, unforgivable death. Sara pictured for a moment the three generations of women in her family taking that last walk together. She imagined being there, with her mother, to close Alice's eyes when she got tired, when she lay down on the riverbank. Instead, Jane was busy throwing people out on the street with Jeff, while she was on a mission to make Utah's best cappuccino. She fell on the couch, put her head in her hands.

"*Mi dispiace*, Nonna Ali."

I am so sorry. Her apology sounded foreign and clumsy in the room.

***

When Sara opened her eyes, her gaze fixed on the floor, she found Una's bare feet, and then moved up to her friend's solid frame, thin waist, and worried expression. Una crouched down, as if talking to a child.

"I went to the café, I thought you were still there. Julia told me. I'm sorry."

Sara nodded.

"Julia told me you didn't know your grandmother's health had worsened so much in the last few months."

Silence.

"... and that you were very close to her."

Both statements were basically correct. Sara nodded.

"I'm sorry... I won't be much company tonight. Maybe it's better if I leave," she finally said.

Don't send me away don't send me away don't send me away.

Una sat down on the couch and took Sara's hand. Since their first excursion to Delicate Arch they had avoided all physical contact. Sara recognized the same flush of heat cutting sharply through her suffering.

"Stay if you want, but only if you want. And there's no need to talk if you don't feel like it."

Sara leaned backwards and rested her head on the cushion. She remained still for a long time, as if all life had drained from her. She heard Una get up and move around, open doors, look in drawers. She seemed busy preparing something. Maybe dinner, Sara thought, and was tempted to tell her to stop, she was not hungry at all. At some point she realized the brightness behind the windows had become muted, it was almost sunset. Una was standing in front of her with two backpacks.

"Let's go."

"Where?"

"Out. This is not the night to stay at home."

Sara followed passively and climbed into the Jeep. From Una's house at the edge of Moab, they took an isolated road that Sara did not recognize. The vehicle bounced up and down on the rough pavement, raising clouds of dust.

"Here we are."

They parked and got out. Una took the backpacks from the Jeep, gave one to Sara and kept the largest one for herself. She started walking on a downhill path, occasionally turning around to make sure Sara was following, until they reached the banks of the Colorado River. Una approached a small pier that stretched into the water, untied a canoe from a pole, jumped in, and stretched her hand out to help Sara.

"You know how to swim, right?"

"Yes, of course."

"Hopefully we won't need to, but just in case…"

Now the canoe cut through dense water, leaving a firm line in its stead. Una kept close to the shore, rowing and looking at the river while Sara crouched down on the deck of the canoe. The rocks began to rise around them, eventually hiding the sight of the setting sun that imbued the frayed clouds with pink streaks and the canyon walls with amber hues. A great blue heron glided softly over the river before resolutely plunging into the water. Sara realized she didn't particularly care to know where they were going. She felt comfortable letting herself be carried by the flow without resisting, abandoning herself to the same river that with infinite patience, for millions of years, had dug the intricate labyrinths that now stretched hundreds of miles, the same river that sometimes became exhausted and dry in the desert, its path to the sea seemingly lost, and yet always managed to resurface and resume its creation of wonders.

Una let the canoe run aground on a tiny beach and jumped nimbly to the shore. Sara handed her the backpacks and looked at her as if waiting for directions.

"Now," Una said, "follow this trail next to the river. It's so overgrown you may not be able to recognize it at times, but all you need to do to find your way is to walk along the shore. Nobody can hear you, and nobody can see you. Run, shout, do whatever you like. I'll wait here."

Sara hesitated, but then realized that Una had done talking and was busy searching for dry branches to start a fire. Sara took a few cautious steps, until a bush hid Una from sight. Her slow pace felt awkward, she lengthened her stride and soon she found herself running, chasing the shifting images in her head, merging them with those created by the river and the current, dancing to the beat of her anxious heart. She ran until she was out of breath and a strange noise rose from her dry throat. She turned a corner and the majesty of the landscape surrounded her on all sides. The sun that had just disappeared bathed the luminous outline of the rock wall in front of her. She glanced at its crevices, its unusual formations, almost like the map of a distant, mysterious land. She located a boulder jutting out slightly, like a stone sentinel over the river. This, she decided, was Cape Nonna Ali, a reference point, a sacred destination for a pilgrimage. Nonna Ali would have liked that, Sara thought. No plaque, no speeches, no funeral procession, just a flight of sparrows at sunset. The contours drawn by the light on the rock wall became blurry as the moon rose into view. A coyote howled to greet it.

After setting up camp in just a few experienced moves, Una crouched by the fire, and doubts descended upon her. Was she making a major mistake? She had never been afraid of the forces of nature, not even as a little girl. Instead she was frightened by unpredictable human reactions, killing as a sport, the equally bloody battle of seduction, the insidious rhetoric of those who never show their true colors, hypocrisy masked by good manners. But maybe her inclinations were not the same as Sara's, as much as she would have liked them to be, as much as she would have liked their thoughts to fit together. She smiled, yielded to her desires, and corrected herself; rather than their thoughts, she wished their bodies would fit together, that was the truth. Since their first encounter at the grocery store, the idea of Sara's body, of Sara's body against hers, had kept her company. She had replayed their conversation by Delicate Arch a thousand times, going over Sara's strange recommendation to follow the moon carefully, slowly. Una struggled to pull herself away from that memory. There was no indication that Sara shared her desires. Quite the contrary. A cheerleader, ready to jump through hoops to entertain the captain of the football team. She imagined her in her environment of rich, spoiled girls waiting for their Thirsty Thursdays and an even crazier weekend. *Una, Una, come back to yourself, you are out of your mind.*

This nocturnal expedition, though inspired by the best intentions, could potentially turn disastrous. Even the canoe felt heavier than expected, Una's forearms were weak and sore. She had never taken anyone to that path, that secret beach that had witnessed her joys, sorrows, and discoveries. The rocks, the river, the sunset, never failed to comfort her, but what made her think they could produce the same effect on Sara? Perhaps the city girl in her, so easily overwhelmed by the sights of nature, would feel frightened and alone in that barren landscape.

The moon appeared from behind the cliff. A coyote howled from a distance, then another, closer. Una put another log on the fire and enjoyed the bright flames. Suddenly, she noticed a discordant note in the animals' cries. She took a few steps down the path, standing in wait with her arms folded. Was someone crying for help? The sound fed her fears. Perhaps Sara, who could barely distinguish the Milky Way from a cloud, was now prey to her ghosts. Perhaps those same shadows that had so many times risen from the river to console Una would instead drag Sara down into their swirling whirlpools. The strange, piercing note was approaching, carried by the chorus of the coyotes. All of a sudden, Sara came barreling out in a screaming run from the nearest turn in the path, looking for her. Una didn't have time to move or speak. She felt the impact of that sweating and panting body against hers and only later, as she softly caressed Sara's hips in the dark, she realized she must have opened her arms to embrace her.

OUT THERE
AFTERWARDS

Dying, truth be told, proved easy. It was like a visit to the dentist that you dread so much but turns out to be painless. She felt a little sore, perhaps, as a result of an awkward feeling that started from her legs and invaded her whole body. It was a new, peculiar sensation... Could it be the awakening of the soul? When Eric bent down to kiss her, his shadow shielding her from the sun as it had done so many years before, the color of his eyes matched the blue of the sky in the background so perfectly that she suspected, in one supreme attempt at rationality, that they were not really eyes but slits, and he a ghostly shade without substance. He approached her slowly, and when their lips finally met, Alice heard a sharp sound, like a branch snapping. She let go, she allowed herself to yield. As she reflected upon it, afterwards, she realized she must have died there and then.

Reflecting upon it... afterwards?

The first consequence of her new condition was a curious change of perspective. Instead of looking at Eric against the blue sky, she was now looking at her own body from above, not from very far away but from above nevertheless. It seemed so natural that at the beginning she felt no surprise but rather a certain satisfaction. That was it then! Ah, how nice it would be to be able to relate her discovery to those who continued to elaborate the strangest hypotheses, like Jane bouncing from one congregation to another, from a sect to an esoteric group. Of all the theories, it was the most basic one that turned out to be true. No light at the end of the tunnel, no archangels with trumpets, no Minos wrapping his tail around the sinner. Rather, that silent suspension.

What an old woman she had become... She felt pity for that shell, abandoned on the grass like an old coat on an armchair. She would have liked to reposition it, because her joy at seeing Eric had vanquished her mature restraint and her legs were spread as if waiting for love. Her desire to make her body more dignified led to the discovery of death's second consequence, namely her inability to interfere in the slightest with what was happening on earth, not even with the events that concerned her most directly. The realization sat uncomfortably with her, but perhaps only because as a dead woman she was still in her infancy and had so much to learn and get used to. An ant crawled over the forehead of the body sprawled on the grass. I hope they find it soon, Alice thought. She had always liked that area because it looked and felt like a forest, despite being so close to the city, but that now posed a real threat. They would soon find her—squirrels, raccoons, deer, stray dogs and then crows, wary-eyed hawks, and maybe even coyotes. But why did she care so much? It was just that old body of hers. It was no different, that was apparent now, from the earth it rested on, from the rain that would soon bathe it, from the roots that would take their nourishment from it. But a little respect, come on, a little respect. Alice had looked after that body, washed it, made it presentable for eighty years. She had witnessed with joy and apprehension its blooming and its withering. But the opposite was also true—that pile of flesh and bones had faithfully served Alice's dreams, accompanied her travels, and embraced the people she loved. And if at times she had resented it as a cumbersome impediment, she now understood that that worn out envelope had instead provided her only chance to ground her ineffable essence in something real, in the world, in life. So much so that now, without that body—Alice realized it right away, and it pained her—she would never be able to dream again.

Without a body to nourish and clean, even her knowledge of time became approximate. She could not tell how many hours had elapsed since she'd changed perspective. The progression of the sun in the sky turned into an abstract, meaningless notion. She wondered how long it would take Liliana to realize the house was empty, and whether she'd be tempted to just disappear for fear of the police looking too closely into her own and her family's papers. Alice understood those concerns, she had been an immigrant herself. She hoped Liliana hadn't done something as stupid as running away, though. Jane and Jeff could make her life impossible. But even if Liliana had alerted Jane right away, they would probably start looking around town first, they'd never suspect that an old woman in her condition could walk such a long stretch of the Capital Crescent Trail. Alice found that unbelievable herself. It was all those people cheering her along, she thought. Celestina, Suor Arcangela, Alberto, Eric… They helped her die just as they had helped her live.

A deer emerged out of the forest and cautiously approached the spilled, cold body, rubbing against it with its dark damp nose. From a nearby bush, a man materialized, pointing a camera at the animal. The deer stared at him for a second before scampering off behind the trees. The man continued to walk, stopped a few yards from the body, framed it with the camera, and took a photo. He then started backing away, casting worried glances all around, and finally, when he felt safe enough, turned his back and began to run. What the hell, I don't bite, Alice thought.

When the photographer overcame his shock and alerted the police, Alice had to deal with a new discovery. She was still tied to that body. When the nurses placed it on the stretcher and loaded it into the ambulance, she went along, as naturally as she did when she was alive.

If death had consisted of a fairly painless operation that brought about interesting discoveries, cremation instead turned out to be a rather undignified procedure. First of all, the body must have been exposed to the elements for several hours, or there must have been some other issues, judging by the nurses' complaints in the ambulance. Once identity and causes of death were established, they had to proceed quickly. But since the Bethesda funeral home did not have a crematorium, the body had to be placed in the worst possible coffin, or rather a cardboard container ("it's going to burn anyway," Jeff pointed out with his trademark pragmatism), to travel to a nondescript suburb where specialized staff carried out their duties with the same indifferent efficiency that fast food workers employ when preparing a hamburger, except that the temperature must have been hellish and the cooking very slow. But the worst part was that their efforts did not result, as Alice had hoped, in a decorous pile of ashes, but rather in a whitish pulp that had to be cooled and inspected by hand—yes, by hand!—by the person in charge of this grisly task. Alice congratulated herself for having earned her living as a librarian, there are so many worse jobs in this world. However, the poor man did not find much among the bones, apart from a titanium tooth—"practically eternal!", the dentist had boasted; Alice regretted not having believed him—and her engagement ring. Jane stammered something about the necklace that she would have liked Alice to wear on her "final journey" but had not managed to find—that was strange, Alice thought, because Jane had put it on in the morning, she remembered it well. However, Jane's concern revealed her lack of familiarity with crematory procedures. Even if the necklace had managed to resist the heat, it would have been recovered by the clerk who, Alice surmised, would have taken advantage of the confusion among the relatives of the deceased to round up his salary. Not to mention the fact that comparing that baking job to a "last trip" was decidedly inaccurate but then again, Jane's metaphors always struck Alice as infelicitous.

But the process was not over yet. The remains had to be subjected to a fine grinding that reduced them to the cinder-like consistency that everyone expected. Eventually, what had once been Alice's body, after having been properly cooked, cooled, inspected, shredded, and even lightly scented, was boxed in a special container that was impossible to call an urn. Jane winced when she saw it, but Jeff explained that since they hadn't yet decided what to do with the ashes, it would be foolish to invest in a precious urn. The model in question, which had been recommended by the funeral home, was hygienic, sanctioned by the Food and Drugs Administration, absolutely hermetic yet easy to open, if necessary. In case the family decided to bury the ashes in Italy, its lightness and compactness would be much appreciated. Approved by the Ministry of Aeronautics, the container was X-ray compatible and could be brought on an airplane as a carry-on. Alice could not help but admire the ease with which Jeff stored new information in his brain, and how excited he became when an object perfectly matched its function. To hear him speak, it was like listening to a representative of mortuary containers or whatever the hell those boxes were called.

If only Jeff would quit stepping on my toes, Alice thought, but the expression soon turned out to be an utterly inadequate way of describing their relationship. First of all, she no longer had feet, let alone toes, and would have done well to relinquish anthropomorphism once and for all. Furthermore, she soon risked being stepped on, quite literally, by Jeff.

Jane burst into tears when the director of the funeral home, sporting an appropriately sad expression for the occasion, gave her the container with the ashes. She seemed to have exhausted her ability to cope with death during Alice's last weeks. She held the box as if she had been handed something unseemly, almost illegal. Despite her small size, Alice felt rather cumbersome. In the car, Jane didn't know where to put the urn, beset by irrational concerns that it would tip over. Jeff, in vain, kept praising the container's sturdy construction and airtight closure.

"There would be nothing left, nothing," Jane kept repeating, as she moved the urn from the trunk to the back seat, and from there to the ground.

Jeff would have liked to remind her that when his parents exploded on the tiny plane that was taking them back to their base at the end of a mission, they disappeared without even leaving their ashes behind. But recently he had to weigh every single word when talking to Jane. She started the car nervously, turning to look at the floor behind the passenger seat, where the box rested. Without saying a word, she stretched her hand to grab it, but she couldn't reach it. Her blazer that had gotten just a bit too tight to allow her to complete the action added to her discomfort. She got out, went around the car, opened the door and, ignoring Jeff's offer to help, lifted the box and put it first between his arms and then, exasperatedly, right between his feet.

This is how Alice ended up between Jeff's shiny black shoes. She found this annoying but he probably wasn't enjoying it much either because Jane kept ordering him to hold the box still and to be careful not to ruin it at the same time. Why had he purchased such a miserable container anyway? Where did he find it, at a garage sale? Was it a special offer, two for the price of one? Jeff looked at her astonished and offended, wondering how far he'd have to go to show his understanding without losing his dignity. Jane had given him control over her family's troubled finances, and it was thanks to him that she, her mother, former husband and children had managed to stave off bankruptcy. It was unfair on Jane's part to now interpret all that effort as stinginess, and attack him at a time when he couldn't defend himself. Besides, the choice of the urn had not been exclusively his initiative. He had shown her the model online, and summarized its features and benefits. It wasn't his fault if she hadn't paid much attention. To be honest, he'd thought himself that the urn wouldn't have looked quite this cheap, but that's the risk you always take when you order something without seeing first, right?

"Because we have to be careful with everything, don't we? We have to calculate our expenses down to the last penny," Jane continued, "…because the insurance paid for the first operation but not for the second, and for the first round of chemotherapy but not the second. And they couldn't keep her in the hospital because she was no longer undergoing treatment, and hospice care was out of the question because our policy doesn't cover it."

Before specializing in real estate, Jeff had worked for a medical insurance company, something Jane wouldn't let him forget.

"And so we were forced to rely more and more on Liliana, though Mom never liked her much. And Liliana, who began as a maid, became a makeshift nurse, and we clearly saw how responsible and professional she was in that role on the day Mom ran away. In the meantime, it was all work work work for us, even on weekends and holidays, to the point that we ignored my mother on her deathbed because we were too busy kicking that poor family out of their home…"

"Oh, don't you start again with that poor family!" exclaimed Jeff who had increased his dosage of Xanax to keep the memory of the camouflaged madman at bay. "Please, let's not start again with the poor people who cannot read the clauses of their contracts, claim to earn double what they actually earn, chase profit at all costs and keep it all for themselves, but are so ready to ask the government for help when things go wrong…"

"Just like the banks, right?" Jane screamed, more and more

exasperated. "You just described the way banks operate! But for the banks, the government was quick to intervene so that their CEOs could continue to receive millions of dollars as a reward for their extraordinary performance!"

"Is that my fault too, now? I am not the one who voted for Obama!" snapped Jeff, but immediately regretted it. Jane's political ideas had always been confused, it was better to avoid being dragged down that rabbit hole.

"Didn't you also say that we had to work hard, to allow your mother to have the best care?"

He looked at the box between his feet, the result of all that top-notch medical care, and gave it a little squeeze to keep it from moving around. Jane was driving too fast, as she always tended to do when she was in a bad mood. Jeff, as well as trying to keep the urn upright between his feet, had to grab on to the door handle.

"And so, my mother died without me. While she was closing her eyes forever, I was busy selling my soul to the banks and the real estate market!" Jane continued to shout.

"Medical insurance, banks, real estate market... you're talking like your starry-eyed ex-husband!"

"Don't you dare talk about Xavier like that, you don't know him!"

"But you're the one who told me that he was starry-eyed..."

To be precise, Jane's preferred expression to define her former husband was "dud," which she alternated with "loser," but Jeff thought it prudent not to be so finicky.

"It's different when you say it, ok? Think of your own family!"

This was a low blow because after his parents' accident, Jeff's family had shrunk to just one aunt, a Jehovah's witness whose house he'd fled as soon as he came of age.

"That was really uncalled for."

Jane did not apologize but did feel somewhat guilty. She stopped talking and pretended to concentrate on her driving.

Alice had found the conversation extremely informative. She couldn't believe she had been so oblivious to all the practical issues concerning her illness. The only thing she remembered about her medical expenses was the first bill she received. Everything was carefully itemized so that, between the fees for the anesthesiologist, the surgeon, the two specialized nurses, a week in intensive care, sedatives, antibiotics, IVs, patches, breakfast, Band-Aids, and other odds and ends, the total was astronomical: $126,434 dollars and ninety-seven cents. It truly was a masterpiece in absurdity and fastidiousness, that reached its apex with the listing of the ninety-seven cents. She remembered laughing about it with Jane. She had even considered sending a single dollar with a letter of explanation: the remaining $126,434 would arrive in due time, and in the meantime voilà the ninety-seven cents, plus a donation of three cents. Just like that, as a joke.

The day they got the bill, they had just come back from a bike ride on the Capital Crescent Trail, stopping at the boat house and discussing whether to rent a canoe. In the end, Alice suggested that they do that some other time. She didn't feel comfortable at the idea of adding more physical exercise to their biking. She knew from experience that the barely perceptible slope, which made the ride so enjoyable when heading east toward Washington, would leave her gasping for air on the way back. They were slowly pedaling home when they saw a fawn near the edge of the trail, eating shoots with such concentration that it didn't even notice them until they stopped just a few feet away. With its head raised, the fawn looked at Alice with eyes that struck her as somewhat ironic under the long eyelashes. Jane stopped—bad move, thought Alice, but it was already a miracle that Jane had joined her for a bike ride in the first place, better not to nag her—and took out her camera. The fawn unceremoniously turned around, showing the white tuft of hair on its behind before taking a couple of slow strides down the hill. Jane followed it while

Alice laughed, unsure if she should join in the photo safari or stay on the trail to keep an eye on the bikes. A middle-aged man who was out walking a beautiful golden retriever stopped to see if anyone needed help and started chatting with Alice while his dog stretched the leash, excited by the scent of wild-life. When Jane reappeared, disappointed and sporting a few scratches, she showed them a photo of an out-of-focus brown stain against a green background. The man laughed.

"Modern art… you should exhibit it at the Hirshhorn!"

Jane, who loved modern art, took it as a compliment.

"Mother and daughter?" the man asked. He wasn't sure, they didn't resemble each other much. They both smiled and nodded.

"Do you mind if I take a picture?"

"Not at all."

The photo came out well and slightly mollified Jane, still resentful at the fawn's lack of cooperation. She stopped at her mother's place for coffee. There were blueberry muffins that Alice had made that morning but Jane, who was wor-ried about her weight, opted for a piece of toast. Alice found some bread lying around and popped a couple of slices in the toaster to try to make them edible. While they were waiting, they took a look at the mail, and it was then that they opened the bill from the hospital and laughed at the cost of the Band-Aids and at the subtle perversity of the ninety-seven cents. Alice's monthly pension was less than two thousand dollars. Jane put the bill in her pocket, she would deal with it.

"That's certainly a lawyer's job more than a retired librari-an's. Sue them for the moral and material damages caused by their letter!" incited Alice.

"Moral damages alright, but what material damages are you talking about?"

"The toast! The toast is burning!" Alice shot up and ran to-wards the toaster, removing a hot and charred slice of bread.

"When are you gonna get a new toaster!?"

Alice mumbled something as an apology, but Jane burst out laughing.

"Fine, we can consider the burned toast and the extra pound I'll put on from your blueberry muffins as material damages. Come on, pass me one."

Snug between Jeff's shoes, that she insisted were stinky—a mean, gratuitous slander, as she no longer had a nose to smell with and Jeff could be accused of anything but being malodorous—Alice started listing her recent, remarkable discoveries. First: a lawyer does not necessarily instill more fear than a librarian. Second: while the ninety-seven cents seemed like a joke, the 126,434 dollars were anything but, and deserved closer attention. Third: her daughter thought her ex-husband Xavier was an idealist, or worse, and had shared that unflattering assessment with the size 12 shoes. Fourth: Jane, the ultimate capitalist pawn, deep down was a communist! This last addition to the list was a joke that only Alice could understand and it would have made her laugh out loud if she still had the necessary equipment—cheeks, lungs, and lips. In the end, all that came out was a tiny gasp, which Jeff misunderstood and blamed on Jane's reckless driving. It took a while for Alice to draw the most important conclusion from that exchange. Fifth, she thought, happy with her long coherent list: her daughter had sacrificed herself for her, she had taken care of that first bill and who knows how many others—the second opinion? The third? The experimental treatment?—without saying a word so as not to trouble her. My daughter! My sweet girl! Alice was so moved that she didn't pause to reflect on her most momentous discovery, which however would soon keep her busy for days at the time. The attention with which she followed that complex conversation clearly proved that, however ashy, crushed, and boxed, she was still herself. In some form, she was inhabiting that little black container. A bit weaker, perhaps, but still there. Would she ever be allowed to die for real?

Alice assumed that they were taking her home, and was disappointed when the car stopped in front of Jane's house instead. It was a two-story in Kenwood, the most elegant neighborhood in Bethesda, a symbol of success for the only child of an immigrant single mother, a statement of what she had been able to achieve against all odds, a testament to the American dream. Jane activated the electronic garage door from the driveway, parked the car and got out quickly to switch the alarm off. She entered the house followed by Jeff, turning back only to take the container from his hands. They were in the basement, which Jane alternatively referred to as the family room or game-room. Alice always found that nomenclature odd, as it implied a family life and a desire to play. That area seemed to her, more than anything, the graveyard of Jane's good resolutions. Amongst the tombstones were a Stairmaster, an easel with paint brushes encrusted with dry paint, and a brand-new dog kennel dating back to the days Jane had considered getting a dog for Sara, which for some reason never happened. There were also shelves that Alice, with unwavering optimism, had filled with books that she hoped her daughter would read one day. Jane looked around the room, walked toward the fireplace, made some space amongst the knick-knacks on the mantelpiece, and placed the container right in the middle. Alice couldn't help but consider that a sign of respect, even love, especially as Jane gave her a brief caress after setting her down.

"I wasn't even with my mother when she died."

This comment came out a bit melodramatically. Alice was familiar with Jane's ways of picking a fight and knew it was better to avoid responding to her provocations, but Jeff walked straight into her trap.

"But how were you supposed to know? It's not like we have a crystal ball!"

"No, I knew it, I felt that it was going to happen. All those stories, the historical past, the door left ajar, all the signs were there, right in front of me, and I was not able to read them..."

"But the doctors said she could have lived another year, they were just worried about dosing the painkillers. What signs? The last few weeks have been a sequence of false starts!"

"What?!"

"I mean, this month we didn't really get much work done, did we? And we didn't go to the movies once, or out to dinner..."

He thought it prudent not to mention the thing he had missed the most, during all that time spent taking care of the old woman. But Jane understood anyway.

"You're right! Now we can finally get back to kicking people out of their homes full-time and eat scallops 'à la Casanova' at whatever new restaurant the *Washington Post* recommends" she retorted, also avoiding mentioning their *other* pastime.

"What's wrong with that?"

"Are you happy now? Well, there's no need to worry anymore, she's gone, the start was regular and the race quite gripping, all the way to the finishing line!"

"Listen, I didn't mean for it to come out that way, but you have to admit..."

"I don't have to admit anything, Jeff, and I think it would be better if you went home now."

Yet, as soon as the words left her mouth, she regretted being so impulsive. The idea of being alone with her mother's ashes was unsettling. Luckily, Jeff didn't seem to take her seriously. He went to the shelves and removed two volumes by Ismail Kadare, creating a small gap from which he extracted a bottle. He poured an inch of Jack Daniels into a glass and offered it to Jane, who took it and slumped onto the couch. Alice was startled. Clearly, all the AA meetings Jane had attended had not been very successful. From the way she guzzled the whiskey, she had clearly never lost the habit, in spite of all her preaching about moral inventory, spiritual awakening, and the twelve steps of AA. Even more offensive, though, was Jane's idea of turning her library into a wet bar. But Jeff's rough nonchalance in handling Kadare's volumes, as annoying as it was, was only a prelude to his next move. He was on his feet for less than a minute, just enough time to down a healthy dose of whiskey himself. Then, he sat down next to Jane and started to caress her hair. Not only did she let him do it, but she also rested her head on his shoulder. Still unsatisfied, he raised her chin with two fingers and kissed her. Despite the darkness, their movements became unmistakable, and Alice regretted no longer having eyelids to lower the curtain over that spectacle. The inverted primal scene unfolding in front of her brought about the last revelation in that eventful day, and sealed her assessment of the situation. She had no nostalgia. She always found the living a touch incomprehensible, she had no desire to hang out with them, and longed for the moment she'd manage to die completely.

Alice spent her first few days on the shelf mulling over her predicament and exploring her surroundings. Like a newcomer in an unfamiliar neighborhood, she paid a great deal of attention to the other dwellers, which included: a little ceramic black robe with the Italian word for "lawyer," *avvocato*, inscribed on its base; a Murano glass ashtray from which Jane had unsuccessfully tried to remove a "made in China" sticker; an hourglass bearing a banner with the erudite warning "Carpe Diem"; and a photo of herself, Jane, and Sara in a decorative frame with little hearts and the caption "girl power." Alice found the cohabitation with all that junk positively irritating. She reckoned she possessed something more, however difficult to define, that put her in a different category from her neighbors. She also suspected that they, especially the hourglass, guessed her feelings and considered her a snob, but she preferred to guard her distance and avoid establishing relationships that she feared were bound to be disappointing. Sharing the space with all these knick-knacks, however, could hardly be defined as gratifying, and Alice developed a touch of resentment toward Jane for keeping her among the clutter.

Being deceased did come with its perks, though. For instance, while she had always been restless in life, she never got bored now. She remained suspended in a sort of dreamless, half-asleep, half-awake state that became more pronounced as time went on. This sensation wasn't completely new to her, she remembered feeling something similar during her illness that, she realized now, had been a bit of a training. She wondered, without fear, if her fading consciousness was a precursor to a permanent shutdown. Her links to the world had become increasingly weak for some time now, the idea that they would undergo further rarefaction left her indifferent. She feared instead the possibility that these bonds would intensify again, that she would regress and care again about her name, her face, all those accidental attributes that used to mean so much to her. Fortunately, such a prospect seemed quite remote.

One day, she heard a litany of "pobrecita" and "qué lástima" and realized that Jane had decided to pardon Liliana. Took her long enough, Alice thought. It was really absurd of Jane to blame Liliana, really. In all honesty, she should have blamed herself for leaving her mother alone. Deep down, Alice suspected that all that animosity toward Liliana originated precisely from Jane's feelings of guilt which, with Jeff's help, had been redirected toward a safer target. Jane had meticulously reconstructed the sequence of events from that day: Liliana had waited a bit before checking on Alice because, she maintained, she was afraid of waking her up; when she finally did and realized Alice was neither in her bedroom nor anywhere else in the house, she tried to reach Jane though she knew she was at work with her phone off. Then, instead of calling 911, she wasted time first by redialing Jane's number over and over again, and then by walking around the block and asking everybody she met if they'd seen Alice. In the end one of the neighbors, the one who had just got home from her trip, put two and two together and alerted the cops. Jane claimed that Liliana's reluctance to call the police had resulted in a fatal delay. She repeated her theory to her children, Jeff, Julia, and just about anyone who would listen or couldn't escape. After convincing her audience of her version of the events, she was able to quell her guilt and look at that strange morning in a more detached way. She remembered finding the orange pill on the bedside table and realized that her mother had somewhat planned her escape. In the end, she died as she had lived. Her face at the morgue was serene, elated even.

"We didn't intervene in any way," the man who accompanied Jane to the stretcher where Alice lay said. "This is exactly how she looked when they brought her in."

Alice was smiling. She seemed much younger than eighty.

After all, Jane reasoned, if the police had managed to capture her—there was no other word, really—they would only have condemned her to suffer a little longer. Once Jane reached that conclusion, she saw no reason why Liliana shouldn't resume working for her. Liliana's reaction to the idea, however, was a baffling silence that left Jane wondering if she had somehow hurt her feelings. She tried to recall whether she had manifested her disappointment too vehemently, and concluded that she hadn't had much of a chance to do that, since Liliana had disappeared right away and they hadn't heard from her since. Jane remembered venting quite a bit with family and friends, sure, but that was it.

But Liliana was not offended, she was scared. When she recognized Jane's voice, she feared a lawsuit was coming her way. Contrary to what she had told the police, in fact, she had realized that Alice had disappeared right away, but her first reaction was to reach out to her family, hoping they would join her in searching the neighborhood. It was only after her husband started screaming that she was going to get all of them deported that she called Jane, although she knew very well she wouldn't be able to get through. At that point she left the house and walked around aimlessly, trying to reach Jane every ten minutes or so, just to pretend that she was actively searching for Alice, instead of calling the police like her whole family kept urging her to do. This is why Jane's call made her nervous. She was afraid Jane had somehow managed to get a hold of those phone conversations where Liliana refused to call the cops for fear that Immigration officers would also show up. "Manslaughter," her American-educated son ruled, "That could be construed as involuntary manslaughter." The ominous sounding word kept her awake at night.

Once she realized that Jane wasn't threatening to sue her, Liliana relaxed and gladly accepted her offer. Standing in front of Alice's ashes, the two women were in a similar state of mind: both felt they had acted somewhat unfairly toward the other, and both hoped that the other hadn't noticed. Besides, they soon realized that taking care of Alice over the last few months brought them together more than they had thought. Liliana, in particular, started to affectionately reminisce about Alice, la *señora* who used to review Italian history through her stamp collection (a *Gronchi rosa*! How she wished she had a *Gronchi rosa*!), who read Mario Vargas Llosa (a Peruvian, like Liliana herself!), who insisted on listening to Janis Joplin and hummed lullabies in Spanish while under the effects of sedatives. This last memory was flattering but clearly apocryphal because Alice's knowledge of Spanish was, at best, approximate and passive. It's possible that Liliana had mistaken for Spanish some phrases that Alice might have mumbled in her Italian dialect during that strange torpor induced by painkillers. Jane, however, did not intervene. Maybe she overestimated her mother's linguistic capabilities or was simply too focused on her goal. From their conversation, Alice understood that a major family reunion was in the works. This required a deep cleaning and some touch-ups, since the house had been a bit neglected lately. Liliana quickly agreed but was stunned by the urn on the mantel. *Pobrecita*, why had they cremated her? Didn't they have a family chapel? What was she doing on the mantel? Despite Jane's explanations, Liliana found Alice's present condition and whereabouts somewhat disturbing. The idea of being alone with the urn made her apprehensive, and Alice regretted not being able to let out a "boo!" to scare her, like any jolly family ghost.

Liliana knew her stuff. The room magically organized itself according to some simple but effective rules. Now that Alice could no longer object to it, the books were arranged by height and color, criteria that perfectly corresponded to their primary function of decorating the shelves and hiding the bottles. The new organization moved Akhmatova next to D'Annunzio—one final, unforgivable insult for the tragic queen. But Alice also enjoyed a small personal victory when the hourglass and the fake Murano ashtray were downgraded and removed, leaving her the undisputed ruler, indeed the *señora*, of an entire shelf. Once Liliana got used to the idea of having the dead woman still in the house, she started to make a little altar out of that corner of the room. Jane made her remove a small plastic statue of the Madonna of Fatima, but did not notice a prayer card with Jesus Christ on the cross hiding under the urn.

The room was so clean, orderly, disinfected, and fragrant, that it transmitted a sense of anticipation. Even Alice felt a tinge of curiosity toward the family reunion that Jane had mentioned. Some small signs—the new evergreen houseplant, the list of completed tasks that Liliana rattled off to an uncharacteristically attentive Jane—revealed that everything was ready for the guests' arrival.

KENWOOD, MARYLAND
NOVEMBER 25, 2010

The first November snow had chosen a bad time to fall, the biggest travel day of the year. From her bed, Jane watched it come down onto the patio and the lawn, the plastic cover stretched over the pool, the trampoline and the tool shed. The greyish hue of the autumn dawn, filtered by the snowflakes, blended together trees and outdoor furniture in the same drab atmosphere. As she lingered between the covers, Jane tried to remember the details of the dream that had woken her up before they dissipated. She was in her mother's kitchen trying to fill a bowl with water, like she had done that morning, right before she had left for work and Alice had gone out for her last walk on the Capital Crescent Trail. But the bowl remained empty. The water that flowed from the faucet magically passed through its base and spilled into the sink. Jane grew anxious, time was slipping away while she could not complete such a simple task. Her mother would die of thirst. The thought was so painful that Jane felt her own throat dry up. She decided she needed a bigger, more solid container and took out a ceramic salad bowl from the cabinet. That seemed to work, the water collected nicely, but the bowl became unbearably heavy, so much so that it took all her strength to lift it out of the sink. She carefully started walking toward the stairs that led to the bedroom, with both arms underneath the bowl, as if holding a baby. But before she reached the first step she heard a noise from upstairs, looked up, and down came her mother, except that she was a child, leaping down the stairs with strap-bound books, sandals, and an apple that she had already taken a bite of. Alice dashed out the door, but she must have seen Jane, because she waved happily as she passed her by. Jane wanted to wave back but she couldn't, for fear of dropping the bowl. Instead, she asked Alice to wait for her, but no sound came out of her mouth, and then she realized she was very thirsty herself, and tried to reach the water with her lips but she couldn't, her neck felt short and stiff, and finally she did manage to call Alice, in a pleading cry that woke her up. Maybe that strange dream was the reason why she sat up and poured herself a glass of water from the bottle resting on her bedside table as soon as she realized that yes, it was just a dream. She looked around her familiar and reassuring bedroom. She got up without making a sound and, still barefoot, crossed the corridor and opened the door to the kitchen, where she started going over the list of ingredients for the festive meal. The turkey left to defrost since the previous evening had a certain watery softness to it. There was, as usual, a ridiculous amount of potatoes—they always lasted for days, she would move them from the oven to the fridge, where they would outlive all the other leftovers, until they became pale and stale and had to be thrown out. The pumpkin pie filled the kitchen with its gelatinous scent of cinnamon and nutmeg. She was so focused on the meal preparation that it took her a while to remember she needed to do her exercises. She stepped away from the countertop, sat down in a corner, and closed her eyes. She imagined the turkey during the night, barely visible. She saw it lose its frozen hardness while a faint, sweet odor of raw poultry became stronger and the blinking microwave clock signalled 2:23 a.m., then 2:24, 2:25… The clicking of the thermostat, the warm air coming out of the vents, a creaking noise—a mouse, or just old wood settling—from the attic.

Jane was so absorbed by her exercise that she did not immediately realize that the soft thump she'd heard did not
come from the kitchen she was reconstructing in her memory
but from the one that was coming to life around her. Taking
advantage of the door that was finally open, Lucy, her old cat,
entered silently on her velvet paws, jumped onto the counter,
licked the plastic, flared her nostrils, and prepared to attack
the motionless and fragrant bird.

"Lucy!"

Jane managed to grab the cat right before she could carry
out her plan. She ignored the cat's complaint and buried her
face in the red, soft fur, feeling ribs and muscles until she felt
a tentative, friendly lick on her neck. She then set Lucy down,
opened the blinds, and looked outside. Everything was in
order; the porch was clean and the birdhouse stocked with
feed. Her eyes were still half-closed, but the spell was broken.
It was pointless. No matter how hard she tried, she couldn't
imagine what it was like not to exist anymore.

"Shall we go over the guest list?" Jeff asked.

He had arrived early, in case he could be of any help. He
was uncomfortable at the thought of finding the family together already.

"I hate to admit it, but I'm kind of nervous."

"Oh, stop! It's not like I have a huge family. Plus, you already know Sara."

Yes, he already knew Sara. He hoped Jane's other kids
would be a little easier to get along with.

"Then there's my son Richard, the scientist, and his girlfriend, Valerie, who works for some company that does something with Latin, or education… I should review my notes;
I haven't met her either. Look, I am the one who should be
nervous!"

"Then there's Kate," Jeff continued, counting on his fingers.

"Yes, my second child and first daughter, Kate, who's six months pregnant, with her husband Mark, a good-natured guy and a hard worker. They are coming all the way from Ohio, an eight-hour drive. Now do you understand why I couldn't expect my children to come home for the funeral? I didn't want to create problems for them, I am sure my mom would have approved of my decision. This way it is much better, and gives us a chance to celebrate Thanksgiving together."

Jeff nodded and looked at his phone.

"The road conditions are improving, it stopped snowing and the temperature is rising. Traffic is heavy, of course, but overall things don't look too bad."

"Great, thanks. I guess I should start working on this turkey."

"How about some coffee?"

"Sure."

Jeff opened the cabinets looking for some cups.

"Have you made up your mind? Are you going to tell them today?" he asked, while scanning the contents of the cabinet in search of his favorite mug.

"Yes, I think it's better this way, otherwise I'll need to have the same conversation separately with each one of them."

"So, you have decided to talk about both things? About us and… you?"

"Why not? In a way, the two topics are related."

"What an eventful year this has been…"

"Yeah… Disgraceful, I'd say, more than eventful. I don't know about you, but I could use some everyday dullness at this point."

Jane opened the dishwasher, took out the mug Jeff was looking for and started washing it by hand. It was decorated with colorful pictures of the sun, a girl in a bikini, and a beach umbrella. The caption read: Spring Break 1980. She dried it and handed it to Jeff.

"Listen, Jeff, if you think we're going too fast, if you don't feel sure about this, or if spending all this time together is raising some doubts..."

"What are you talking about?!" Jeff hastily protested.

"... if you're finding out things about me that you don't like," continued Jane as if she hadn't heard him, "we can take it slowly. The announcement, today or another day, doesn't really matter, what's important is whether we are ready to take this step. Maybe we're going too fast. Also, the test results are a legitimate concern. You don't have to commit right now to share your life with someone who might need help, assistance. We just went through my mother's illness, you must feel hostage to these complicated family affairs... Look, I understand."

Jeff opened his mouth to answer, but the radio started to broadcast a traffic update, and Jane raised the volume to listen. Once it was over, they silently agreed to change the subject.

The turkey was cooking very slowly, perhaps it wouldn't be dry this time. A barrage of shouts and exclamations came from the family room, where the men were watching the football game—Jeff, Mark, even Richard. Kate was doing her best to help out, although pregnancy slowed her down. She shuffled between the kitchen and the dining room, setting the table, arranging flowers in vases, bringing some beers to the guys sitting in front of the flat-screen TV.

On her solitary shelf, Alice was beaming. She had finally realized that it was Thanksgiving and was delighted that her condition spared her Jane's famous turkey, tough as leather, and the cloying cranberry sauce that, sure as death, would accompany it. Jane, ever the conformist, had made a point of learning how to cook turkey. She must have suffered a lot as a kid, when she had lasagna on Thanksgiving and then pretended with her classmates that she'd eaten the traditional all-American meal instead. One year, Jane was so insistent that Alice decided to cook the massive bird, and even invited Eric's relatives, just to pretend they had a family. When the turkey was half-cooked, Jane, on her tippy toes, opened the door to her friends, went to the kitchen and showed them that they celebrated Thanksgiving like everyone else, with turkey and all the trimmings. Alice was so struck by the scene that, from then on, she always made turkey for Thanksgiving, even though it never came out very well, until Jane took on the task herself. Jane's roast, however, wasn't any better than her mother's, which made Alice come to the conclusion that it wasn't their fault but rather the indigestible bird's. The year before, she used her illness as an excuse to avoid both the turkey and the family reunion, stopping by only for a brief visit that allowed her to sense the tensions around the table. Jane would never give up turkey, it was her passport to normality. Back in the day, Alice called it conformism, but with death she had become more indulgent.

Football was a whole other story though. There was absolutely no way she could bring herself to watch it. Especially with those buffoons Jeff and Mark "ooh-ing" and "ahh-ing" every time two helmets clashed. And Richard, unrecognizable, was joking, laughing, and drinking, pretending to be a real manly man! It was hard to believe that this was the same person who, when watching his first football game as a kid, started crying because those madmen were doing all the things that his teacher told him not to do, like grabbing the ball and hitting each other. He did try to play football at school, though, but he was immediately singled out by his teammates who would purposely pass the ball to him in parts of the field where he would be easily tackled, or ignored him and never passed him the ball for an entire game. Richard wasn't sure which of his teammates' strategies hurt him more. Luckily, before long, that fight in high school brought his career as a halfback to a sudden halt.

Also Jane noticed Richard's interest in the game, but her reaction was completely different. She had worried about the interaction between Jeff and her firstborn but now, as she watched them share a few beers and talk football, she felt not only reassured but also proud. If only Xavier and Alice could see him now, so at ease, so comfortable with himself. They always loved Richard's sensitivity, his being different, unique. They didn't seem to understand that it was precisely his difference that got him in trouble. The other boys started calling him Piaf when they heard him sing *La vie en rose*, and not as a compliment. It was easy for Alice and Xavier to downplay Richard's issues; they weren't the ones dealing with their consequences. They certainly weren't the ones who met teachers and therapists, or strove to avoid the gaze of other mothers.

He didn't fit. He was a nerd, a snob — that's what his classmates thought of him. He was beaten up by neighborhood kids and humiliated by high school bullies, who told him where to sit on the bus, what to bring for lunch, what to wear. Once, Jane went around the neighborhood and talked to the other parents, begging them to get their kids to leave him alone, to let him grow up and live and be the way he wanted to be. She met looks of commiseration and generic reassurances, punctuated by the refrain "boys will be boys." Boys are like that, it's just their nature, a bit bullyish, quick with their fists. Better than having them turn out like misfits, or worse.

Richard was so embarrassed by his mother's intervention that he refused to go to school for a week. He lifted weights and checked out a handbook on wrestling from the library. When he finally went back to school, he was ready to try a move on the first kid who sneered at him. He didn't have to wait long. He threw the boy to the ground and went straight for the pressure point between his ear and his jaw, squeezing on it until the kid's body became limp and his face pale as a ghost's. All the while, other students were pulling Richard's arms, back, and hair, trying to tear him off his victim.

So now he wasn't only a nerd and a snob. He was also a troublemaker, an expert in potentially lethal wrestling techniques. The first born and the only boy, his mother surely coddled him too much. These are the kind of kids who end up on the front page after a school shooting. When Jane decided she had heard enough of the other parents' tirades, she excused herself as if she was only going to the bathroom. Instead, she crossed the parking lot, started the car and drove away, leaving Lincoln High School behind, never to return. She told Richard that she agreed with his decision to be home-schooled. Xavier was not happy, he thought some socialization would be good for his son. Then, good results started pouring in, one after the other, until Richard became a researcher at an important pharmaceutical company and an assistant professor of genetics. A few months earlier, at the university, he had even met a girl, another box ticked off the normality list. There he was, her son. Funny how people's judgement had evolved over time. Now, all those things that made him weird were mentioned only as early manifestations of his genius.

The food thermometer registered 165 degrees. The turkey was ready.

In order to escape the game, Kate had taken refuge in the cat's favorite room, the warmest one in the house. Her mother called it the little library, to distinguish it from the family room where she kept most of the books. The volumes in the little library were mostly textbooks and encyclopedias, that nobody ever touched anymore. Plus, it was difficult to read in there because of another television. For Kate, this was an irresistible temptation. At home, when she had nothing to do, she would flip channels until she began to fall asleep. While waiting for Mark to come back from work, usually late in the evening, she could spend four or five hours in front of the TV, just like that. She wasn't used to all this time away from him, but they were lucky that he found work, especially during a recession and with a baby on the way.

Kate and Mark always bickered, but only for the pleasure of reconciling later on. Their main cause of disagreement was sports. Mark was immovable during football games; he would not even let her flick through the channels during the commercials. Kate always gave up but often ended up accus-ing him of being selfish at one point or another. Every time she went back to her mother's home she found it more com-fortable, this TV for instance was brand new. She didn't dare tell Mark about that, for fear that he would bring up again how spoiled she was or feel bad because he couldn't provide the standard of living she was used to, or both. Who knows, perhaps her grandmother had left them an inheritance that would allow them a little luxury, including another TV. She thought it would be insensitive to inquire about that so soon, but a house in downtown Bethesda, however modest, was quite an asset. At any rate, these two days at Thanksgiving would be her only vacation that year, better take advantage of them. She started watching a talk show with a woman sport-ing a real beard. She had subjected herself to various forms of waxing and hair removal procedures before accepting herself for who she was.

"Mark, come look!"

Between the match and the commentary, the volume was fairly high in the adjacent room, and before Kate could yell louder there was a commercial break. She changed the chan-nel and fell upon Mr. Manlone, a man with a curiously fixed gaze, who was complaining about the government's silence on his experience. Four times already, when he was 7, 14, 21, and 28 years old, he had been abducted by aliens who held him prisoner for hours on end in a room with porphyry walls, where they abused him with electromagnetic probes. His 35th birthday was only five days away and he, understandably, was more than a bit concerned. The talk show host interjected to point out that not all of the scientific community was ignoring him. In fact, Mr. Manlone was in close contact with Dr. Boward, from the University of Santa Catilina. Kate went back to flipping channels until she found one of her favorite infomercials. She lowered the volume. She knew that Mark didn't approve of her purchases and complained that they only sat around the house. He seemed to believe that you had to start using everything you bought right away. On the screen, a blond woman slid from side to side on what seemed to be a metal mat. Her make-up was impeccable, her movements effortless, and her leotard fit her perfect figure like a glove. Despite hours of exertion, she showed no sign of perspiration. In the background, other women mimicked her movements and smiled, all thanks to their metal mats and their special footwear. At the stroke of 3 p.m., a special offer would begin where the first hundred callers would receive not only the metal mat, the footwear, and a booklet, but also a thirty-minute instructional video and free lifetime access to the company's helpline, a two-hundred-dollar value right there. There was also a chance to win an additional prize through a raffle. Kate automatically reached for her handbag and looked for her credit card.

"And the offer starts... now! The first hundred callers will receive our *Slimhips* Thanksgiving special!"

Kate hesitated for a moment. It was true that she had put on some weight after her wedding, especially around her hips. It was also true that this mat was a pretty original concept and it wouldn't take up much space, it could even fit under the bed. It would allow her to get back in shape right after giving birth. It was better to make these purchases now, while she still had some free time. It was a toll-free number. If she called from her mother's phone, there was no danger that other companies would start harassing her with their offers.

"Hello, welcome to *Slimhips*, your passport to the land of fitness."

The doorbell rang. Kate quickly gave her name, address, and credit card number.

"Gather your family, we'll put you on live!" encouraged the voice on the other end of the line.

"No! I mean, thank you but I'd rather not, it's a surprise, I would prefer them not to know for now."

"That's too bad! Oh well, as you please ma'am. Either way, you can still participate in our 'Thanks for being what you are' sweepstake. The prize is a hundred dollars' worth of products from our catalogue for the whole family, delivered today. All we need from you is your current house address."

"What? Oh, yes, sure, definitely."

Voices from the hallway announced the arrival of the rest of the family. Kate hurried to give Jane's address. If she spent fifty bucks and got a hundred as a price, Mark couldn't possibly complain.

"Excellent. Thank you for calling *Slimhips* and have a wonderful Thanksgiving!"

"You too."

Kate walked to the front door where everybody was sharing hugs and laughing, even if the men seemed impatient to get back to the game. There was Valerie, Richard's mysterious girlfriend—it was a miracle that someone went out with her brother, even if he had lightened up a bit since he was a kid. Also Sara had just arrived, with a dark-skinned friend — probably Mexican, Kate thought.

"Finally everyone's here! The turkey was getting cold!" said Jeff, trying to mask his discomfort at being surrounded by strangers by raising his voice and playing the role of party host. He even walked right up to Valerie to welcome her, trying to remember what Jane had told him in the morning.

"You are an expert of Greek and Latin, right?"

"Yes, mostly Latin, really."

"Nice, nice, that's great! Do you teach, then?"

"Yes, that too. I am an adjunct at the University of Texas, which is how I met Richard." She wondered whether Jeff would understand what "adjunct" meant. "But I mostly work for a start-up, Toga, Inc. I help create educational material, structure course content, organize field trips, things like that..."

"That's so great!" Jeff repeated. He didn't have anything else to add so he excused himself and retreated to the kitchen.

By the time Richard finished carving the turkey, Mark and Jeff were back sitting in front of the TV, and Kate offered to go get them. It was the perfect opportunity for her to check whether those *Slimhips* people had honored their promise to the first one hundred callers, she was afraid they wouldn't follow up on that. However, first there was an ad, and then a long interview with the woman who had been exercising on the mat, talking about this and that but mostly trying to catch her breath. By the time Valerie came looking for her, Kate wasn't sure if she had been ripped off or not. She had no choice but to follow Valerie back to the dining room, where everybody was already sitting around the table. They had to give thanks, which was always a bit tricky. Jane thought it was her duty to break the uneasy silence.

"I'm thankful to be with all of you here today," she began, "and I'm grateful to my mother for the gift of life and for doing so much for all of us."

"Speaking of which..." Sara interjected.

Kate hoped that her younger sister would bring up the issue of the inheritance, but Richard cut her short, afraid that the dinner would turn into a commemoration.

"Not now, alright? There's time for that later."

Sara looked at him, already annoyed.

"Not now," repeated Jane. "Let's eat."

She smiled as she spoke. Sara lowered her head.

"So, what were you guys watching that was so interesting?" asked Jane once the plates were full. "It was a chore to get you all around the table!"

"We have it better, right Kate?" said Mark. "At least our place is so small that we can watch TV from any spot in our apartment."

"I do think we need another little TV here in the kitchen," interjected Jeff.

"Yeah, then there'd be no place where we'd be safe from all its bullshit," quipped Sara.

"Sara!" Jane exclaimed, in a reproachful tone. "I can't wait until you start college. Your vocabulary isn't getting any better out West."

"I'm actually learning a ton 'out West,' as you say. I feel as if I were already taking classes at Princeton. I'm learning to look at things from a different perspective."

"Different doesn't mean rude and unreasonable," Jane replied. "Look at Kate, she didn't start cursing when she left home. However, since we have an expert in education in our midst, maybe we should ask her."

Everyone turned towards Valerie.

"I... I'm not really a specialist..." Valerie seemed a bit uncertain as to what exactly she had been asked to comment about. "But I do agree that education helps to process experience and look at things from different perspectives."

"I think we can all agree on that," said Richard, a bit disappointed to hear that platitude from the woman whose intelligence he had praised to his mother for months. "But what does 'different' mean?"

Valerie got instinctively defensive.

"Different means being informed and as unbiased as possible. It means having your own point of view and not just going along with that of those around you," she replied, looking at Richard.

"Doesn't sound like much, considering the price of tuition these days!" Mark exclaimed. "The more I think about it, the happier I am that I stopped studying after high school. Plus, I have a job and Kate doesn't, even with her fancy degree."

"You're the one who doesn't want me to work!" complained Kate.

"And I don't think you should look at it that way, Mark," Jeff intervened, feeling suddenly invested with the authority of a father figure. "Education is always useful. Girls, even if they won't work outside their homes, become better mothers, and can always pass on their knowledge to their children."

"If that's the point of education, Mom can spare my tuition," said Sara dryly. "I'm not planning on getting married or having kids."

"You'll be singing a different tune, Missy, when you meet Mr. Right," Jeff responded with a conciliatory smile on his face.

"I wouldn't stay home to knit socks and iron clothes, not even for Prince Charming."

"What are you saying, Sara?" said Kate, offended. "You have to make sacrifices for your family. Love changes lots of things; I was like you before I met Mark."

"Really?!" Mark said with fake incredulity. "Thank God I met you afterward!"

His booming laughter was outdone only by Jeff's.

They hadn't stopped eating during the discussion. Richard, sitting with his perfect posture, cut tiny pieces of meat, put his knife down, and passed his fork from his left to his right hand to bring food to his mouth. Valerie took long pauses between mouthfuls and, with both hands on the table—a European habit that she had not managed to shake off—was eyeing the others with a scrutinizing curiosity. Una kept eating with a healthy appetite, seemingly undisturbed by the conversation, while Sara barely touched her food, nervously spreading the mashed potatoes on her turkey. Mark and Jeff had already gone for seconds. Jane watched them attentively, her plate nearly intact, searching for the right moment to share the matters that weighed heavily on her heart. The delay had dried up the turkey beyond recovery.

"Do they celebrate Thanksgiving in France?" Mark asked tentatively in an attempt to resume the conversation.

Valerie seemed surprised by the question, but responded with a polite "no." The big national holiday, she explained, was July 14th, Bastille Day.

"Why would they have Thanksgiving if they aren't American?" Kate asked, glad to show the importance of education.

"Fair enough," interjected Jeff. "Thanksgiving is the ultimate American holiday. I bet Valerie already knows: Today, as Americans, we thank God for letting us survive our first winter on the New Continent, and the Indians for teaching us how to harvest the gifts of the land..."

"...So that we could comfortably exterminate them."

Sara completed Jeff's sentence.

"This is a great example of what we were talking about earlier, different ways of looking at the same thing!" Jeff replied, laughing.

"I would say the only possible way, in this case," Valerie quipped.

"Hey, hey, wait a minute!" bridled Mark. "If we hadn't killed them, they would have killed us!"

"Yes, as they should have. Sometimes self-defense is a duty even more than a right."

It was the first sentence that Una had spoken since entering the house, and left everybody speechless.

Jane wondered why her children didn't seem to be able to share a meal without getting at each other. She also felt her determination to make her announcement fade away. They didn't seem to realize that, while they talked away as if they could repopulate the continent with Native Americans, the cells in their bodies kept feeding, growing, multiplying.

"Well, there was a lot of self-inflicted harm as well. Nobody forced the natives to start drinking alcohol," Jeff intervened, happy to throw in a surreptitious allusion to the reason for Sara's exile. "Since the dawn of time, this is the way things work in this world. The Romans, were they not the first imperialists? What do you think, Valerie?"

Valerie found herself in the awkward position of having to defend, or at least describe, the Roman Empire in thirty seconds. Based on the rhythm of the exchanges and the attention span of the audience, she doubted she'd be granted much longer than that. She tried to buy time, hoping that the conversation would somehow move onto a different topic.

"They weren't the first."

Then she found a better argument.

"At any rate, I'm French, not Roman. I descend from Vercingetorix, if anything, not from Caesar."

"From what?" asked Mark.

"From Vercing… Never mind. In any case, the Romans invaded Gaul, which is modern day France, and therefore I descend from the invaded, not the invaders, if we want to think in those terms."

"Yes, but we can't think in those terms, right? Isn't this what you are saying? Well, I couldn't agree more! Centuries later, who knows who invaded whom… I may also be part native American, but it's no big deal to me."

The thought of having Valerie on his side comforted Mark.

Some cells die, others live longer than they should…

"I could have gone to a college on a great scholarship, just because I have a quarter of Cherokee or whatever blood in me, but I said no thanks, I'm an American."

"If I were you, I would take the money from whoever is willing to give it to me," Jeff suggested. "A college degree may always prove useful in life."

…Until poof, a small distraction, a bad photocopy, an imperceptible error, and you start to secretly nurse your treasure, the little cancer that will kill you.

"Listen…"

Jane shifted uncomfortably in her seat. She felt sweaty under Richard's gaze.

"I have something to tell you."

"Me too," echoed Sara. She suddenly stopped fiddling with the food on her plate.

Mother and daughter looked at each other. Jane nodded encouragingly.

"I am discovering so many things in Moab," Sara began slowly. "I am having time and space there to reflect, to question the things I always took for granted."

The men around the table looked skeptical.

"… But the most important discovery has been about myself."

"Really? And what would that be?" asked Jeff, impatient but trying to come across as encouraging.

"I'm gay."

She lifted her defiant gaze. Una was startled. She feared that the rest of the family would make the obvious connection between her presence at the table and Sara's announcement. From the moment they arrived in Kenwood, Sara had transformed into a different person. Her reflective and shy demeanor had been replaced by a challenging, resentful attitude that had caught Una by surprise. Yes, fine, Sara may have had her reasons to be mad at her family, but why did she drag her into this reunion? And why bring up their relationship like this, almost out of spite? She wished she had her own car to drive away as fast as she could.

After a few long seconds, Richard's calm voice broke the silence.

"How did you find out?"

"It was pretty simple, I'd say. I fell in love with a woman."

Everybody looked at Una.

"So, it's because of her!" blurted Kate.

"*Thanks* to her, if anything," responded Sara.

Jeff opened his mouth as if he were about to say something, then got up and brusquely left the kitchen.

"You see?" Kate said with small, mean eyes that reminded Sara of her childhood.

"Don't worry, he'll be back for the pumpkin pie, I know him," Jane tried to smile.

Mark could not wait to be alone with Kate to comment on this new drama unfolding. He always thought Sara was a bit bizarre, but today she had proven to be just weird. He didn't need a degree in psychology to see that something wasn't right with that family. Kate would have to acknowledge that all those complications led to disaster, that life was simpler for them back home, and that moving closer to Jane, as she mentioned once in a while, was not a good idea.

"Well, if no one has anything else to say, I'm going for a walk," Sara announced.

Una automatically followed her, if only to avoid being left behind with the rest of the family. Jane also got up, trying to escape Mark's smug look and likely comments. She had barely reached the door when she heard Richard's voice.

"Mom, didn't you have something to tell us too?"

She turned around to look at him. Her son's eyes always seemed able to uncover secrets, fill pauses, decode silences. She felt strangely relieved at the thought of not having to give the little speech that she had prepared so carefully.

"Oh, nothing important. It wasn't a matter of life or death."

The snow from the day before was turning into grayish puddles as the brisk cold gave way to warmer, damp air. Mark took a few steps outside, leaned against his car and lit a cigarette. Unbelievable, what a Thanksgiving. He breathed deeply, looking at a small delivery van coming up the street. It slowed down as it approached Jane's house, turned into the driveway, and stopped right behind Mark's car. The driver checked the address on his notes, got out, and walked to him.

"Does Kate Baldwin live here?" he asked Mark.

"No, not really, it's her mother's house. Why, what is it?"

"She won the *Slimhips* prize 'Thanks for being what you are'."

"Look, there must be a mistake. We don't live here and my wife didn't participate in any contest."

The driver opened the back of the truck, went over his list once again, and shook his head. Working on Thanksgiving was miserable enough, he didn't need to waste time chatting.

"So you're her husband? The address is right, the name is right, and here's the prize. Can I leave it with you?"

Mark had instinctively opened his arms to receive the box that the driver was handing him. There were some big letters before his eyes that he couldn't quite make out. He shifted his head back a bit to bring them into focus. *Guaranteed fun!*

"What's inside?" He yelled from behind the package.

"You'll see, you'll see… There's something in there for everyone!"

And it was true. The contents of the package, emptied out onto the kitchen table, turned out to consist of: a plastic herring that gave off a fishy smell (for cats); a "cleaning thermometer" that, when grasped by dirty hands, magically revealed the word "wash us" (for children); a notepad for the grocery list, with pictures of vegetables and the words "let's not vegetate!" (for the lady of the house); a checkered blanket that could double as a chessboard (for the grandfather); a saxophone-shaped tie (for the father, assumed to be a failed saxophonist); finally, a multicolored bag of popcorn (for the whole family in front of the TV). The box also contained a detailed catalog of similar wonders, the *Slimhips*, and a receipt. Mark's attention was particularly taken by this last item.

"More of this crap...!? Fifty dollars for another one of these shitboxes!?"

"Come on Mark, I am sure there is something useful in there..."

Richard had followed the scene and eyed the checkered blanket.

Mark stared at him for a moment, then made his way downstairs in search of Kate who, unaware of her good fortune, continued to flip through the channels.

When I was little and I was hurting and afraid, I always said to myself: if I am alive tomorrow morning, it's nothing serious and I will survive. I wish I could do the same today. But I know that tomorrow will only bring more uncertainty. It isn't death that is unbearable, but fear.

Jane is finally alone in her room. She just failed another exercise. She thought that the events of the day would make things easier, she believed for a moment that it would be even reassuring to envision the world without her. But she noticed something on the floor and she bent over to pick up a plastic fishbone with a pungent smell. She turned it over in her fingers, without understanding, when Lucy's glowing eyes greeted her. One of Kate's prizes had clearly been much appreciated.

She had prepared a nice but firm, serious speech. She wanted to tell everybody to enjoy life, to avoid giving too much importance to petty concerns, to love each other while they could, until their muscles tired and their hearts exploded. She had begun to doubt her resolve as soon as the family gathered under one roof, together with all those strangers that for some reason they had brought into their lives. In the end, she was relieved that Sara, in one of her most accomplished scenes ever, had stolen the stage.

She went over the rest of the day. The pumpkin pie was excellent, perhaps the best she ever made, and helped calm everybody down after Sara's bombshell and the arrival of the *Slimhips* box. They returned to the table. Surprisingly, it was Kate who, somewhat clumsily, tried to bring everybody together. She said she did not completely understand, that she hoped Sara was just going through a phase, but that no matter what, they would always love her. Remarkably, neither Sara nor Una replied. The conversation slipped into politics, but that turned out to be a minefield, because Mark was a hardline conservative and Kate backed him more vehemently than usual to make up for her latest purchase. Valerie was stunned by their smug ignorance of international politics, combined with a very rough knowledge of the domestic. Aided by Richard, Jane struggled to keep the conversation civil. Love each other, it's easy to say. These are the things that only those at life's threshold understand, and even they are prone to distraction. A plastic fish bone is enough to summon you back to the fray, make you pay attention to that noise from another room. Was someone watching television that late at night? Jane opened the door, listened for a moment, and walked through the dark corridor.

The person sitting on the sofa had their back to Jane, who approached without making a sound. It was a film about a group of men, a bit battered, with ragged uniforms, but in a good mood, joking with each other in front of a lowered curtain, while a band was getting ready to play. On the other side of the curtain there was a woman getting ready for the show, adjusting her dress and the regal crown on her head. The musicians concentrated on their instruments, then the curtain rose and the singer entered with arms raised. The music started cheerfully but something strange happened, the singer didn't begin her song. The musicians looked at each other, bewildered. At a signal from the conductor, the guitar player restarted the introduction. The woman looked down, and the camera that followed her gaze rested on the young soldiers, on their wounds, their scraggly beards, their bandages. She seemed dazed, then tore off her dress, threw away the crown, and remained with nothing but a knee-length undergarment. She said something to the young man with the guitar, who nodded and consulted with the others. A new song began, much different from the bold intro they had just played. The woman began to sing, lowering her voice and almost reciting her lines at times. Her voice seemed about to crack and falter but always recovered, overcoming the temptation to surrender.

Jane could not understand all the words, but she sensed what they meant to the attentive soldiers—something dear, warm, delicate and strong, like the life that seemed to slip a little further away with each note, each line. There was a refrain that they all seemed to know, and after each refrain Jane thought that the singer was too overwhelmed to continue, and yet she started again, whispering and crying her lines. She finally surrendered and ended the last refrain in a sob. She covered her face in her hands, her shoulders shaking as if shivering with cold. A huge applause broke out, and a smile brightened the guitarist's face.

To get a better view, Jane had gotten closer to the screen, and ended up being next to the sofa. She turned only at the end of the scene, and saw Valerie there, with trembling shoulders that resembled the singer's, her eyes bright and burning. She hadn't heard Jane approaching, but didn't seem surprised to find her there. She stopped the video.

"I'm sorry I woke you up."

Jane shook her head.

"I was still awake."

Jane sat on the armchair in front of Valerie.

"That scene is very moving, no matter how many times you watch it."

"I took your invitation to feel at home literally... I saw this old Italian film on the shelf, I couldn't resist."

"*La sciantosa*... It was one of my mother's favorite movies. It's basically the reason why I still own a VCR."

They were unsure of what to do or say next. The buzzing of the rewinding tape filled the air.

"So, you studied classical literature," Jane said finally.

"Yes."

"Too bad you didn't meet my mother, I'm sure you'd have gotten along. She was just a librarian but she was a great reader. I used to tease her and say she only worked at a library to have all those books around her all the time. She was born and raised in Italy and I understand they take literature seriously over there, or at least they did when she was young."

Valerie shifted uncomfortably on the sofa.

"I don't know what Richard told you... Yes, I have a Ph.D. in Latin literature, but here in the States it is not easy to make a living with this kind of thing. Perhaps it is not easy anywhere, I don't know. I work for a company, Toga, Inc. We write lesson plans, we try to spread the love for the classics, we organize trips..."

"Where?"

"Well, in Italy and Greece, when things work out. When they don't, we go to the Parthenon in Nashville, Tennessee... A cheaper and more colorful alternative, with plenty of clean restrooms. I'm not kidding."

"You don't look very happy with your work."

Valerie smiled bitterly.

"It's always a struggle to preserve some dignity. Once in a while people complain because we never organize trips to Latin America... Some schools would be happy with the Toga Parties. Anything that attracts students, or that they think can make students excited, is fine. We even debated dressing up as gladiators for our presentations. So I guess you are right, I am not very happy about my job, and sometimes I'm afraid I got everything wrong."

Valerie hesitated a moment before asking a question in turn. She sensed Jane's reticence, the same reserve that she noticed in Richard. But the night seemed ripe for communication. Hermes, the messenger god, darted across the skies, winged and unstoppable.

"I am sorry about your mom. From what Richard told me, I assumed she was Italian-American. I didn't know she was actually born and spent a long time in Italy."

"Yes, she was. She came here when she was in her twenties and never went back, not even on holidays."

"With her family?"

"No, alone."

"She must have arrived in the fifties, then. A brave choice, back in those days. May I ask you why she decided to move?"

Jane looked at the urn on the mantel.

"For reasons that seem straight out of a novel, or a movie. She gave a ride to my father who was hitchhiking across Europe. He got in the car and never got out, my mother used to say, every time she told us the story. From the little I know about him, I have the impression that he was the one who thought he had been trapped. My mother had a tendency to take everything seriously, I'm not sure he had given the same importance to that chance meeting. Add the fact that she barely spoke English, and he didn't speak Italian at all, and you wonder how they could possibly communicate. But long story short, when she joined him in the States, a few months later, she was already pregnant. I suspect that he no longer remembered much of that ride, but he did his part. Perhaps he could not find a way to back out. His parents must have thought that starting a family would help him straighten up. But he didn't have the time. He died before I was born, in a car accident, maybe drunk. You must have seen the photo on the fridge. That's them, Eric and Alice, the day they met."

Funny to think of them as "Eric and Alice." What a couple, what a story. Was she really alive because of them? That required quite a leap of faith.

"And your mother, after he died, didn't think about going back to Italy?"

"I asked her the same question a few times, but she didn't like talking about it. It wouldn't have been easy to go back home with her tail between her legs, bringing the evidence of her wrongdoing—that would be me, by the way—into a traditional, Catholic country. She always said that things do not happen by chance. It wasn't by chance that she'd given a lift to that hitchhiker and followed him to the States."

"Chance is a common nickname for destiny," Valerie said thoughtfully.

"Who said that?" asked Jane.

Valerie laughed.

"What do you mean who said it? I don't only speak through citations. I'm the one who said it! Chance is a common nickname for destiny. But now that you mention it, it's a catchy sentence, isn't it? I can picture that on a bumper sticker."

Jane laughed too, but when she started talking again her tone was serious.

"It's the same for you. Don't believe it is by chance that you are here tonight and we are having this crazy conversation in front of my mother's ashes."

Why crazy, this conversation? Alice had enjoyed Jane's story immensely. It was so clear and coherent—beginning, middle, and end. It took death to turn her ordinary life into a novel, and not a bad one either.

"And then, fundamentally my mother was an introvert," Jane continued. "She never needed the pleasantries, the parties, the thousand rituals that people officiate to pretend they are not alone. In this, as in many other things, I am very different from her. She loved solitude, and she found it easy to keep on her own here in the States."

Lonely, alone, a loner. Valerie thought of her American life, with or without Richard.

"I mean," Jane concluded, "she never felt at home here, but she also knew she'd be a foreigner in Italy. The only home that she truly inhabited was the Italian language. The subjunctives were the pillars of her identity. Grammar tenses punctuated the seasons of her life."

Jane remembered her last evening with her mother, Alice's last attempt at clinging to life.

"Here it is, in just a few words... a life."

She felt Valerie's eyes on her.

"I miss her a lot," Jane confessed, biting her lips. "It makes no sense to be in this world if there is no one left who saw you as a child."

Her tone struck Valerie.

"Do mothers feel that way too? I mean, doesn't having children protect, at least a little, from emptiness, from meaninglessness?"

"I wouldn't say so, at least not in my case. Maybe I'm not a good mother." She smiled bitterly, thinking of Sara's reproaches, her resentment. "Having children only made me more vulnerable. And then we women are always caught on this seesaw, we are mothers and daughters at the same time, it's not easy... Lately I have been feeling a lot like a daughter. Do you know that spiritual, *Sometimes I feel like a motherless child*? Here I am, I'm over fifty but I feel like that, a motherless child, and not just sometimes."

Jane could not remember the last time she had spoken so openly with someone. Perhaps her mother was right to complain about the Anglo-Saxon cult of privacy. By using generic modes of politeness with everybody, by calling discretion what is only indifference, people learn to lie even to themselves. It felt good not to weigh every word, for a change.

"And you don't have to feel like you are in exile because you left home," she continued. "If you do go back, you will find that you are still in exile. We are all in exile."

"This is an almost religious idea," Valerie observed.

"No, it's a uterine idea. Exile begins when they tear us away from mothers. We can never go back."

I'm here, I'm here! When two have been together like you

and me, how can they possibly be separated!? Alice called in vain from the mantel. Her feelings were so intense that she felt herself torn apart, as if she were giving birth to Jane once again. She remembered the story of those people who shouted from one shore of an iced river, in a winter so cold that their words froze before reaching the people on the other side. They then decided to make a fire in the middle of the river and behold, their words began to liquefy and came murmuring down, perfectly intelligible, like mountain snow turning into flowing water at springtime.

At the thought of no fire and no spring ever thawing her words, of that insurmountable river that separated her from Jane; at the thought of all she hadn't told her before winter came upon them, Alice for the first time regretted being dead. As if responding to a call, Jane stepped closer to the mantel. Something in her fixed stare made Alice suspect and hope that her daughter had discovered her secret, her precarious and illogical persistence. But it was over in a moment. Jane waited until she felt she could control her moist eyes, pursed her lips into that expression of self-restraint that Alice knew so well, sighed deeply and turned around.

"We better go to sleep; we have another tough day ahead of us."

The next day Alice saw them enter one by one into the family room and take a seat on the couch and the armchairs. Jane had hidden the remote to stop them from watching television, while Mark had slept with the car keys in his pocket to prevent Kate from rushing to the Black Friday sales. The nearest mall opened at three in the morning, and until four o'clock there was a 50% discount on plasma screens. The year before, the salesclerk who opened the doors ended up killed, crushed by the crowd hunting for the deal of the century. Not a place for pregnant women, really. Jeff was unusually quiet, Richard was the only man who had found time to shave, Valerie looked much more relaxed, and Sara and Una sat as if holding hands, even if they didn't dare to. Jane stood for a moment in front of the mantel, as if gathering her strength, then turned around. I got your back, Alice thought, though she was not quite sure about the purpose of the gathering.

Everyone seemed curious to know why Jane had called the meeting. She waited for Kate, the very last one, to enter the room and take a seat, then began.

"You'll receive an official letter from my lawyer, but I thought it was better to discuss some details while we're all together."

What details?

Jane waved a yellowish envelope, took out a sheet, and began to read.

"I, Alice Arienti, of the town of Bethesda in the state of Maryland, being of sound and disposing mind and memory, nominate and appoint my daughter Jane as executor of this will. She will divide all my assets between her and her children, as she sees fit. Before making any allocation, however, the sum of five thousand dollars is to be detracted from said assets and donated to the Bethesda public library for the purchase of large format books."

How pedantic, how selfish, Alice scolded herself. Why "large format?" Wouldn't it have been better to invest that money in initiatives that encouraged children to read? She must have written that will after her sight had begun to deteriorate. Strange that with all the time the disease had granted her, she hadn't thought of taking another look at it. She barely remembered all the details. At any rate, it's not like she had an estate to manage. It seemed obvious that Jane would take care of everything. After all, she was a legal expert.

"Now you must know," continued Jane, "that I want to divide everything between the three of you, keeping nothing for me."

Laudable, very generous.

"You must also know, however, that the inheritance is less than you might think. Medical expenses have eaten everything up, there is a mortgage on the house."

"But she had insurance..." Kate protested.

"Your grandmother saw it fit to change insurance after the diagnosis because they wouldn't allow her to get a second opinion. I can't blame her, but she overlooked the small print regarding pre-existing conditions. When she relapsed, it was easy for her new insurance to take advantage of that technicality."

Jane realized she had taken on a very professional tone. She tried to get to the point.

"In short, she was required to pay a big chunk of the expenses related to the illness out of pocket—the second surgery, chemo, radiation, and home care. I am not sure she ever found out about that. When the first bill came, I told her I would take care of it, and I did. I started checking her mail, and took the letters from the insurance company before she could see them. But I've had my expenses too—between your college tuition, the divorce, and some investments that turned out to be less profitable than I thought. We should have mortgaged Nonna's house, but I couldn't do it without speaking frankly about the economic troubles she had gotten herself into. She had plenty to worry about, I didn't want to add one more thing. Stubborn as she was, I was afraid she would refuse treatment. In short, I decided to put a mortgage on my house, not hers. Now, however, we have to rectify the situation, sell Nonna's house, pay off the mortgage on this one, and divide whatever is left between the three of you. As you can imagine, this is going to take some time and effort. Luckily Jeff will continue to help us…"

She looked at him gratefully.

Alice had the impression her urn was the object of some resentment. Actually, sweet daughter of mine, I am sorry to say, but I am not sure all your efforts paid off. All those expenses, the entire family on the verge of bankruptcy, mortgages and debts, to end up boxed up like a Chinese take-out? The kids are right to feel cheated. Look at Kate who can't buy the latest iPhone, just because her grandmother wanted to enjoy the luxury of one last round of chemo!

"Is that all?"

"No, there are also some small… gifts, I imagine, for each of you. There is no indication of how to pay for these, but it doesn't matter, I'll take care of it."

"Presents?" Kate asked.

"Yes, but don't get your hopes up…"

"Come on, tell us!" Sara urged her.

Jane lowered her head and resumed reading.

"I leave my grandson, Richard, an annual subscription for dance classes at the Austin Ballet School."

"But Richard doesn't like to dance!" Kate interjected.

Richard received the announcement without flinching, stiff in his chair.

Alice was quite pleased with herself. Of course, she could have spared Richard that gift, but still, she never quite understood why he didn't drop all that pretense of masculinity. "Free the Piaf inside you!" she wanted to exclaim every time he was scrambling to imitate what he thought real men did. Now she understood why she never had the courage to tell him such a thing while she was alive. Even now that she was dead, she feared his reaction.

"For Kate, a lifetime subscription to *The Progressive* magazine," Jane continued.

"Which magazine...?" Mark asked.

"Never mind..." Kate replied, annoyed. Her grandmother always strove to influence her political ideas and was clearly committed to keep on trying even from the grave. She made a mental note to trash the magazine without reading it and above all before Mark even saw it, that liberal junk really got him mad.

"Don't take it personally, Kate," Jane consoled her. "I really don't know what to think of these last wishes. Do you know what she left me? A recipe... here it is. Turkey stew (recipe for Thanksgiving)."

Complicity and relief brought her entire audience together for a moment. Jane didn't like Sara's smile one bit.

"Of course," she added dryly, looking around the room, "I'm ready to hand over the recipe to anyone willing to organize the traditional family reunion next year."

"Come on, Mom," Richard encouraged her, "please continue, let's finish this reading."

More than last wishes, those gifts struck Jane as Alice's last chance to get on everybody's nerves. She felt that reading them made her look a bit like an accomplice. And the worst part was yet to come.

"Finally," Jane resumed "I bestow the necklace with the rose window of Santa Maria di Collemaggio to little Sara."

"What?"

"Santa Maria di Collemaggio is a church in Nonna's hometown in Italy. She had a necklace with a pendant that reproduced its central rose window."

Finally, Alice thought. She had been a touch impertinent, good thing that at least she had reserved a real gift for Sara, and what a beautiful gift that was.

"Unfortunately, the necklace is lost," Jeff intervened hastily.

"We couldn't find it," he corrected himself. Jane looked at him hesitantly.

"Thank you, Jeff" she said, "but the truth is that I gave it away. By a strange coincidence, just as my mother was dying, I felt the urge to give her necklace to a couple of poor wretches we were kicking out of their home."

"A couple of psychopaths! And their home stopped being theirs the moment they defaulted on their mortgage," snapped Jeff, annoyed that Jane, instead of complying with his version of events, had gotten entangled in that explanation. She still didn't seem to realize that things had to be simplified in her family, rather than always trying to find arcane meanings in everything.

"At any rate," Jane said, "the necklace is gone. I'm sorry, 'little Sara.' Of course, you can choose another jewel among the few that Nonna Ali left."

"That's not exactly the same thing," Sara said sourly.

"If you want, I can give you the dance lessons," Richard offered. It's true they would have been good for Sara too, Alice thought, she was becoming a little gruff. Sara decided to ignore her brother's comment.

"So that's it? Can we go?" she asked.

"Well, there is only one last wish, but it's not binding," Jane said.

"Since these are Nonna Ali's last wishes, it seems just fair that we read all of them, whether they are binding or not," Sara insisted.

Brava, granddaughter, dammit, you only get to express your last wishes once.

Jane put her glasses back on and continued.

"As for me, I would like to be cremated, and that my ashes fly from the top of the Corno Grande, on the Gran Sasso. However, should this turn out to be too difficult, I would at least like them to be scattered in the historic center of L'Aquila."

"What?!"

Alice understood their reaction. True, at some point she had entertained the thought of going back to L'Aquila, at least after death, but she was no longer sure it was a good idea. She found that her location on the shelf wasn't too bad after all, especially now that she had managed to have the hourglass exiled to a drawer. Besides, looking at the group gathered there, it was hard to imagine who could fulfill that wish.

"Laguìla? What is that?" asked Mark.

"La-ki-là!" Valerie corrected.

"The name rings a bell…"

"Let me guess… it must be a place where the Romans won a battle," Richard said ironically.

"La-ki-là, La-ki-là…" Valerie mused, "Now I remember! There was an earthquake some time ago, it was in all the newspapers for a few days. Wait a minute, I think a documentary just came out…"

"L'A-qui-la, 'qui' as in 'queasy'," Jane said, trying to provide the right pronunciation and some geographical coordinates to facilitate the discussion. "L'Aquila is the capital of the Abruzzi region, right in the middle of Italy. And yes, you're right, Valerie, there was an earthquake, my mother did mention it. But the Italian government intervened quickly and efficiently, and now everyone has a roof over their heads again."

"The Italian government... Who, Berlusconi? I'll believe it when I see it. If Berlusconi said so it cannot be true," said Valerie indignantly.

"Let's not start with politics again, please!" Richard exclaimed.

"Yes, please, don't start arguing about Sarkoni, Berluscazzi, and Puttan again!" said Kate exasperatedly, harkening to the conversation from the day before.

Valerie looked at her icily.

"You're right. Why waste time with foreign heads of state who insist on going by unpronounceable names, especially today, with all those sales going on?"

"Exactly!" Kate exclaimed, missing Valerie's sarcasm.

"Stop it, Valerie," said Richard, and he was surprised at his own resentment. Later, he would look for a way to hurt her. "And you are amazed that the rest of the world considers you French a bunch of snobs," he would say. And, from very far away, "And you are amazed if the rest of the world knows for a fact that you Americans are a herd of fools," she would reply. Harsh words. It is not uncommon, however regrettable, for estranged lovers to resort to national prejudice and stereotypes.

"And please do not forget, however, that we also have a certain experience with foreign heads of state and their unpronounceable names... Have you heard of Barack Hussein Obama?"

Only Kate echoed Mark's roaring laughter, more out of conjugal duty than anything else.

"I've already consulted other lawyers," Jane said, trying to keep the discussion on track. "This last wish, as I mentioned, is in no way binding. I think my mother, as I know... knew her, would be the first to not want to create problems with what was perhaps a fleeting whim."

"Yes, indeed. Jane sought another opinion just to make sure, but we could have told you the same thing ourselves.

You are under no obligation whatsoever to do what's written in the will," Jeff intervened.

"Especially when a wish is so darn impractical. How do you even get there? It wouldn't be a cheap or simple journey..." added Mark.

"I'll do it."

All eyes turned to Sara.

"Do you speak Italian?" asked Valerie.

"Italian is my first language," said Sara proudly, even if the conversations with Italian tourists in Moab had shaken her confidence.

"I don't think language is an issue, everyone in the world speaks English these days," Jeff added.

"How do you hope to finance this trip, pray tell?" Richard asked.

"Didn't we just hear about our inheritance?"

"And it would be appropriate if those who don't want to participate in this expedition personally, at least contribute financially," Valerie added. Her French accent was particularly noticeable. She realized that and reacted by going a step further. She turned to Sara.

"If you want, I could join you. I wouldn't mind going to that region. You know, that's where Sallustius and Ovid were born..."

Richard couldn't help but smile ironically.

"No thanks, Valerie," Sara answered without hesitation. "I really appreciate your offer and your support, but I have to go alone. In fact, if you don't have anything else to say, Mom, I'll go online and look for a ticket."

Without waiting for an answer, she got up and left the room.

MOAB, UTAH–WASHINGTON, D.C.
JANUARY 5–6, 2011

Everything was different from what Sara had imagined, everything. First of all, regardless of her proud announcement at Thanksgiving, she didn't really think she would have to travel alone, as she assumed Una would join her. She almost regretted not accepting the offer from Valerie, the only one who could have accompanied her. But she was tired of having strangers around and she felt everyone in her family was a stranger at this point. Jeff never had a passport and didn't see any need to cross the border anyway; Jane, after Nonna Ali's death, was terrified of losing Jeff too; Kate was more and more pregnant, and Richard... Never mind. Of course, no one had told her that they would not go, but it was all "we'll see," "later," and "maybe." Her grandmother was the only one who said yes or no in that house, it was one of the things they had in common. After making that promise at Thanksgiving, she was basically obliged to go. The others seemed to think that she was two years old and that they could easily distract her, make her forget things. Clarity, putting all your cards on the table: maybe that was the quality that attracted her to Una, so now she couldn't in all honesty reproach Una for having said, loud and clear, that she didn't want anything to do with that adventure. If Sara really felt the need to respect that wish, without taking into consideration that perhaps it had been, as Jane suggested, a fleeting whim, that there were objective difficulties, and that the dead should not impose their desires upon the living, she had to do it alone. Sara had not taken it well. She suspected that Una was still recovering from the Thanksgiving trip, and she couldn't blame her. Even Sara was surprised at the anxiety that her mother and her siblings induced in her. She had the impression that everyone played a part and demanded that she do the same, and this was unbearable. It was an impression that came from far away. When she was little she thought that the other family members had reached an agreement before her birth, that there were shared secrets from which she was excluded. It was one of the fixations that had led Jane to resort to a therapist for the first time, when Sara was still in elementary school. The only result was that Sara learned early on not to share her discoveries with her mother. Although she now realized that suspicion was absurd, she could not completely shake off the impression that the others were bound by a sort of pact that allowed them to tolerate, or even welcome, those family reunions where they never said one single meaningful or sincere word. In these situations, she always felt she was on the verge of exploding and sometimes, like that last Thanksgiving, she exploded for real. She could not resist the temptation to pierce the veil, to lay bare all the hypocrisy of their family life. There had been no premeditation, though. It had been an impulsive decision, and Una was wrong to be angry with her for not having been forewarned.

But there was something else, more serious, more substantial. On the eve of Sara's departure, Una went back to their first meeting at the grocery store. She confessed, all in one breath, that the cart incident had not been a lucky coincidence, but a tried-and-true ploy.

"It hurts me to tell you this," she added, "but I can't continue to let you believe that story, no matter how beautiful."

Sara felt abandoned and betrayed. She accused Una of all sort of things, of being a predator and a liar, of having kept silent all that time but, also, of having spilled the beans at that precise moment to get rid of her, because she obviously didn't care about her, she had never cared about anything or anybody, and couldn't wait until Sara left so she could be free to go back to the supermarket and fill her cart with bait for the next catch. Una tried to convince both Sara and herself that she'd done the right thing.

"I could never find the right time... I wanted to tell you before Thanksgiving. Come to think of it, maybe I should have. I couldn't wait any longer, couldn't let you go away like this."

A ruthless winter night had fallen as they talked. Sara insisted on walking back alone in the freezing cold. Julia was asleep, like the cat, and the only sign of life was the buzzing of the refrigerator on the ground floor. She took one last look at the suitcase and thought of the inevitable stop in Washington that awaited her. She had asked Jane to meet her at the airport only to bring her Nonna Ali, or whatever was left of her, but the complications of the itinerary had forced her to transfer from the national to the international airport, making a prolonged face-to-face with her mother inevitable. She pulled the covers over her head, curled up and plunged into a dreamless sleep.

When she woke up and lugged her suitcase downstairs, Una was already there, talking to Julia who disappeared into the kitchen muttering something about the cranberry orange bread and the temperature of the oven. A few customers lingered around. The tourist season was long over, now it was mostly locals.

"Hi... I didn't expect to see you," Sara said. "Shouldn't you be at work?"

"I'll go later. I had to see you. I have something to tell you."

Una had prepared that "something" during a sleepless

night. She just blurted it all out. It was not easy to correct the image that Sara had of her as a coherent woman, in touch with herself and with the world. That was an ideal, far removed from a reality made of missteps, approximations, painful memories. As Una spoke, Sara realized how little, after all, she knew about her, how little she had asked, absorbed as she was in her own problems. Yet, Una continued, Sara had made her reflect on her absurd attempt to catch the moon in a trap, in its moment of maximum splendor. Did she remember? She had used those exact words. "In a trap." She also had a request for Sara, something she would like Sara to think about. She wanted Sara to erase from her mind that image of Una as the embodiment of harmony and instead believe in her desire to create something beautiful together.

"Come back," she concluded, and there was trepidation in her voice. "Come back to me, and I will be worthy of you... worthy of us."

Sara didn't remember ever hearing Una talk for so long. The speech was confused and betrayed all the preparation that it had required of her. And yet, Sara only had to go back to their first night hiking to understand it perfectly.

"Like the phases of the moon?" she asked. "Should we follow the phases of the moon?"

Una nodded.

"Like the phases of the moon."

As the plane began its descent towards National Airport, the city seemed so close that Sara could make out the Washington Monument, the Lincoln Memorial, the Capitol. National Airport. Nonna Ali refused to call it by its official name, Ronald Reagan Airport. She used to remind everybody how Ronald Reagan had fired the air traffic controllers who were striking for better working conditions—an ominous sign of what his presidency would entail, and the damage it would bring to working people across the country. To name the airport of the nation's capital after him meant to add insult to injury. The others could call it whatever they wanted, for Nonna Ali it would always be National Airport. She was truly revolutionary, Nonna Ali, always on the side of the working classes and against capitalism. Sara smiled at that colorful language—so twentieth-century, really.

"Rebellious... always," Jane confirmed, while the gate raised in the parking garage.

"Do you remember?" she continued as soon as they came out of the darkness. "Only a few months ago, she bought posters of Che Guevara and Janis Joplin for her bedroom... Can you imagine your grandmother, at eighty, with Che Guevara and Janis Joplin on the wall, like a teenager in the Seventies?"

"*Summertime, child, your living's easy. Fish are, fish are jumping out and the cotton, Lord, cotton's high, Lord so high,*" Sara sang softly. "Her favorite, she sang it to me often... Under her breath, she sang it almost like a lullaby. *Hush, baby, baby, baby, baby now, no, no, no, no, no, no, no, don't you cry, don't you cry...* I know, I sang out of tune, but it is not an easy piece, and then she sang it out of tune too, didn't she?"

Out of tune indeed! Jane laughed, and Sara thought that it was nice to be able to laugh again about Nonna Ali's eccentricities. For a while, it seemed that death had triumphed over everything and that you couldn't remember her without feeling sad, while in reality she was quite a funny lady when you thought about it.

"Do you remember when Obama won the election and she forced us to go all the way to the White House at midnight? We kept complaining that we had school and work the next day, but she didn't want to hear about it! And then she didn't know what to bring. In the end, she chose that ridiculous Italian alarm clock, that old, noisy piece of junk. She would make it go off and chant 'What time is it? It's time for you to go!' What a character..."

"Or when we insisted that she buy a pair of fancy shoes for Kate's wedding, and she couldn't find anything she liked, so she came back with yet another pair of sneakers..."

"Fancy sneakers, though, and red! Wedding sneakers, she called them!"

How angry Jane had gotten! Now she felt guilty about that, especially as she remembered her mother in front of her, small in her memory, who feebly protested, "As if these were real problems..."

You were so right, mom, what kind of problems were they?

Sara didn't notice Jane had gotten pensive.

"...and that time we came back from Disneyland and she picked us up, but then didn't have the faintest idea of where she had parked? We had to rent a car and go through all the airport parking lots before we found it... She could be so absent-minded! Speaking of which, where is... it?"

She was referring to the urn, and Jane understood immediately.

"In the trunk."

That exchange was enough for death to reassert its power. Sara looked for the right words. The closer she got to taking off, the more nervous she felt.

"This trip is important, isn't it? Perhaps once we set her free, as she has asked us to do, we will also be able to cope with her loss. She'll be a gentle presence again."

"Let's hope, Sara, let's hope... It's generous of you to take it this well. I, on the other hand, cannot stop myself from holding a bit of a grudge against my mother for that will, half a riddle and half a mockery... *The Progressive* for Kate, the dance lessons for Richard, the turkey recipe for me... Incidentally, the meal wasn't that bad this year, was it?"

Sara nodded politely. She remembered Jane reading the will. What a memorable scene! Nonna Ali managed to reveal to everybody a bit about themselves, even from the grave. Sara rushed to her grandmother's defense.

"You shouldn't resent her will. Don't we all have the right to be honest and sincere, at least in our wills? Sometimes I get the impression you didn't understand your mom much..."

It must run in the family, Jane thought, and she bit her tongue not to say it out loud. The therapist had been clear about that. She needed to think before speaking, weigh a sentence and determine whether it contributed to the conversation or, rather, fostered resentment and confusion. More than anything, she needed to avoid sarcasm, be wary of the fact that pointing out the logical flaws in her daughter's arguments sometimes did more harm than good. What a shame that Sara had always refused to do family therapy, and therefore was oblivious to those communication strategies. Jane felt the full weight of that injustice, as if only one of the boxers in the ring was bound by the rules, and the other could keep on hitting below the belt without even realizing he was doing something wrong. Jane held back her bitter comments and was immediately rewarded, because Sara was deep in thought and continued.

"I do understand you, though. It is difficult for the living to deal with the dead. Nonna Ali knew something about it, remember? *Non dee guerra co' morti aver chi vive*, she used to say."

"*The living must not wage war against the dead*," translated Jane, always more at ease with English than with Italian. "Yes, she did say that, and perhaps I'm finally beginning to understand what she meant. It's difficult. Death is so revolting, isn't it? I mean, even biologically, the rotting, the decay... How can the living contemplate death without disgust, without fear? Those who believe in God can console themselves by thinking they will resurrect, meet again, but not us..."

There was something else that she had discussed with her therapist and wanted to share. It was a discovery that she hoped would be useful to Sara, if not right away perhaps one day, when she would have to mourn her own mother.

"But after all I am not sure that even religion can make a big difference. There is something else. We blame the dead for deserting us, which is of course irrational. So, since we can't really complain about that, we cheat. We accuse them of other sins, of true or presumed misdeeds. They are not there to set us straight anyway."

"Sins, misdeeds… What can you possibly reproach Nonna Ali for?"

"Oh, a little bit of everything. I have already told you about my issue with her final wishes. But the list is long. I blame her for growing up without a father, for never feeling at home here in the U.S. but not having another place to go to either, for refusing to cook a proper Thanksgiving meal for so many years, for not taking us to church…"

"You, on the other hand, took us everywhere, didn't you? Methodists, Universalists, Jehovah's Witnesses… Boy did we shop around!"

"Yes, alright, perhaps I exaggerated. I was hoping a church would give us a sense of belonging, a community… Seriously, it works for so many people. Why didn't it work for us?"

"Because fundamentally we are atheists, remember? Like Nonna Ali."

"Atheists, atheists… That's a big word! Who knows what we are… You do need to make some compromises in life. There, I blame my mother for not having taught me how to compromise."

Sara looked at her mother in disbelief.

"Sure, I did make a few compromises," resumed Jane who was in one of her moments of grace, when she seemed to be able to read her daughter's mind, "but without conviction, without ever being able to fully believe in them. I mean, sure, I made them, but I was always aware that they were compromises, which is a way of undermining your own effort, really…"

It was never easy for Sara to follow the acrobatics of Jane's logic. She was so absorbed by the conversation that she only noticed they hadn't taken the highway when her mother parked in front of a restaurant.

"But my flight..." she protested.

"Your flight is in five hours... You don't want to spend all this time at the airport, do you? And then you'd better eat, otherwise you'll be poisoned by the food on the plane."

It was a Lebanese restaurant, elegant without being pretentious.

"Do you come here often?" Sara asked.

"No, I have never been here, but I read an article, I saw photos and menus on the Internet... In other words, I did my homework. I thought you would like it."

The appetizers were indeed excellent, varied and very fresh. From the tabbouleh to the stuffed vine leaves, Sara ate everything with the satisfaction and appetite of her eighteen years. Jane felt a tinge of maternal pride. Her baby was hungry; her baby was eating. That didn't come as a surprise. Opening a bed and breakfast surely hadn't turned Julia miraculously into a chef. The cranberry orange bread must have remained her greatest achievement.

"How is Una?" she asked while waiting for the kebab.

Sara tensed up immediately.

"Good."

"I'm glad. And how are things between you two?"

"Good... What is this, you've decided to play the part of the modern mom?"

Jane looked at her with surprise, then burst out laughing.

"Look at you, you're unbelievable! You told us about you two, and you told us in that way, hoping that we would react badly, so that you in turn could hold it against us, and blame our closed-mindedness and lack of understanding! And because we're not actually shocked, you get all upset... If you must know, I don't find anything strange in this relationship of yours."

"And Richard, Jeff, Kate…??"

"Go ahead and call them whenever you want to know how they feel about it. I will certainly not play the mediator. As far as I'm concerned though, I'm happy for you."

"Because you think it's a phase, as Kate so eloquently put it!"

"Everything is a phase; our life is a phase."

"Mom, please don't start with the clichés!"

"I don't know if it's a phase. You don't know it either, for that matter. And then, not to bring up unpleasant memories, but your straight phase kept me pretty busy. Whatever it is, I am happy for you, for both of you, I didn't like thinking of you all alone in Moab. And then, instinctively, I like that girl. Well, she is not exactly a communicator, that's for sure…"

"What do you mean?" asked Sara, again on edge.

"What do I mean? Exactly what I said. With your grandmother, you always talked and talked, everything needed to be looked at from various perspectives. What did she say? The unexamined life is not worth living."

"Socrates said that, not her."

"Whatever, now don't be nitpicky… Anyway, first you get on everybody's nerves for analyzing the explicit and implicit, the understood and the implied; then you get into a relationship with someone who says one word every hour, and you get annoyed when somebody points that out…"

"Una has other ways of communicating."

Jane decided not to investigate Una's forms of nonverbal communication. Modern mom alright, but let's not exaggerate.

The thought of Una brought Sara back to her recent sorrows.

"Who knows, Kate may be right, maybe it is a phase after all," she said sadly, "and maybe it's over already."

She impulsively related her conversation with Una the night before. Just the night before! Moab already felt very far away.

Jane did not seem to find anything reprehensible in Una's pick-up strategy. She thought it charming, in some strange way.

"It's like being at a bus stop and asking everyone what time it is, right? It's a request for love, normal and innocent enough. What counts is what happened after, what you are now."

Sara felt like the sensitive child that she used to be, who cried inconsolably about the death of the spider in her favorite fairy-tale—"but it's a story... and it's a spider!" Richard would tease her. She got even more defensive.

"Perhaps it's normal for straight people..."

"Now this! You are already throwing blanket statements about 'straight people'!"

This time Jane wasn't able to restrain herself.

"That's all we needed, a new label, as if your arsenal was not well-stocked enough already: children vs. parents, sisters vs. brothers, women vs. men... Let's add gay vs. straight to the list!"

Sara attempted an uneasy smile.

"Listen," Jane resumed, encouraged by her daughter's silence, "I know that these four years of difference between you and Una may seem like a lot to you, and I also understand that, in her environment, she might seem full of certainties to you, a rock..."

Sara nodded.

"...but trust me, I do have a bit more experience than either of you, and I watched you both, you know, at Thanksgiving. You are two young women in search of your place in the world. And Una was right to abdicate her role as a guide."

Sara had continued to play with a piece of pita bread. The waiter arrived with the dessert menu.

"A baklava for me," Jane ordered.

"But mom...!" Sara protested. She ordered a rice pudding, just to keep her company. She waited until the waiter left to resume talking.

"But mom, a baklava is a million calories! What's happening to you?"

"Nothing is happening to me, I am in a celebratory mood, I don't often have the chance to spend a little time with my daughter. And anyway, since I had that scare, I've decided to be a little more indulgent toward myself."

"What scare?"

"That's right, I didn't get the chance to tell you. It happened right before Thanksgiving, they found a marker in my blood that seemed to indicate ovarian cancer. My mother's death had already thrown me into a state of absolute confusion, the fear that I was about to follow her so soon messed up my brain a bit."

"I bet! And then...?"

"I was so convinced the end was approaching that I started to have the most bizarre conversations with Nonna Ali's little box. I even began to do some exercises. I was trying to imagine the world without my presence. Isn't that strange?"

"...And then?" Sara repeated.

"Have you ever tried it? I bet Buddhists do something like that. Maybe I have to try Buddhism. At any rate, I was trying to develop a complete indifference towards the world, let it go on without my emotional investment... A complete failure. The phone rang, the cat jumped on me, the washing machine finished and I needed to put the clothes in the dryer..."

"Mom! Please, let's get to the damn point!" Sara burst out, exasperated. "The blood test, the marker, the ovarian cancer... Have you found out anything more? How are you now?"

"Ah... good, thanks. They did a biopsy, an annoying little thing, the general anesthesia gave me a bad reaction, I spent a night at the hospital. But the results came back negative, I don't have anything! You can't imagine, I felt born again!"

"I bet you did!" Sara exclaimed, relieved. "But why didn't you say anything?"

"I wanted to, you know. I had in mind this great conversation around the Thanksgiving table, on the importance of love, of understanding... A bit of a sermon, now that I think of it, more than a conversation. But the turkey had already dried out a little and then we started to talk about something else. I decided the time wasn't right."

Despite Jane's cheerful tone, Sara felt guilty. She remembered all too well how she had hijacked the conversation at Thanksgiving.

"I'm sorry," she whispered.

"What are you sorry for? I'm fine, I told you!"

"I'm sorry that I didn't realize what was going on, that I didn't give you time to speak..."

She stopped, as a suspicion went through her mind.

"Did you tell Richard?"

Jane broke into a bitter smile.

"Go ahead, let's add this to the list of complaints! Richard who always had a newer bike, a better report card, and could run faster; Richard who is privy to his mother's secrets on her deathbed... Thank God I was an only child!"

Sara fell silent for a moment, but the infinite anguish of the neglected daughter got the better of her.

"So, you told him."

Jane stopped smiling.

"It's pointless for me to answer a question, or rather, an accusation like that. I'll leave you with the doubt. But please stop blaming me for your aching need for affection. It wasn't my indifference, or my neglect as you would say, that caused it. And do not overwhelm others with the task of satisfying it, this need for affection. Perhaps this is what Una is trying to say. Take charge of the pain of others, of their weaknesses, and see how it goes."

There, she had done it again, she had given up on caution and protocols. For a moment Jane was afraid Sara would yell and storm out of the restaurant. But instead she remained silent, absorbed in thought.

"I miss Nonna Ali so much," she finally said.

She was not trying to change the subject, quite the contrary. All of a sudden, she realized everything was connected.

Jane struggled to keep her anxiety at bay. She told herself that this trip was just her daughter's European grand tour, albeit under rather peculiar circumstances. Wasn't this what young wealthy Americans used to do, back in the 19th century? And not only men, just think of Margaret Fuller. True that she got in some serious trouble and ended up drowning in a shipwreck, they couldn't even find her body. Not a happy precedent. Jane tried to think about somebody else, but she couldn't remember any specific case. At any rate, thousands went and came back just fine. Maybe this trip would open up new horizons for Sara, shake her up. Jane was beginning to abandon the great plans she had in store for her daughter. So what if she didn't become a lawyer like her mom, a surgeon or a politician? She glanced at Sara's determined profile on the Dulles Access Road. Let's just hope that she learns how to live with herself, she concluded.

Sara could tell her mother was worried.

"Don't worry, Mom. For a foreign country, Italy is as familiar as it gets. And that old acquaintance of Nonna Ali's promised to help me out. And then after all that time in Utah I am a mountain gal, I am sure I'll find myself at home in Abruzzo!"

The elegant outline of Dulles airport appeared all of a sudden on their left as they approached the main terminal. Glass, steel, and concrete combined to suggest the shape of a wing, the idea of flying. Sara was excited and terrified.

"Let me park, I'll accompany you to the check in at least."

"No, thanks, I'll be fine."

The conversation with her mother had been surprisingly enriching, but now Sara felt she needed some time on her own. She was also eager to check whether Una, disobeying her recommendations, had sent her a message, even if just to wish her a safe flight.

"Why not? I can help you with the bags!"

"No, really, thanks mom, don't worry, I don't have much stuff, and it's a shorter walk to the counter if you just drop me off at the entrance."

"I can leave you at the entrance, park the car and meet you at the check-in.

Jane realized her plan didn't make much sense and that her anxiety was only increasing her daughter's.

"Never mind," she concluded.

She opened the trunk and handed Sara the small black box with a conspiratorial air, as if they were smugglers. Sara quickly slid it into her backpack. The suitcase was Valerie's, whether a gift or a loan, she did not quite know. It was red with white dots, impossible to confuse with somebody else's luggage at the baggage claim, unlike the thousands of black suitcases that always ended up in the wrong hands, at least according to Valerie. Yes, she was checking only that, while the backpack was her carry-on. Her precious secret cargo made her feel like a spy in a movie. She wandered through the halls, taking in the sight of people rushing to their flights and the sweet aroma of pretzels and low-fat yogurt. She feared her inexperience as a traveler. The weekends in Montreal with Nonna Ali and her stay in Moab seemed like short getaways, now that she was about to cross the ocean.

L'AQUILA, ITALY
JANUARY 7, 2011

Good thing I mapped out the itinerary ahead of time, Sara thought, as she tried to find her way around the terminal after retrieving her suitcase. From the airport, a rattling train plastered with graffiti took her through a nondescript suburb all the way to Rome's Tiburtina Station. The station itself was clean and modern but its surroundings were drab and uninviting, and in order to reach the bus terminal Sara had to walk under what looked like a highway suspended over huge cement pillars. A fleet of buses was waiting in a busy area that resounded with foreign languages she couldn't identify. It reminded her of the set of one of those movies Nonna Ali used to watch, about the Soviet Union or Eastern Europe. Most of the buses were setting off for far away destinations, from Poland to Romania. She felt embarrassed about her apprehension as she moved her backpack from her shoulder to her chest so that she could keep her eyes on it at all times. She was uncomfortable about the instinctive mistrust that she felt once she realized that she was, unequivocally, in a foreign land. The jet lag contributed to her sense of unreality. She had not slept at all in her cramped seat in economy class, wedged between a middle-aged man who ordered a cocktail every hour and a woman in the aisle seat who got up only once during the entire flight. The lack of movement and the rush from the sugar-loaded breakfast increased her sense of displacement.

She had just missed the coach for L'Aquila, so she bought a ticket for the next one and she leaned on a railing by the departure booth, too tired to read and too wary to enter the small cafe with all her luggage. When the bus finally arrived, she realized it was a double decker and her seat was on the top floor, right above the driver, in front of the wide windshield that provided a 180-degree view. On its way out of Rome, the bus went through another gloomy suburb that made Sara feel as if she had entered a postmodern vortex of advertising bill-boards and high-rise buildings. She pulled herself away from negative thoughts and tried to concentrate on her task, taking a step at a time, as her grandmother always urged her to do. She closed her eyes, easing herself into her seat. When she reopened them, the landscape had changed completely. The bus had eased out of the city traffic and was climbing between little hills dotted with villages. They spoke of attachment to life, the cycle of the seasons, resistance. The horizon had broadened, and Sara's eyes swept over a panorama graced by cultivated fields, manicured farms, soaring bell towers. She felt her breathing calm down, her tension fade away. All of a sudden she thought of her luggage. She remembered handing her suitcase to the driver. How about the backpack? She got up to make sure it was in the rack above her head. Since no one had taken the seat next to hers, she put it there, almost hugging it. It's alright Nonna Ali, we're going home.

Sara was not the only one to notice the change in scenery. Imperceptible signs (lower humidity? a brighter light?) alerted Alice that she was on her way. *Ad Aquilam! Ad Aquilam!* She seemed to hear Saint Bernardine's cry echoing across the valley. Sara had not lied, they were going home! Suddenly Alice's last wish no longer seemed meaningless to her. She recognized those proud villages, signposts along the hikes and adventures of her youth. She remembered them separately, each the destination of a different journey. The highway that now connected them lined them up in a coherent sequence, like beads in a necklace, like the frames of a film. With its distinctive fortress, Castel Madama came into view, honoring with its very name duchess Margherita, governor of Abruzzi; higher up they encountered Carsoli, the border town; climbing further still, Pietrasecca rose on the edge of a vertiginous cliff, with its doorways opening directly onto the abyss and its mysterious caves below. Frequent tunnels interrupted the view. The first one caught Alice by surprise, making her doubt that the glimmer of consciousness she had preserved was now abandoning her, precisely when she was just beginning to feel a resurging interest in life. But she soon got used to those pauses and took advantage of them to situate the bus route within the landscape of her memory. At the end of the longest tunnel, the distinctive profile of a dark mountain dusted in snow came into view. The *Pandoro*! She remembered Fulvio opening a box to show her the elegant cake he had carefully guarded on his knees all the way from Verona. He posed like an expert as he put confectioners' sugar in the bag, shaking it vigorously until, voilà, the powder uniformly embraced the sticky surface. The resemblance made them both laugh. Yes, the *Pandoro* was like the Tornimparte mountain with its fresh snow gently evaporating under the sun. From then on, that would be its nickname. So many of the peaks had monikers that referred to their adventures or their readings, creating a private map that only the two of them could decipher. But if that was the *Pandoro*, then they couldn't be very far. Already the massive chain of the Gran Sasso loomed on the horizon. Its summit, the Corno Grande, seemed to invite and defy her now as it did when she was young and alive. How many miles left, then? Sara, don't sleep, don't you feel the air is changing, can't you interpret the signs? The semicircle of one last tunnel framed L'Aquila, resting there in its valley, crowned by the Apennines. Then the bus shot out into the sun, amid glorious heaps of fresh snow.

I've come back to my city. These are my own old tears,
my own little veins, the swollen glands of my childhood.

"Hey, we have arrived."

A sharp voice awoke Sara. She was the only one left on the bus. She jumped up and instinctively reached for her backpack. It was still there. And the rest? She hurriedly got off. The driver had already removed her polka dotted suitcase from the baggage compartment and was back in his seat, eager to leave. She moved out of his way quickly, without knowing which direction she needed to go. She had slept soundly on the bus, comforted by the view outside the window. What a strange feeling, though. She could have sworn that someone was sitting next to her.

She remembered the plan she had discussed with Jane. A taxi. In fact, there it was, a single white taxi. She hurried inside, afraid that somebody might take it but realizing soon after that there was nobody else around. She handed the driver a piece of paper with the address, choosing not to trust her Italian for such an important task. The man stared blankly at her.

"Is this where you are staying?"

"Huh?"

For a moment Sara feared she had gotten off at the wrong stop, after all she had only gone from one parking lot to another. The man rephrased his question.

"What is it, one of the C.A.S.E.?"

What a strange inquiry, Sara thought. Of course it was a house, a *casa* or, as the driver said, one of the *case*, houses.

"Yes, it is a home, a house…"

Or perhaps he was asking whether it was a house as opposed to an apartment?

"I am asking whether this is the address of one of the buildings in the C.A.S.E. Project."

The man noticed Sara's confusion, seemed to decide that

she couldn't help him, and made a couple of phone calls before starting the car.

"Is it far?" Sara asked, mindful of all the stories about
charming but dishonest Italians and determined not to be immediately taken in.

"Ten kilometers."

Sara did not like taxis. The fear of finding herself at the
mercy of a stranger, dragged to a nondescript suburb where
she wouldn't be able to orient herself, gave her the courage to
formulate an objection.

"I... I thought this was an address in L'Aquila."

The driver raised his eyebrows.

"Where are you coming from?"

"From Rome."

The man looked at her, skeptical.

"The United States," she confessed.

"That's what I thought... No one lives in the center of
L'Aquila anymore, don't you read the papers in the States?
There was an earthquake."

"The earthquake was two years ago," Sara retorted, determined not to be intimidated. "I read that everything has been
rebuilt."

"You didn't read very carefully, did you? Or perhaps you
did, but you read a lie. The truth is that nothing has been rebuilt, everything has been built anew. Do you know what
L'Aquila means in Italian? It means the eagle. Well, L'Aquila
is no more, but if you want I can take you to our fancy shopping mall. To add insult to injury, do you know what its name
is? L'Aquilone..."

"The big eagle!"

The man burst into an uncontrollable fit of laughter.

"No! I see what you mean, but no... Aquilone means kite.
Quite a leap, don't you think? From L'Aquila to L'Aquilone,
from eagle to kite... This is the miracle you must have read
about! They even had the guts to put up a sign welcoming

shoppers to 'the new center of town,' though they were forced to take it down right away."

Sara was embarrassed about her mistake; she should have known better. Then again, her confusion seemed to have made the man more amenable towards her. He was still smiling and muttering "the big eagle!" under his breath. She decided it was a good time to gather additional information.

"And… what about the 'case' then? They are not 'houses'?"

"Well, yes and no… It's another little masterpiece of theirs… Let me explain it to you. They kicked us out of L'Aquila. Our homes are still in ruins, but they took over the land around the town and built some ugly apartment buildings. But they didn't want us to feel displaced or anything, so they thought really hard and came up with the perfect acronym—C.A.S.E. It sounds like the plural of "casa," home, but actually stands for… wait, I can never get it right… Complessi Antisismici Sostenibili Ecocompatibili. In Italian it's a mouthful… Perhaps it sounds better in English?

"Eco-compatible Sustainable Anti-Seismic Complexes…"

Sara translated the acronym as best she could. A mouthful indeed, kind of redundant. She wasn't completely sure what it meant.

"Beautiful, that's just beautiful," the driver commented ironically. "It sounds weird in any language, doesn't it? Pretty soon they'll try to convince me that not only am I surrounded by C.A.S.E., but that I live in a city, a C.I.T.T.À. Ah, what a sweet life, what a dolce V.I.T.A.!"

Sara didn't dare ask the driver whether the last two acronyms really existed or he'd invented them himself. All of a sudden, he seemed tired of that strained conversation, turned the radio on and drove off.

Ten minutes later Sara stood in front of an apartment building resting on what seemed like stilts but were actually, she quickly realized, support columns that created a cavernous hall at the ground level, where cars were parked. The building was not very tall but rather long. Sara took a few steps backwards to take a better look. Another building stood right in front of the first, and a third one was perpendicular to the other two. So, these were the C.A.S.E. the taxi driver was talking about. The space between the buildings was quite desolate. The color of the brown grass was barely distinguishable from that of the soil, and the few little trees planted here and there seemed to be struggling. Sara's glance instinctively turned to the majestic snow-clad mountains in the background. She unwrapped an energy bar, chewed it slowly while looking around, alternating bites and sips of water. She didn't realize she was being watched until she finished eating and turned around. A small, grey-haired woman smiled at her.

"You must be Sara! *Benvenuta...*"

One of Alice's old schoolmates, Concetta, had agreed to host Sara for a few days. Sitting at her kitchen table, Sara quickly realized that English was not really a lingua franca like Jeff seemed to believe. Proving her mother's new partner wrong always gave her some sweet satisfaction. In this particular case, however, that pleasure was soon overshadowed by major communication problems. After two or three ow-r-u and some awkward pauses in the conversation, Concetta switched to Italian and proudly showed her the picture of a young man in shorts and a T-shirt, covered in mud from head to toe.

"My son, Alessandro plays scrum-half for L'Aquila Rugby! But he's always done great in school too. Now he studies astrophysics at the university. His older brother, Aldo, is an engineer, imagine how busy he is after the earthquake! He has helped me so much to navigate all the paperwork for getting this place, I don't know what I would have done without him. They'll be here soon, both of them."

Sara was forced to resort to her Italian, something she would have gladly avoided because she noticed during the preparations for her trip that the language they used to speak at home was somewhat old-fashioned. Their first phone call to Concetta had been painful.

"How do you say *ashes* in Italian?" Jane asked with a panicked look on her face, covering the receiver with her hand while Sara mentally scanned her grandmother's books.

"*Cenere*," she finally said, with a hint of pride in her voice.

"Is it feminine? *La cenere*?" Jane asked dubiously.

"Masculine: *Il cenere*," Sara clarified. Then, making an even greater effort, "*Il cenere muto*," she added. Jane's explanation that Sara needed to go to L'Aquila to scatter *the cenere muto dell'avola*, her forebear's mute ashes, met with stunned silence from the other end of the line. Jane even thought for a moment that Concetta had hung up, and regretted not having insisted that Sara, whose Italian was so much better than hers, make that call herself. Her daughter had never liked phones, though, and Jane herself thought it would be a good idea to get personally involved, just to show that Sara's trip to L'Aquila had the support of the whole family. By the time Concetta replied that sure, Sara was welcome to stay at her place, Jane had broken out in a sweat, and couldn't wait to hang up.

Sara pointed out that "cenere muto dell'avola" sounded too much like a line in a Romantic poem, and tried to remember where exactly she had heard the expression. The whole thing had been rather embarrassing. In order to avoid behaving like stereotypical ignorant Americans, they had overcompensated and may have ended up looking like snobs.

"That's possible, but what did you want me to say? Isn't it always better to err on the side of politeness and propriety when you first meet somebody?"

Jane's question didn't really require an answer, and both agreed that the conversation, however awkward, had reached its objective, which was to find lodging for Sara in what was essentially a disaster zone. Jane didn't dare offer monetary compensation for fear of offending Concetta, but had a case of wine delivered to her address, and made sure Sara had enough cash to contribute generously to the daily expenses.

Now that she could no longer rely on her mother to sort out the practical side of her mission, Sara realized she needed to become more comfortable with the language. She started paying attention to every word and tried to get used to the song-like inflection of Concetta's speech. She decided to keep a language journal of her discoveries. She wished she had recorded the cab driver, what a character! She was sure she'd never forget the Italian word for "kite" for the rest of her life.

That labored conversation must have felt awkward to Concetta as well.

"Feel free to use the Internet if you'd like. The password is on the fridge."

"Thanks, that's great."

Sara felt as if she had been away for a long time. She had promised Jane only a text once in a while, as astronomical roaming charges and the time difference made calls impractical. Sara was determined to keep communication to a minimum. She wanted a break from everybody, and had explicitly asked Una not to contact her. She still needed time to go over their last evening together and Una's confession. She hadn't anticipated feeling so lonely, though. Deep down she hoped Una would ignore her request and write. But when she finally managed to go online, Sara found only ads, reminders from Princeton, and special offers from various stores. She was almost about to log out when she saw a message from Valerie.

"By the time you read this, you will be in Italy already. I hope you had a smooth trip. I have been thinking a lot about your grandmother's last wish, and about your decision to honor it. It made me think of Antaeus, the giant that draws strength by touching his mother Gaia, the earth. Hercules managed to defeat him because he held Antaeus between his arms as he fought him. This way, he lifted him off the ground and prevented him from reaching back to the source of his power. The story reminded me of your grandmother. She must have felt like Antaeus in Hercules's grip. She wanted to go back home, to her mother earth. Her last wish was not a whim. There is something more, I am sure, and I am sure you'll find out what it is. Good luck with your mission!"

There was also a P.S.: "Your brother and I broke up as soon as we got back to Austin."

Sara drummed her fingers on the desk, barely convinced, then wrote:

"How can she regain strength if she's already dead?"

She added a P.S. in response to Valerie's. "Good for you." As soon as she pressed "send" she regretted it. Poor Richard, that was mean of her. She was almost tempted to send a message to her brother who was now single again, alone as usual, but she didn't know what to write, and was afraid of deepening the rift between them. It was not a message to send on the spur of the moment, better to think about it.

"Do you want something? Tea, coffee, a snack, a drink?" Concetta asked from the kitchen.

"No, thank you. I've almost finished, sorry..."

"I know, the connection is slow. Take your time."

Soon Concetta's apartment filled with people, or at least that was the impression, given its small size and the volume of the conversation. Alessandro arrived, tall and athletic, with a couple of friends.

"Mom, you probably remember Francesca and Giulio, the social workers."

Concetta rushed to put a bottle of Montepulciano wine and some glasses on the table. The three were already talking spiritedly before they entered, and once in the apartment they continued to debate the allocation of public funds and the rebuilding process. Then Alessandro spotted Sara's suitcase.

"What's that? Do you have guests?"

"Oh, yes! I told you about her, remember? She's the grand-daughter of Alice, a high school friend, who went to the States half a century ago and worked as a librarian…"

"Worked…?"

"Yes. She died a few months ago, and she asked her granddaughter to scatter her ashes from the top of the Corno Grande."

"*Oh temé!*" They all looked at her with surprise.

"I know it seems strange. I told her that in this season it is almost impossible, unless you are very well trained, which she isn't, and have professional equipment, which she doesn't. But Alice must have thought about that, because she suggested as an alternative plan that her ashes be scattered in the center of L'Aquila.

"*Oh temé,*" they repeated all together.

"Now this!" Giulio burst out.

Francesca was outraged.

"Now we've heard it all! First there were those who wanted to send a brick from the collapsed Student Dorms into orbit, then the organizers of the Ferrari show in Piazza Duomo, then the meeting of the G8… How can people be so insensitive and turn tragedies into tourism? Not only did the center of L'Aquila turn into a grave for so many people, now we even have to put up with Americans who want to join the party and scatter ashes amidst the ruins!"

"Does she know about the earthquake?" Giulio asked ironically.

"This just goes to show how little people around the world know about what's going on here," Alessandro said pensively.

"I would have thought that an Italian-American with a grandmother from L'Aquila would know something," sighed Giulio.

"Maybe they could scatter the ashes somewhere else—in the countryside, or in that field by the mall, you know the one I am talking about," Francesca ventured.

"In any case it's absurd for a complete stranger to suggest such a thing," Giulio concluded.

"My grandmother is not a complete stranger!"

Sara felt herself blush as she stood at the door, but did not lower her gaze. Everybody else in the room turned toward her and fell silent. It hadn't been easy for Sara to make sense of the conversation, but the more she understood the more incensed she became. That final comment about her grandmother had been the last straw. Forget it, Alice tried to warn her from the little box. Forget it, they are like that. Not mean, but a little over-sensitive when it comes to their town, especially now. *Oh temé, temé, temé.*

"My grandmother was not a complete stranger here. She was certainly not crazy, and if she asked to come back here she must have had a reason."

She lifted her eyes to meet the expressions of her audience, ranging from skeptical to embarrassed, and searched for a more convincing argument.

"Like Antaeus who had to lay on his mother to regain his strength, my grandmother needed to return to L'Aquila," she said, hoping that her translation would not transform a learned reference into some vile allusion. Francesca's puzzled look was anything but reassuring.

"So, who was your grandmother?"

"Her name was Alice... Alice Arienti."

"Arienti...? That's not a name from around here," Francesca diagnosed.

"Are you sure?" said Alessandro. "Because you're right, it's not a common last name, and yet I could swear I heard it somewhere... but where?"

"Wasn't there some Arienti who married one of the Mancini girls?"

"Mancinis who? The ones who had the bakery on Via Cimino?"

"No, those were the Placidis. No, the Mancinis I am talking about were three brothers..."

"Nooo! Those were the Marconis."

Sara was stunned to witness the creation of an elaborate genealogy that stretched back a couple of centuries linking her grandmother to Mr. Mancini, the notary public, who had managed to snatch up a plot of land from the famous Torlonias, the barons. Except that then his son, the gambler, lost it at Montecarlo along with the rest of the family's fortune. Following along with the speculations of Concetta and her guests, she learned of Carbonari movements, Nazi retaliations, instances of brazen opportunism, precipitous falls from grace, unspeakable depravations, Masonic lodges, and genetic predispositions. The problem was that, with the exception of Concetta who didn't seem to remember much, everyone present was much younger than Alice. Sara couldn't provide much information. She had no idea what school Nonna Ali had attended, her address in town, exactly when and why she left. Perhaps Alessandro and his friends felt some remorse for dismissing Alice's last wish so hastily, but they certainly showed great passion in trying to recreate her lineage. Sara liked that, she already felt less of a stranger. She didn't understand most of the references and certainly didn't know any of the people mentioned, but didn't dare interrupt.

"Alice and I studied together with the Benedectine nuns," said Concetta, "but we are talking about something like sixty years ago, when Suor Arcangela was Mother Superior. What a character she was, that Suor Arcangela! Then I got married and moved while Alice went to college. I really don't know why she decided to transplant herself overseas.

"To transplant...?" asked Sara.

"Yes," said Alessandro, who seemed to understand Sara's efforts to follow the conversation. "Like a plant, when you move it from one plot of land to another. Or wait, even better... like an organ, get it? Heart transplant, kidney transplant."

Sara understood what he meant, but the expression still didn't feel right in this case. It wasn't only Nonna Ali, but not even her daughter and grandchildren seemed to have been successfully transplanted. Rather than sprouting sturdy roots, they kept drifting around. If they were plants, they were not oaks but tumbleweeds, the shrubs without roots that spend their life bouncing around in the desert. Yes, that's what they were, perhaps because the land had turned out to be too hard and dry, or their roots too picky and fragile.

"So, back to square one," Francesca concluded, discouraged.

"Do you at least know when your grandmother left L'Aquila, and if she left alone?"

The latest lead—Celano's municipal secretary, who during the war hid an American who turned out to be a Getty and later on gave him enough money to take care of the whole family—had proven inconclusive. Sara shrugged her shoulders.

"She left on February 12, 1958, on an Alitalia flight from Ciampino to New York and yes, she was alone."

"Professor!" Concetta exclaimed, welcoming the newest arrival.

Fulvio! A flash of emotion stunned Alice.

They were all so engrossed in the conversation that they hadn't heard the man come in the door that had been left ajar. He was quite old, with white hair and a peculiar way of moving and speaking, a bit nervous and twitchy. He was obviously a man of stature. Alessandro jumped up to offer him his chair. The Professor thanked him, sat down, and made two strange gestures. He raised his right thumb to the sky and then rotated it toward the ground, like he was imitating the gesture the Roman crowds used to signal they wanted a gladiator to be put to death. Then he completed the movement with his thumb and index finger horizontal and parallel, about one inch from each other. It was only when Concetta hurried to pour him some Montepulciano that Sara understood that he was asking for a drink and indicating the desired amount. Nonna Ali's ironic words came back to her mind: "Italy is a great country for men!" Indeed.

But Alice didn't even notice, she was not in the right mood to make anthropological observations or criticize patriarchy. What a memory, Fulvio! February 12, 1958? True, or at least plausible. It must have been the beginning of '58, and it was so cold... Yes, it probably was February. Fulvio, do you still remember?

"I remember it well. 1957 had been awful, a year to forget. On the one hand, there was the Italian Communist party clumsily trying to justify the Soviet invasion of Hungary; on the other, Gaetano Azzariti, the former president of the anti-Semitic tribunal for the 'Defense of Race' during Fascism, became president of the Constitutional Court in place of Enrico De Nicola... Crazy times, I tell you! But precisely for this reason it was necessary to stay, resist, save the salvageable. But Alice gave a ride to a hitchhiker and decided to follow him to the States."

"Her father!" Francesca exclaimed, pointing at Sara.

"My father... no, wait... that was my grandfather!" Sara said, a bit confused herself.

"Yes, your grandfather, that's right. Sorry, it's all so confusing."

The Professor ignored the interruption.

"Well, there were also some signs of hope, if you knew how to read them. Things move slowly, but Alice was young and impatient. At any rate, since I couldn't talk her out of leaving, I offered to take her to the airport. When we arrived in Rome, I insisted that we visit the bookstore in Piazza Esedra to buy a copy of Renato Poggioli's anthology, *The Flower of Russian Poetry*. Have you read it? It's an authoritative, indispensable work that opened new frontiers, made the poems of Stalin's victims known to us. And to think that Alice, at the beginning, had refused to read it, because she believed it was counter-revolutionary! But then she kept me company as I read it, at the Tommasiana Library, and she grew more and more passionate about those poets. Blok, Yesenin, Akhamatova, Mandelstam... The true flower, the broken flower of Russian poetry. We spent hours copying down our favorite poems, we took turns dictating and writing, whispering so as not to disturb the other patrons, day after day, until closing time. A magnificent book, magnificent. If you read the correspondence between Cesare Pavese and Renato Poggioli, you get a pretty good idea of the opposition that such a noble project had to face in post-war Italy..."

An embarrassed cough introduced Francesca's attempt to bring the conversation back on track.

"I am sorry to interrupt, Professor, but let me get this straight. When you arrived in Rome you thought that it'd be a good idea to have your own copy of the book, since you liked it so much, so you went to the bookstore. Is that right? And then what happened? Did you go to the airport with her?"

The Professor looked at her absent-mindedly, as if he were still lost in the memory of his trip to Rome.

"Yes. Alice was so afraid she'd miss her flight that I had to insist that we at least stop at the bookstore, but she wasn't in the mood to visit Rome. We got the book, went to Ciampino, and so long Alice. That was the last time I saw her."

Sara thought that if her grandmother had missed that flight, she wouldn't have been born in the U.S., or perhaps wouldn't have been born at all.

"So, then Alice's story moves overseas..."

Everybody looked at Sara, who cleared her throat.

"Um, I don't know much more than what I already told you. She arrived, got pregnant almost immediately..."

"Oh!" Concetta exclaimed.

Sara decided to be frank. They were in the third millennium after all.

"To tell the truth, if you pay attention to the dates, she must have been pregnant when she left... already pregnant, I mean."

"Aaaahhhh!"

"Yes, and I understand that something like that was a bit of a scandal back then. Eric, my grandfather, the hitchhiker, died in an accident before my mother was born."

"Probably drunk," Jane always added at this point, but Sara opted to omit that detail out of a sudden concern for the family's honor.

"And why didn't she come back here then?"

"To return with a child out of wedlock, with her tail between her legs... She'd never have done it," the Professor interjected. "She had too much pride, and then objectively it wouldn't have been easy..."

"Saint Agnes, patron of gossip!" Francesca exclaimed, looking up.

Everyone laughed, to Sara's surprise. Alessandro, with a glance, encouraged her to ignore the interruption.

"Apart from the problems with her visa and the language barrier, I think that staying abroad was easier for her in that situation. You know, the U.S. is kind of..."

She was about to say "free," but held back. Even her sister Kate would understand that was not the right moment to brag about the good old U.S.A.

"And don't forget that we are talking about something that happened over fifty years ago. People were pretty uptight about these things back then," the Professor added.

"Half a century ago! It's incredible, when you think about it. How quickly life goes by..." Concetta whispered.

Wise words, Alice thought. Beware, mortals, life goes by quickly. You barely have the time to open a window, complain that the weather is changing, and sneeze.

"However, by law, ashes cannot be released in populated areas," concluded Concetta's older son, Aldo, who'd arrived in the meantime and had been silently following the conversation.

"Now, now, to define downtown L'Aquila as populated strikes me as somewhat anachronistic," Francesca commented.

"Things are moving along. Piazza Palazzo just reopened to the public and other areas will soon follow. You shouldn't take risks where public health is at stake," Aldo retorted.

"With all the asbestos still lying around from the collapsed buildings, I'm sure that this poor woman's ashes are not the worst public health hazard in town!" Alessandro protested, suddenly irritated.

"You can't do it, I tell you!" Aldo insisted. "Not to be too fastidious about it or anything, but have you thought about the details? Do you plan on going during the day, pretending to smoke and sprinkling a few ashes here and there? Or maybe you are dreaming up a clandestine night-time expedition? Just try not to end up in jail, will you?"

They all looked at each other hesitantly.

"I'll help you."

All eyes shifted to the Professor, who was in turn staring at Sara.

"I'll call Concetta's number tomorrow, okay? And we'll find the right place, don't worry."

The Professor rose, held out his hand.

"We have not been introduced. My name is Fulvio Innocenzi."

"Sara... Sara Westbridge."

As if their exchange had signaled the end of the evening, everyone got up. Concetta got worried as she looked at them. She would have preferred for someone to stay over and spare her the embarrassment of resuming her one-on-one conversations with her English-speaking guest, but after a quick survey of her refrigerator's contents she realized she couldn't invite them all to stay for dinner. The goodbyes went on for a long time. After everybody left, Concetta quickly cooked pasta with tomato sauce, with a little salad and sliced mozzarella. Sara found everything delicious, especially the mozzarella.

"Buffalo mozzarella?" she asked.

"No, you need to go further south to find that. This is made from cow's milk, but it's a local specialty. How do you like it?

"It's wonderful."

It truly was. It oozed a tasty, rich, slightly salted cream.

The sound of the television, that Concetta had rushed to turn on as soon as the door closed, saved both of them from having to carry on a conversation.

On the screen three women on a sofa were discussing the challenges of cohabitation.

"Beeg Broader," explained Concetta.

"What?"

"Beeg Broader, 'Il grande fratello.' You have it in America, don't you?"

Sara squinted, trying to understand what was going on.

"Yes, sure, Big Brother! Sure, we do have it in the States, but I don't watch much TV."

She was about to add something to justify her ignorance, but Concetta was very absorbed by the events on the screen.

"Ah, they eliminated them!"

"Who?"

"Those potty-mouths. It was all over the papers. Some of the contestants swore too much. I can't believe it! True, they exaggerated, but it's not fair to eliminate participants just because of that, a warning would have been enough. Only six of them are left at this point. What a shame, I liked that guy, what was his name… Matteo!"

Spending her first evening in Italy watching Big Brother seemed surreal to Sara but then again, she was also happy to avoid more conversation. She volunteered to do the dishes to give Concetta time to enjoy the rest of the show. She cleared the table and poured what was left on the plates—a piece of bread, a lettuce leaf, an apple peel—into the sink, pushing it all down the drain.

She let the water flow from the faucet and turned on a switch next to the sink. A sconce on the wall lit up. She looked around while the liquid filled half of the sink.

"Concetta?"

"Yes?" muttered Concetta, distractedly.

"I can't find the switch for the, um… ah, that thing that breaks the garbage into small pieces…"

"The what?"

Sara scanned the walls again. Perhaps it was a safety issue, the switch for the garbage disposal must be far away from the sink. She walked around the kitchen and even ventured back into the living room, operating all the switches she could find. Lights flickered on and off. The water in the sink was about to overflow. She shut the faucet off.

"What's going on?" Concetta asked.

"Nothing. We can talk about it later."

The episode of Big Brother ended with the elimination of Concetta's new favorite contestant. When she entered the kitchen, she noticed the sink was filled to the brim with reddish, greasy water.

"Oh my…"

"Do you have Drain-O, by any chance? Or perhaps…"

"What?"

Sara made a snaking gesture with her arm, feeling a bit awkward. Concetta looked at her perplexed.

"We need a plunger, that's what we need," she said, "but we don't have one. The apartment came equipped with a champagne bucket, but not a plunger. I guess they were expecting more sophisticated tenants. I will ask around tomorrow. I am sure one of the neighbors must have one."

"I'm sorry," mumbled Sara. All of a sudden she felt like crying.

"Don't worry, these things happen. Let's go to bed, we'll figure it out tomorrow."

In bed, Sara tried to reorganize her thoughts, review the names of the people she had met, analyze her feelings. The thought of Una suddenly slipped into her mind and made her shiver. She imagined feeling her as close as during their first night by the Colorado River. She brought a hand between her legs, uncertain of whether to follow the flow of her desire or to let it all melt away in her sleep. She would have given anything to know if Una was also thinking about her now. She wanted to believe that a similar current was bringing her closer, so that their thoughts would meet above the ocean, halfway between those six thousand desolate miles that separated them. No, she couldn't get any sleep without first consoling herself somehow. But the light filtering through the shutters fell right onto her backpack and she felt guilty for having those thoughts in front of her grandmother. She got up quietly, opened the door to the living room, carefully placed the backpack on the couch, and went back to bed.

She remained a moment with her eyes open in the dark, wondering whether she had done the right thing. What if Concetta woke up, found the backpack in the living room, and put it away somewhere? Or maybe Sara was just creating problems for herself, as usual. Perhaps she was having all these concerns just because it didn't feel right to be thinking of nothing but Una when she was in what was still a disaster zone, with an important mission to accomplish. Processing her reactions didn't calm her down. The thought of leaving Nonna Ali alone bothered her. She tip-toed back into the living room, retrieved the backpack and placed it under the bed.

"I'm sorry," she whispered.

Sorry about what? Alice was astonished at all this action in the middle of the night and at finding herself shoved under the bed, but then a gasp above her revealed the reason for her hustled displacement. What a family! First she had to witness Jane's amorous entanglements with Jeff, now this... Such intense erotic lives, the lot of them, who could have imagined? As far as she was concerned, that chapter of her life was over after that episode with Eric. How intense, though, that season had been! Such a storm, such fireworks! After his death, she acted like traditional Southern Italian widows, who can mourn for a lifetime. Her progeny, though, sure were making up for that. Sara was still a girl, though, who was she thinking about?

L'AQUILA, ITALY
JANUARY 8, 2011

It was still early in the morning when noises from the kitchen woke Sara up. A little man with a mustache was talking animatedly to Concetta while trying to clean up the drain that Sara had clogged the night before. It was not an easy job.

"Darn it, how could someone stuff so much junk into this drain, did they mistake the sink for the garbage bin?"

"I'm sorry, I didn't know there was no *tritarifiuti*," Sara apologized, glad to have had time to consult the dictionary and find the word for garbage disposal.

"The what?"

"The *tritarifiuti*…"

She repeated the word slowly, articulating each syllable.

"*Tri-ta-ri-fiu-ti.*"

The man looked even more puzzled. She tried to explain.

"It's a thing, a bit like a grinder. It breaks down solid kitchen scraps so you can wash them down the drain with water."

"And what's the point of such a fancy machine? They don't have garbage cans in America?"

Concetta's gaze moved from the sink to Sara's bare feet. She shivered.

"What happened to your slippers?"

"What? Oh, yes, I forgot to bring them from the States."

She didn't have the courage to confess that she had never worn slippers in her life.

"Let me take you to the mall later today, then. I need to do some shopping myself."

When the man finally left, after warning her not to throw anything else in the sink, the two women got into Concetta's car and took a straight road punctuated by frequent round-abouts.

"This is L'Aquilone, our biggest shopping mall," Concetta said with a hint of pride in her voice. "You should hear Alessandro's complaints when people refer to it as L'Aquila's new downtown! But sometimes even he must admit that it is quite convenient."

A loud and upbeat melody welcomed them to the parking lot. *Vamos a la playa, a me me gusta bailar, el ritmo de la noche, sounds of fiesta.* At the supermarket, Sarah insisted on buying the groceries on Concetta's list—bread, sausage, mozzarella, wine. She added some fruit and was making her way towards the checkout when Concetta walked up to her with some plaid slippers.

"Which size do you wear? Is 37 ok?"

Sara couldn't come up with an excuse fast enough.

"Perfect, thank you," she lied.

She wasn't sure what to do for the rest of the day. The Professor hadn't called and Concetta didn't have his phone number. Sara's mission was turning out to be more difficult than she had thought. However, garbage disposals and plaid slippers aside, she was intrigued by the people she was meeting and the situations she found herself in. Everything seemed bizarre, yet strangely familiar.

She decided to turn her cellphone on. Concetta insisted that they have lunch at the mall, and Sara had to admit that the pizza was delicious and reasonably priced, as strange as it seemed to her to eat in a mall, something she tried to avoid back home. L'Aquilone was no regular mall, though, Concetta kept explaining. The offices and the stores that the earthquake had displaced from the center of L'Aquila had reopened there, creating a strange mix of people. Lawyers, insurance agents, and government workers hurried to their jobs while housewives looked for post-holiday sales and bored teenagers loitered in small groups.

Her cellphone rang. For a moment she hoped it was going to be the Professor, but then she remembered that he didn't have her phone number. "JW." Jane Westbridge. Sara apologized to Concetta before taking the call.

"Mom, didn't we agree that you wouldn't call me? It costs an arm and a leg. No news is good news, ok?"

"Sara, thank God I got a hold of you! Yeah, no news is good news, but there are many shades between good news and bad news. You could have sent an email, you know. How are you?"

"Fine."

"Have you done what you needed to do?"

"No, it's not quite so simple."

"How is L'Aquila? Do you like it?"

Sara repressed a laugh. She would have liked to say that L'Aquila was just like Montgomery Mall, the shopping mecca of Bethesda that Nonna Ali considered to be one of the circles of Dante's Inferno, but didn't want to get roped into a conversation.

"I can't be on the phone, I'm at lunch," she said.

The idea of her daughter having lunch in Italy stirred up plenty of images in Jane's mind, all rather removed from L'Aquilone Pizza Special.

"How are things with Concetta? Have you met other friends of Nonna's?"

"No. Well, maybe one. An old man, a professor who is passionate about Russian poetry. He promised to help me."

"How come you need help?"

"Apparently it's illegal to scatter ashes here."

"Illegal?!" The expression tickled the lawyer in Jane.

"But I'll find a solution, don't worry."

"What's his name?" Jane asked after a brief pause.

"Whose name?"

"The professor who loves Russian poetry."

"I don't know, everybody simply calls him 'Professore.' No, wait, he told me... His name is Fulvio, Fulvio Innocenti, or Innocenzi maybe, something like that."

Jane paced nervously around the family room, walking from the fireplace mantel, where the hourglass had reclaimed its position of privilege, to the stairs that led to the top floor. She stopped in front of the shelves. They were much more crowded now, overflowing with the books from her mother's house that she couldn't quite bear to give away yet.

"I'm asking because I found a book on Nonna's night table. Wait a minute, here it is... It's an antique! She must have read it a lot, it's falling apart."

"What book is it? Take me off the speaker phone, I can't hear a thing!"

"OK, wait..."

Jane positioned the phone between her ear and her shoulder while delicately opening the worn-out volume.

"Here it is. *The Flower of Russian Poetry.*"

"That's the one!"

"What do you mean?"

"Nothing, it's just... an important book."

Sara tried to remember the details of the Professor's speech the night before. The flower, the broken flower, the library in L'Aquila, the bookstore in Rome, the airport, a magnificent, magnificent book... Another conversation, or rather a monologue, that she wished she had recorded.

"Thanks, mom."

"Of course," Jane replied mechanically, leafing through the book as if she were looking for other clues. "Wait, there's also a handwritten dedication, but it's from a woman, a certain Osia. *Per sempre*, it says. Forever."

"Really?! Did Nonna Ali date women too?"

"I feel I can safely rule that out," Jane responded dryly.

Sara did not appreciate her mother's abrupt reply. She took advantage of the fact that Concetta could not follow their conversation in English.

"First you say that you don't find anything strange about my relationship with Una, and then look how you react if someone makes a joke that threatens the family's heterosexual lineage! Because that's what it was, you know? A joke!"

Jane tried to make up for her hasty reaction. She had forgotten for a moment that she needed to weigh every word with Sara.

"I didn't mean for it to come across that way, I'm sorry," she said, "but I didn't finish reading it. The complete sentence reads *A Nadia, per sempre, Osia*. To Nadia, forever, Osia."

"Nadia? And who's she?"

"I really have no idea. Perhaps the book belonged to somebody else at some point. Perhaps Nonna Ali found it in a second-hand bookstore."

Sara was tempted to explain to her mother why that was not the case, but she didn't want to spend more time on the phone.

"Don't worry, mom, I'm alright and I don't need anything. This is probably going to take longer than we thought but I don't mind spending more time in L'Aquila instead of visiting other Italian cities. Everything will work out in the end, I'm sure."

"I don't want to bug you too much, but let's keep in touch. After all, we've never been this far away from each other."

"Sure. I need to go now. Don't worry, okay?"

Jane sure seemed to have gotten more fragile after Nonna Ali's death and her health scare, Sara thought. She hung up and apologized to Concetta. Now that it had cooled down, her pizza no longer seemed very appealing.

"How can I contact the Professor?" Sara asked.

"Didn't he tell you that he'd show up, or call?"

"Yes, but what should I do? Just hang around and wait?"

"Sure. If he said he'd show up, he'll show up."

They went out into the damp cold of the early afternoon. The snow that still lingered in the puddles had become dark and muddy, melted by a sun that didn't manage to warm up the air. The upbeat music continued. *Vamos a la playa, a me me gusta bailar, el ritmo de la noche, sounds of fiesta.*

Once they got back to the car, Sara surrendered to fatigue and jet lag. She leaned her head against the window and closed her eyes.

She only woke up when Concetta turned the engine off. The Professor walked quickly toward the car and opened the door on Sara's side.

"You haven't done it yet, have you?"

"Done what?"

"Scattered the ashes."

What a strange question, Sara thought. Scatter them where? At the mall? Unsanitary indeed, this time Aldo would have a good reason to complain. What would happen to the Pizza Special?

"Listen, Miss, I know you are in a hurry to complete this task so that you can continue your grand tour and toss coins in the Trevi fountain, but I'm not quite ready yet, understand?"

Sara got out of the car and looked around. It was too cold to continue the conversation outdoors, and she wasn't sure it was appropriate for her to invite the Professor to Concetta's place.

"Why don't we go downtown?" she asked.

"But we were just there!" Concetta protested.

"I mean the actual downtown. When my grandmother wrote that she wanted her ashes to be scattered in the center of L'Aquila, she couldn't possibly have been thinking of L'Aquilone, right?"

"But I just told you I'm not ready yet!" the Professor complained.

"I don't intend to do anything. I just want to see it, this famous downtown."

"I see… That makes sense. Let's go. But no rash decisions, okay?"

Sara wondered if the Professor had ever seen an urn before. He was looking at her with suspicion, as if he thought she carried her grandmother's ashes in her pockets and could scatter them on the sly.

"I promise," she said, fighting back a smile.

Barriers. Scaffolding. Police. An occasional passerby. Silence.

"This is the most important square in the city, as big as Piazza Navona in Rome. It's called Piazza Duomo from the church of Saint Maxim, over there, the patron saint of the city. Nothing to write home about, that church, even before the earthquake. The square, on the other hand, used to be wonderful. It was always packed with people, especially because of the farmers who came from neighboring villages with the best produce you can imagine, and of the artisans with their crafts. The market took place even during the winter, when it got so cold that some sellers burned their wooden crates to keep warm, and when nobody was as popular as the old man selling roasted chestnuts. Too bad you are missing all of it because of this darn earthquake… Come on, let's get some coffee."

They entered a café. From the vaulted ceilings an amber light, warm and welcoming, illuminated the austere columns and the marble floors. The wooden shelves displayed local specialties—saffron, almond candies, gentian and herbal liquors.

"This place was the first to reopen after the earthquake," the Professor said, pointing at a hand-written sign on the cracked wall. The first part was written in what looked like a black marker, and read "Closed from 4/6/2009. Reopening…?" The second part, in a different handwriting, in green ink, read: "December 8!!!"

"Black and green are the colors of the city," the Professor explained. "It wasn't always like that though. Centuries ago, the city colors were red and white. Then, in 1703, there was a disastrous earthquake and we switched to black and green. Black for mourning, green for the hope to rise again."

He pointed at the shelves.

"You know about our nougat, right?"

Sara shook her head.

"Well, then, you absolutely have to try it!" the Professor exclaimed, almost indignantly. "They make it right here, you know."

The nougat had nothing in common with what Sara had tried back home. The deceptive softness of the chocolate hid whole, flavorful hazelnuts. She savored it, alternating small bites with sips of the cappuccino that she found delicious, yes, but also minuscule, and made her regret Julia's unorthodox coffee creations. Sitting in a corner, she could look at the entire café which, unlike the desolate square, was lively and crowded. The Professor had not been able to sit down yet, busy as he was greeting the other customers and discussing book presentations, submission deadlines, and school visits.

Sara was happy to have some time to reflect and collect some expressions for her journal from all the conversations around her. She concluded that "Ricostruzione partecipata," a phrase that she had already heard from Alessandro and his friends the evening before, meant that citizens needed to take an active role in the rebuilding process. Its opposite was "ricostruzione dall'alto," from above, that relegated common people to a passive role. But what really threw her off was the dialect. She still couldn't figure out what "temé" exactly meant, but she had heard the expression so many times since her arrival that she figured it indicated surprise. "Quatrani" and "quatrane" meant something close to "guys" and "gals," respectively, but it frequently lost its last syllable, like so many other words, becoming a generic exhortation, "quatrà." "Let's go" was not "andiamo," as in standard Italian, but "jamo," with "quatrà'" added for emphasis, and it thus became "Jamo, quatrà." It's so complicated! I'll never be able to master this language, Sara concluded, discouraged.

Finally tired of the conversations, the Professor turned around and sat down so that he could directly face Sara, with his back to everybody else in the café.

"So, you are Alice's granddaughter. What can you tell me about her? How was she when she was fifty, sixty, seventy years old?"

Sara tried to recover the woman inside the shell of her grandmother, pushing aside the painful memories of her illness.

"It's hard to tell. She was beautiful, in her own way. For those who understood and loved her, she was stunningly beautiful."

"Brava, that's exactly the way she was. A unique beauty, uncompromising. The absolute."

He looked at Sara with a strange, poignant expression.

"You look a lot like her, you know. When I saw you at Concetta's I was shocked. I had the impression I had gone back fifty years."

Sara was not surprised. She knew she strongly resembled her grandmother. Mediterranean genes had skipped a generation. Dormant in fair-skinned Jane, they had imperiously resurfaced in Sara, shaping her dark hair, petite figure, and pronounced cheekbones.

"Yes, we do look alike, though I must say I only saw a few photos of my grandmother from when she was young. She didn't care for them. She used to repeat they didn't look much like her."

"That's what Sibilla Aleramo wrote to Dino Campana about her pictures."

"What?"

"Never mind. More names for you to add to the list of your

grandmother's youthful passions. And since we are talking about it, did she ever tell you why she left?"

Sara shrugged, realizing once again how little she knew about her own family history. She tried to explain.

"I know it must seem strange, but I always saw her there, with us. I never asked myself why she didn't settle somewhere else. She never talked about it, she never seemed unhappy or nostalgic. She always had something to read, something to discuss."

"How about her wanderlust? Did she travel often?"

"Mostly in her imagination, I'm afraid. She did travel when she could, first with my mother and later with me. Nothing too exotic, though, we had no time and no money. We did go to New York, Miami in the winter, San Francisco once, Canada..."

"So she had assimilated completely."

"I wouldn't go that far. She was always critical of certain aspects of life in the States."

"Such as...?"

"Well, the list is long. The health-care system, the death penalty, the right to bear arms. Also, she never lost her Italian accent, so everywhere we went people asked her where she was from, which gave her a chance to say she was Italian, from Rome."

"Rome?!"

"Well, yes... It was an approximation to avoid having to give a geography lesson every time. But you shouldn't think that she had forgotten L'Aquila. Wherever we went she said, 'It looks like my Abruzzo,' or rather, simply, 'my Abruzzo,' and sometimes even, in dialect, 'J'Abruzzu me!' We made fun of her, it became an inside joke. No matter where we went, from the Florida Keys to the Empire State Building, we'd say: 'J'Abruzzu me!' and we'd burst out laughing. We thought it was the funniest thing, especially because none of us had ever been to this famed Abruzzo. She didn't mind, she laughed along with us."

She hadn't realized she still held onto that memory.

"And now here you are."

"Yes, here I am."

The Professor's attention spurred her to continue.

"I spent a lot of time with her as a child because my mother was very busy, first with law school and then work. Then, when I was twelve, the bus that took me to school got into a bad accident. I needed a year of physical therapy before I was able to walk again. I spent most of the time with Nonna Ali, she came to pick me up from school and took me to the library, where she worked."

That too. Once she started talking about Nonna Ali, memories gushed out like water from a mountain spring.

"And why, do you think, she wanted to come back here after her death?"

Sara shrugged.

"We had no idea, we only found out when we read her will. I guess the connection was stronger than we thought."

"What did she tell you about her family, the Arientis?"

"She never said anything. The few times somebody asked, she would say they were all dead and changed the subject. Now I wish I had asked her more. We must have gotten used to considering us Americans her only real family."

"And what about 'you Americans?' How many of you are there?"

"She only had one daughter. That's my mother, Jane, who as I said last night must have been born soon after Nonna Ali arrived in the States. Jane had three children: Richard, Kate, and me. We haven't kept in touch with my grandfather's side of the family. Of course, since Nonna Ali's husband died so young, not even my mother got to meet him, but he must have been very handsome. In the two or three photos that we have of him, he looks like that actor, what's his name, the one who also died young..."

"Gérard Philippe?"

"Who? No, an American, with a leather jacket..."

"James Dean?

"Yes, that's him, James Dean."

"An imbecile."

The words had slipped quickly out of the Professor's mouth. Sara realized that the insult was not directed at James Dean. She instinctively rushed to defend her daredevil grandfather.

"No, why an imbecile? He was an instrument of fate, it's not his fault if things went the way they went. He did his part, and in a dignified way, if you think about it. He was just unlucky."

"Let's not get into it. Better to say that he was very lucky and he did not even realize it."

"He was lucky to die in his twenties?"

"Why? Am I lucky because I'll die in my eighties, or nineties?"

The Professor got up, as if that conversation had worn him out.

"Enough for today. I'll take you home."

Sara pictured herself confined to Concetta's forty square meter apartment, waiting for a new episode of Big Brother.

"No, I want to keep walking," she said.

"Then how will you get back?

"I'll find a way. I'll take a cab."

"A cab? Where do you think you are, back in New York City?"

"Worst comes to worst I'll walk back, it's still early. Besides, from the moment I arrived in Italy I haven't seen anything other than depressing suburbs, parking lots, graffiti, and an ugly mall. This café is the first thing that corresponds somehow to the idea I had of L'Aquila. It makes me feel like taking a walk downtown."

The Professor seemed to hesitate.

"When will we see each other again, then?"

"Whenever you want, Professor."

"Tomorrow. I'll come by tomorrow."

"Alright, see you tomorrow."

Once she stepped outside, Sara felt the winter chill sink into her bones. She took a brisk walk around the square, walking close to the buildings that framed it. The names of the streets that led to Piazza Duomo didn't mean anything to her—via Roio, via Sassa, Via Patini… They were all cordoned off anyway. Peeking beyond the fences she saw dilapidated buildings and debris. She thought of the night of the earthquake—people running away in fear, screaming the names of their loved ones in the darkness, not knowing if and when they'd be able to go back to their homes. Then, her mind conjured another image, that of the square as the Professor had described it to her, with people gathering around improvised fires, the smell of roasted chestnuts in the crisp air. A girl approached a stall, chose some vegetables, handed money to the seller and turned around to look at Sara, as if she knew she was being watched. Nonna Ali? Sara blinked and the ghost disappeared.

She completed the tour of the square and started walking on the only other road that was open to the public. It was an imposing avenue, flanked on one side by columns that formed a covered passage. They were badly damaged, however, and were supported by elaborate scaffolding of steel pipes that turned them into a sort of modern sculpture. As she walked along, she noticed more streets that were cordoned off. Dozens of house keys that the earthquake had rendered useless hung on metal fences. Make-shift signs conveyed promises, demands, and prayers, like "Reopen the City," "We Want L'Aquila back," and "You Will Not Shake Us." The few pedestrians looked up while they walked, as if to check the extent of the damage, or to make sure that nothing would fall on them. Sara saw a statue in the distance, at the end of the avenue, and kept walking in that direction until familiar voices made her turn around.

"There you are! Happy to see you found your way to L'Aquila's real downtown! Where are you going?"

Alessandro was grinning, next to Concetta.

"Nowhere in particular," Sara answered. "I was just thinking I'd go see that statue down there."

"A statue?"

Alessandro followed Sara's gesture and looked at the end of the street.

"Ah, you mean the Fountain of Light!"

"Is that what it is? A fountain?"

"Yes, though I bet there's no water now. It used to be a big attraction, especially for kids, because it lit up in all different colors in the evening. A bit tacky, in a way, but cool. I bet there's no light either these days. So there you have it, the Fountain of Light, without water and without lights. I guess you were right when you called it a statue."

"He convinced me," Concetta said, as if she needed to justify her presence. "I haven't been back downtown since the night of the earthquake. I haven't even seen Piazza Palazzo since it reopened, Alessandro has been asking me to go take a look for days now."

"Piazza Palazzo?" Sara asked.

"You haven't seen it either, I imagine. Come on, let's go."

While they walked, Alessandro explained that L'Aquila had been devastated by earthquakes throughout its history. The one in 1703 had been catastrophic, but it was by no means the only one.

"A very strong earthquake struck in the 1300s, less than a century after the foundation of the city. Imagine the shock! The people, terrified, wanted to go back to their home villages and abandon L'Aquila. But the governor ordered that all the doors to the city be guarded, the breaches in the walls patched right away with wood. Those who were trying to flee were turned away at the gates and forced to stay."

"And this time? Where did the Aquilani go?" Sara asked, looking around.

Alessandro smiled bitterly.

"This time, too, the city is closed off, but in a different way. Just a few hours after the earthquake, all the downtown was declared a 'red zone,' access forbidden to citizens. What a name, don't you think? Like Amsterdam or other places of that sort, with their 'red zones,' a special neighborhood for sex, a forbidden quarter. Already the idea of designating the heart of the city a 'red zone' should have put us on alert. It should have warned us that the government was getting ready to play a dirty trick on us. Anyway, long story short, this time all the barriers you see were not meant to keep people in, but rather ward them off, make sure they stayed in the outskirts, in their little apartments with their plasma TVs, like my mother's..."

"What are you talking about? My apartment may be small but it's actually quite lovely, thank you very much!" Concetta protested.

"They gave us everything we needed, you know?" she continued, turning to Sara. "Glasses, sheets, even an ironing board..."

"Yes, and don't forget the champagne bucket... Mom, do not start again! Look around, see what's going on downtown, and realize how much your sheets and ironing board have actually cost you."

He went on to explain to Sara that they were walking on Corso Federico II, L'Aquila's main street. Everybody used to take a stroll there in the evening, back in the day. Now, however, every hundred yards there was a jeep filled with bored soldiers. They were meant to make sure that the few chilly pedestrians still around didn't try to sneak into the cordoned-off and blockaded side streets. Alessandro seemed restless.

"It's not completely true that *everybody* walked up and down the Corso, though. I, for instance, could not bear the strolling, the shuffling along, everybody putting themselves on display. I preferred to seek refuge in the side alleys, with a few buddies and a bottle of wine. Look, behind that fence is my favorite, *Sdrucciolo dei poeti*, the Poets' Slip."

"The earthquake did bring some advantages, then!" Concetta exclaimed. "At least you can't sneak away to get drunk in those damp alleyways anymore. *Sdrucciolo dei poeti*, what a name. They don't call those alleyways "slips" for nothing, do they? They are steep and slippery, especially when they are wet."

"They certainly are," Alessandro conceded. "But wouldn't you like, though, to be able to sit in a little piazza? With trees, benches, a fountain in the middle... Like the Piazza of the Nine Martyrs, just around the corner."

But the alley leading to Piazza of the Nine Martyrs was fenced off too. Alessandro caressed the metal with his gloved fingers.

"Which piazza?" Sara asked, mostly to avoid being completely cut out of the conversation but also to interrupt their quarrelling.

"Piazza of the Nine Martyrs," Alessandro mechanically repeated. Then his face brightened up. He stared at her, struck by a sudden thought.

"Wait... What did you say your last name was?"

"What?"

"What's your name? Sara what?"

"Westbridge."

"No, I don't mean your American name... Your Grandmother, what was her name, her last name?"

"Arienti. She was Alice Arienti."

"Aha! That's where I heard the name! I read it on a plaque in honor of the Nine Martyrs of L'Aquila. I swear that's where I saw it. There's an Arienti, now I remember. It's not a common name around here."

"The martyrs...?" Sara asked, perplexed, trying to remember the name of the saint pierced with arrows in her art history book. She looked so confused that Alessandro felt compelled to give her a quick history lesson.

"Yes, you know… It was 1943, that mess of a year. Mussolini resigned, and the king had him arrested and taken to the Gran Sasso."

Alessandro pointed in the direction of the statue at the end of the Corso.

"You can see the Gran Sasso from the Fountain of Light, but also from my mother's place, for that matter. Beauty endures, they can't take it away, no matter how hard our dear government tries."

Concetta rolled her eyes, and Alessandro went back to the events of the war.

"At any rate, on September 8, Italy signed the armistice with the allies. Only four days later, the Germans freed Mussolini from his prison on the Gran Sasso and took control of Northern and Central Italy, including L'Aquila. That's when the Resistance began. Thousands of people, all over the country, left their homes and formed armed groups to fight against the Nazi occupiers and their Fascist accomplices. And one of the first episodes of the Resistance took place here, in L'Aquila. A group of young men went to the mountains, hoping perhaps to meet with a larger and better organized contingent."

"Nine hotheads," Concetta interjected.

"Nine heroes!" Alessando retorted. "If only there were some Aquilani like them these days, Berlusconi and his gang wouldn't have had the guts to kick us out of our city!"

"And then what happened?" Sara asked.

"They were captured, forced to dig their own graves, and murdered."

"Captured, murdered… by whom?"

"Well, by the Nazis, officially. Except that many of the details are still quite mysterious. It's doubtful that the Nazis could have found them so easily without the help of someone who knew the area. The Germans were generous in their rewards to spies. Keep in mind also that those who were Fascists before September 8 had not suddenly converted, they were still Fascists. Chances are they were very much involved in the massacre. This could also have played a part in the decision not to divulge the news of the killings. The families only found out almost a year later. There was even a trial, after the war, but guess what? The proceedings are still classified! Doesn't that sound kind of shady to you?"

"And one of those young men had the same last name as my grandmother?"

"I believe so, yes. Ardenti, Arienti, something like that... And the first name also began with an 'A.' Antonio, Alessandro? No, not Alessandro like me, I would remember that. But something similar. Listen, you know what? No need to rack our brains, why don't we go and take a look ourselves?"

Under the puzzled gaze of the two women, Alessandro pushed away the cinderblock just enough so that he could slip through between the fence and the wall, nimble as a cat.

"Where are you going? It's dangerous! It's off limits!" Concetta protested.

Alessandro placed his back against the wall so that he could push the cinderblock a little bit farther with his feet and make an opening big enough for Concetta and Sara to follow him.

"I'm so sick of this... Everything around here is officially dangerous, illegal, off-limits... Let's go, *jamo, quatrà!*" chuckled Alessandro, panting from the effort but thrilled by the adventure. Sara started to ease herself in behind him.

"Where do you think you're going?"

The soldier materialized behind Concetta's shoulders. People peering into the side streets always make a dumb move sooner or later. The soldier was glad he had kept an eye on that group.

"I think I'm going to Piazza of the Nine Martyrs to look at the plaque with the names of our heroes," Alessandro readily replied. "Unless, of course, you can recite them off the top of your head."

"Instead, how about you come out of there immediately and we can pretend that I didn't notice you?" the soldier replied sternly.

"Why? Who gives you the right to decide where we can and can't go in our own city?"

"I am not sure I would consider this exclusively your city at this point."

"I agree, especially if we keep leaving it to you guys and we start forgetting its history. I'll be back soon, ok? Keep the women as hostages until then, Sergeant."

"Should I come over?" another soldier yelled from the jeep he was leaning against, cigarette in hand. The one next to Alessandro made a generic, irritated gesture with his hand, but his gaze became harsher. Every day he had to deal with a few cases like this. It was mostly young people, both male and female. They were arrogant, aggressive, always complaining that L'Aquila had been taken over. As if it gave the army much joy to be assigned to spend the month of January in Italy's coldest city, or whatever was left of it.

"It's a matter of public order, young man. Come out of there right away if you don't want to end up in jail."

"Jail?!" Concetta interjected, a note of desperation in her voice. "Don't do anything silly, Ale, I beg you. We'll check the plaque some other time, when this street reopens. Now, listen to the officer, get out of there!"

Alessandro pursed his lips. Sara realized that he was making a big effort to control himself. He stepped back over to the other side of the fence. The soldier tried to put the cinderblock back, muttering something under his breath, then waved at his colleague to come and help.

"This time you were lucky, you ought to thank the *signora* here… Don't let me see you try something this stupid again. There's plenty of information about L'Aquila that you can find on Google, in the safety of your home, without breaking the law."

"Can't you see that's exactly my point? We've turned into a virtual city!"

The two soldiers were already walking back toward the jeep, eager to get back to the warmth inside. They didn't bother to reply.

"Let it go, come on."

Concetta grabbed her son's arm. The look on her face instructed Sara to do the same. The two women on the sides, holding Alessandro in the middle, looked like two police officers escorting a thief. But Alessandro did not resist. Sara felt his tense muscles relax under her touch. They continued to walk straight ahead, then Concetta made them all turn left.

"I'm sorry to remind you, but didn't you promise to bring me to see Piazza Palazzo? If you had told me that you wanted to sneak into little squares and alleyways, break into the red zone and the like, I would have stayed at home."

"What's in Piazza Palazzo?" inquired Sara.

"Well, the palace, the *palazzo*, obviously. I mean Palazzo Margherita, the town hall," Concetta explained.

"And that's not all. We are also going to see the bell tower," Alessandro rattled off, "the statue of Sallustius, the Roman historian, who was born only a few miles from here. Not to mention the great regional library, the Biblioteca Tommasiana. That's where your grandmother and the Professor read Russian poetry, remember? And I bet that when they got thirsty they drank from the Fountain of the Silent Angel, right at the corner. We'll see that too."

Without even realizing it, he accelerated his stride, as he continued to list the wonders that awaited them. Concetta trotted along happily.

"And before the earthquake, there were many stores and cafés as well. Like that cool store where you could find specialties from all over Italy. Do you remember, mom? The best burrata, and my favorite wine, Anarkos, from that workers' cooperative in Puglia…"

Their walk had almost turned into a jog, until they stopped in a large square. Concetta's eyes fell upon the statue at the center.

"Holy Sallustius?!" she exclaimed.

Alessandro let out a laugh.

"Great! You have just managed to transform even a pagan Roman writer into a Christian... That's a true miracle!"

"Well, he's a patron saint of sorts, or at least I always thought of him that way. Otherwise, why erect a statue in his honor right here?" Concetta shot back, irked to be treated like an ignorant person in front of their American guest.

"But what have they done to him?" she asked.

Sara looked closer and noticed that the statue of Sallustius was proudly holding a shovel in his left hand, a bucket in his right. Alessandro grinned.

"You know, as he watched us shoveling the debris, he looked like he wanted to join in! Maybe at night, when nobody can see him, he does descend from his pedestal to do a little cleaning, who knows? If he is a saint, he can easily perform a little miracle like that!"

But his laughter sounded hollow. Concetta looked around disoriented. Elaborate iron and wood scaffolding held up the windows of the buildings around the square. The now familiar sign that prohibited access to the Red Zone marked the alleyways leading to the square from all sides except the street that had taken them there. Sara's attention was captured by an imposing building and a stone tower that stood out in the desolate urban landscape.

"There it is, Palazzo Margherita and the civic tower," Alessandro said, anticipating her question.

"You know, its bell used to toll 99 times at sunset. My mother could even sing you a whole song about it. Isn't that right, mom? How did it go? 'And the bell rings out, ninety-nine, ninety-nine'!"

Concetta chimed in softly.

"Ninety-nine, the city's magic number," Alessandro explained.

"But the bell doesn't toll anymore," Concetta said, looking around.

An eerie silence followed her words. Not only did the bell not toll anymore, but the Fountain of the Silent Angel, with its cast-iron statue of a child with unruly curls, was now truly silent. It no longer spouted the water that quenched the thirst of generations of students on their way home from school. And you could no longer smell the aroma of freshly-baked bread, roasted coffee, and salami, from the grocery store at the corner.

Concetta glanced at all the sides of the square.

"I was right not to want to come back to L'Aquila," she finally said. "And you know what? I don't ever want to come back here. Never again."

"Come on, Mom," Alessandro tried to console her, "you used to complain even before the earthquake. Don't you remember? Piazza Palazzo had lost all its charm, you used to say, with all those foreign students getting drunk at all hours at that bar over there, the Farfarello."

They looked at a building in front of the statue. Its windows were reduced to mere holes braced by wooden beams. Metal bars prevented the walls from collapsing. The sign depicting Farfarello, a devil laying down with a mug of beer in his hand, remained miraculously intact.

Concetta looked as though she could still see, outside the bar, students congregating with glasses in their hands, leaning on parked cars, spilling out into the square, clustering around the railings of the flowerbeds. Loafers, layabouts, she used to call them. She never missed a chance to point out how carelessly they wasted the money their parents struggled to send them every month from Taranto, Greece, Hungary, Nigeria. Dozens of those students had died on the night of the earthquake, in the shaky downtown buildings or in the student dorms. I am so sorry, kids, I didn't mean it. How was I supposed to know?

Alessandro looked pensive too, his mother's silence and fixed gaze weighed heavier on him than her habitual grouchiness. He couldn't find the words to console her or to explain to Sara what L'Aquila used to be, before.

They stood still for a couple of minutes, in the cold wind that whipped through the abandoned streets.

"Don't get upset, Ale," Concetta finally said, without looking at her son. "I appreciate your good intentions and the tour of downtown L'Aquila, but I'd like to go back home now. I'd hate to miss tonight's episode of Big Brother."

"So he decided to build a church here, where he had that vision. And this is it, Santa Maria di Collemaggio."

Alessandro's words echoed in the huge basilica. The seven-hundred-year-old story of Celestine V, hermit and Pope for just four months, crowned right there, fascinated Sara. He quit the papacy to regain his serenity, Alessandro explained. Power and spirituality, he had quickly found out, were incompatible.

They kept talking as they made their way across the central nave towards the altar. The massive columns were supported by yellow bands. Once they reached the transept, Sara was stunned to see that instead of a ceiling there was a complex structure of metal and Plexiglas. The terse winter sky above was clearly visible, and looked very distant.

"The transept collapsed, as you can see. Celestine's corpse, which is usually there, on the right, in a Renaissance monument, had to be moved, but it wasn't damaged."

Something in Celestine's story struck Sara as odd.

"It wasn't a particularly noble idea to renounce the Papacy, though…"

Alessandro didn't agree.

"Of course it was! He chose his conscience over worldly ambition, there are plenty of people who wouldn't do that."

"That's for sure. But if he was so committed to serenity,

why didn't he turn down the offer to become pope in the first place? Once you're in, you're in. You have to play your part."

She smiled thinking of Nonna Ali raising her finger as she ended that sentence. *There all the honor lies.*

There were times Alessandro had the impression that Sara came not simply from another continent, but from another planet altogether. How could Celestine's greatness be lost on her? He decided to try again.

"You are reasoning like Dante, who put him in hell for his 'the great refusal.' But he was wrong. Once Celestine understood that power had its own logic, and that he would only be but a cog in the machine, he decided to give it all up. This is why he is exceptional not only as a pope, but as a human being."

"Well, if you put it that way, it's easier to understand. But you're actually talking about a miscalculation. Celestine had overestimated himself..."

"What miscalculation?! Celestine was everything but calculating."

"Ok, perhaps he was not calculating, but he was definitely a 'quitter.' How would you say that in Italian?"

"What? How do you spell it?"

But Sara was distracted by the hypnotic rose window at the center of the façade.

"Wait a minute, what did you say this church is called?"

"Collemaggio. Santa Maria of Collemaggio, to be exact."

He followed Sara's gaze.

"Yes, that rose window is a masterpiece in and of itself. It's a miracle it wasn't destroyed in the earthquake. If you stay until August, you'll see that at twilight the sun rays filter through that window and create some amazing reflections."

Sara remembered Nonna Ali's will, the necklace that she meant to leave to her and that Jane had given away.

"A miracle indeed," she said with a smile.

***

The photo was grainy and faded, only part of the face was visible. Alberto Arienti had a wide forehead and thick and wavy hair. There was something still boyish about his features—warm gaze, naked neck, plump lips that seemed to be just about to open in a smile. Sara instinctively brushed her fingers over her own lips, and she needed no other confirmation. Yes, it was him. The photo was framed in an oval, it most likely belonged to Alberto's tombstone. His parents must have had the picture taken for some other reason, they certainly didn't think they'd need it so soon and in such circumstances. But who were his parents? Once again Sara ran into the shadows of her family's history. And what about Nonna Ali? Where was she when the family chose the picture for her brother's tombstone? Was she old enough to understand what had happened? Did she realize Alberto had been murdered? That was a question of simple math. Born in 1930, she was thirteen when Alberto was executed, in 1943. Knowing her, she must have understood everything.

But why had Alberto landed himself in that situation? The information Sara had managed to find on the Internet did not provide any answers. Right after the armistice, Albert Kesserling, the Nazi commander, ordered that all men aged 18 and older register with the German authorities. But Alberto was born in 1926, so he was only seventeen at the time. He was in no immediate, personal danger of being enlisted to work or fight for the Nazis. Yet, he had decided to go into hiding. His face looked even younger beside those of his companions in adventure and death who displayed greater wisdom and resolve. The title of martyr had been attached to the whole group for some reason, but he seemed more deserving of it than the others. Sara was puzzled by that terminology. It was bizarre how they tended to Christianize everything, like Concetta had done with "Holy Sallustius." In the States, she thought, Alberto would be known as a Freedom Warrior or something like that, and the square dedicated to the group would be called "Patriots Square."

The soldier who had stopped Alessandro was right. Google did provide some essential information, there was no reason to get into trouble just to read the names of the nine victims on the wall. A lot was missing, though. "No information available," read the caption underneath Alberto's photo.

It was getting dark in the apartment. Sara got up from the kitchen table, looked at the mountains dusted with snow and the villages on the hills that had just started to glow in the twilight. It was like a nativity scene coming to life before her eyes. She regretted not even knowing a prayer to say for Alberto. She tried to make something up, but nothing better came to her mind than a generic "rest in peace, Alberto." Not much for a martyr, a hero.

A buzz from her computer announced a new message. She went back to the table. It was from Una, and took a while to download because it wasn't a text, but a photo. The subject line read "First Quarter." Sara closed her eyes and counted to ten. When she opened them, a picture of Delicate Arch filled the screen. To the right of the rock, a thin moon crescent. The picture had been taken at dawn on a frigid day. The nighttime wind had chased away the clouds and the sky was now an ethereal azure. The sun had just reawakened the sandstone and, in the background, bathed the La Sal Mountains in pinkish hues. In order to witness that event, Una had left Moab while it was still dark. She set up the tripod and camera under the fading stars, then turned on her camp stove and brewed some coffee, placing her hands around the flame to protect it from the wind and keep warm at the same time. She wrapped herself up in the blanket. With her hands tight around her thermos, she waited for the moon's first quarter to show up for its scheduled appearance. Good luck, Sara, come back soon.

L'AQUILA, ITALY
JANUARY 15, 2011

"How did that happen? How did she die?"

Sara was beginning to get used to the Professor's abrupt questions. He seemed to be following his own train of thought, using Sara's testimonies just to fill in the gaps of the story unfolding in his head.

"Cancer," she said, a bit surprised she needed to repeat those details. "A very aggressive one, unusual in a woman of her age. She had two surgeries, but they only bought her a few more months."

"Yes, you told me that already. But how did she pass away? What were her last words?"

Did she remember me, he wanted to ask, but he wasn't sure Sara would understand.

"Did she ask for a priest?" he asked instead.

"No, no priests. One morning, when she was accidentally left alone, she got up and started walking on a trail near her house, she went down to the Potomac…"

"The Potomac?"

"Yes, the Potomac. It's a majestic river that flows through Maryland and Washington, D.C. She loved it. They found her laying on its banks."

"When did they find her? Who found her?"

"An amateur photographer. He was following a deer and got closer to take a picture. The deer was sniffing something, then saw the photographer and ran away, and that's when he noticed the body."

The photographer must have been quite shocked. Not only did he tell the story at the police station, but he managed to get in touch with Jane and repeated it to her, more or less with the same words. Jane, in turn, related the story to the rest of the family. The images were so vivid that Sara sometimes had the impression she had witnessed the scene herself.

"That's not a bad way to die."

No, it wasn't, Sara had to agree. It was hard to remember why they had all found something tragic in it.

The cold had loosened its grip, and the Professor and Sara were sitting on a little bench in front of a wine bar, alternating sips of Montepulciano with bites of pecorino and salami. It was early in the afternoon and the sky, framed by the scaffolding, had taken on a most perfect shade of blue. More than a week after Sara's arrival in L'Aquila, she still hadn't put together a concrete plan to carry out her mission. The Professor kept repeating he wasn't ready yet. So what? Why was she letting that stranger interfere with Nonna Ali's wish?

"Professor, do you mind if I ask *you* a question?"

"Huh? Yes, of course, fire away."

"Did you and my grandmother stay in touch after she went to the States?"

"What do you mean by 'stay in touch'?"

"Did you write to each other? Call? Things like that..."

"No, nothing of that sort, no."

But we were always close, he would have liked to add.

"You see," Sara continued, "you ask me all these questions, but I also have some questions for you. You'd like to complete the image you have in your mind, but so would I. The more we talk, the more I realize how little I knew about Nonna Ali."

"That's normal," he replied. "You got there too late. How can you know people if you didn't see them when they were kids, and then young adults, before they entered life in the middle?"

"Life in the middle... Do you mean middle age?"

"No, I mean the life you lead once you reach adulthood and start obsessing about career and prestige, and become fake and cautious. That long farce between youth and death, that's what I call life in between."

As soon as the shade fell on their bench they started getting cold. They moved to another bench that was still in the sun to continue their conversation.

"How did she get along with you and your family?"

This question bothered Sara. Sometimes the Professor seemed to consider Jane and her children mere guests in Alice's life. He seemed to think everything she did in the States was a mishap, a curious misunderstanding.

"We are the family she created. It isn't by chance that things turned out the way they did. We are the life she had chosen, the life she embraced."

The Professor looked at her skeptically.

"She ran away."

"Ran away from what? Why?"

He waved his hand in front of his face, as if to chase away a fly.

"It's Celestine's Syndrome," he continued. "When times get tough, get out as fast as you can."

Sara mentally thanked Alessandro who had told her everything about Celestine and his "great refusal." There must have been so many other expressions that were still going way over her head. The list in her journal was growing longer, but so was the number of entries marked by question marks.

"It's much easier to believe that the world exists only in black and white..."

Sometimes Sara had the impression that the Professor was losing his marbles.

"Simpler, more comforting," he kept mumbling.

Could it be the effect of the Montepulciano? Perhaps the Professor guessed what Sara was thinking, because he checked his watch and got up.

"It's getting late, I need to go. Can we continue this conversation tomorrow?"

He left with his characteristic, resolute gait, in spite of a little limp. Sara soon began to feel uneasy sitting with her wine glass on the sunny strip of the bench. She ate one more bite of pecorino, washed it down with a last sip, and walked a couple of hundred meters north, where the Corso ended and opened up onto a circular square. At its center stood the Fountain of Light that Alessandro had described to her a few days before. The massive slabs of marble that formed its base created an intriguing contrast with the sculpture at the top—two slender and intertwined women joined in the effort to lift a large inclined vessel over their heads. Sara guessed that it was from there that the water used to fall. But now, as Alessandro had anticipated, the Fountain of Light was dry and lightless. A few stray dogs lay sleeping at its base, lazily taking in the little heat released by the stone. Sara's attention was attracted by a hotel right in front of the fountain. She remembered trying to reserve a room there, when she had started planning the trip with Jane's help. They had called a number of places but nobody ever answered. Those who did only stated dryly that they were full and did not anticipate any cancellations. Luckily Jane then had a stroke of genius and found Concetta's number in Alice's notes. Now Sara fully understood how naive their request of a single room with a bathroom must have sounded. The hotel in front of her was the first one she had seen in town that was still operational, one of the few still standing in the whole area. It didn't serve tourists or occasional visitors, but housed some of the 70,000 people who had been displaced by the earthquake. It was a little past lunch time, and some of the guests had come out to smoke, a bit disoriented in their shapeless clothes. There was something peculiar about their metamorphosis from city residents into long-term tourists. Sara looked away, afraid to seem indiscreet. In front of her the Corno Grande rose, white with snow, clearly traced out in the sky. She sat on the edge of the dry fountain to reflect. Breaking away from the group of people in front of the hotel, a man slowly walked towards her.

"Do you have a cigarette?"

He must have been between forty and fifty years old, with a dark complexion, and a proud gaze above his unkempt beard. Sara shook her head.

"In that case, do you want one of mine?" he continued, taking a pack of Camels out of his pocket.

Sara couldn't help but smile.

"No thanks, I don't smoke."

"Well, do you mind if I sit here and smoke one? Otherwise I'll be stuck with the same old folks all day long. They're not mean, don't get me wrong, but we always end up having the same conversations. On a scale from A to E, how badly damaged is your house? What were you doing the night of the earthquake? Did you hear Berlusconi is coming to town today? And of course, there's always mention of the seismologist who had predicted the earthquake by measuring the levels of radon, and the special committee that met at the end of March just to tell everybody that there was no danger at all... You have no idea what I'm even talking about, do you?"

His tone was ironic but, Sara decided, not aggressive.

"Not exactly. I do understand what you are talking about, but I can't quite grasp all the details."

"*Brava*, that's just fine, no one really understands everything. So, does it bother you if I smoke here?"

Sara consented for fear of seeming rude, even though she wouldn't have minded staying alone and avoiding the chit-chat. But the man seemed no longer interested in talking. Sitting by her side on the cold marble step, he lit a cigarette and smoked in silence, as though the Corno Grande was a TV show and the two of them an old couple. The scene really did change every few minutes, a cotton cloud seemed to get stuck on the mountain's peak. The man stubbed out his cigarette and got back on his feet.

"Well, thanks for the company, and take care, *quatrà*."

Sara instinctively got up too. He was already walking away.

"Thanks, you too… *quatrà*."

The man turned around, and smiled.

Sara insisted on going downtown every day now, so that Concetta could have some space and time on her own in her little apartment. Visiting L'Aquila, Alessandro had told her, was like going to see a friend with an incurable disease. You can't postpone your visit, because nothing guarantees you'll get another chance. The comment awoke Sara's guilty feelings for not having been closer to Nonna Ali during the last months of her life. Her walks through the struggling city became a sort of pilgrimage, her way to honor her grandmother.

By now she knew every stone along the main street. Glancing down the alleyways, it seemed to her that as each day went by, grass and mold conquered more space between the cobblestones. She was beginning to understand and share Alessandro's frustration about the city's conditions. Since most of the streets were fenced off, her itinerary tended to be the same every day. She walked along the Corso, all the way to the Fountain of Light, and passed by the abandoned booth at the bus stop, where a group of old people occasionally gathered to play cards. From there she continued on a street outside the city walls, packed with cars and lined with some of the cafés, restaurants, and stores that had relocated there from downtown. It was rare for anyone to speak to her, people seemed very occupied or absorbed in their thoughts.

The real problem about going into town was that she didn't have an easy way to get back. There were no buses, taxis were expensive and hard to find. Sometimes she left early enough to walk home on foot, and that was obviously seen as inappropriate. Cars slowed down, people would yell the occasional obscene comment, and Concetta grew very concerned. She got into the habit of putting a couple of rocks in her pocket, just in case. But she liked walking. Her thoughts marched along with her legs, and everything seemed to proceed in harmony, for a change. Walking also made her feel closer to Una. They had learned to know each other while walking side by side, exploring passages between the rocks, helping one another when the terrain was particularly rough. When Sara thought of Una, she always pictured her in a natural environment, against the cobalt sky and the sandstone arches. Sara kept replaying one of their excursions in her mind. Una, ahead of her on the path to Island in the Sky, turning to say something to Sara, she couldn't even remember what. They were walking uphill, so Una was looking at Sara from above when she asked her if everything was alright, with a look of such care and concern on her face that for some reason touched Sara more than any love letter ever could.

Maybe Una, just as Sara was climbing the hill for her daily visit to the wounded city, was on her way to her meeting with the moon. It gave Sara a dizzy feeling to think that the celestial body that Una loved so much was the same one she could see from Concetta's apartment, however dampened by the lights and enveloped by the sounds of the city. The pictures that Sara received every few days proved that Una was following the January moon closely, from the first quarter on. Some of the images were night shots. Looking at them, Sara could sense the cold of the surrounding landscape and Una's body as the only source of heat. She couldn't find the right words to reply to those emails and maybe a reply wasn't even necessary. No message accompanied the images. Every time she received one, Sara remembered Una's serious expression during their last conversation in Julia's café, as they stood among the odd guests who were organizing the itinerary for their day out hiking. *Like the phases of the moon.*

L'AQUILA, ITALY
JANUARY 18, 2011

The evenings at Concetta's were often lively and loud, especially when her guests needed to drown out the background noise of the television. The conversations examined various issues related to the earthquake: the lack of prevention, the absurd rules of the makeshift encampments, the military control over the population, the shortcomings of the central and local government, the slow pace of the reconstruction. Sara soon overcame her surprise at hearing so many conflicting versions of the events. There were those who believed the government knew an earthquake was imminent, which explained why several units of firefighters had intervened right away; others instead swore that on that same night only fifteen firefighters were on duty. She heard complaints that the city was too heavily patrolled, but also that it was left to itself, easy prey for vandals and looters. What surprised her even more was that the same person could hold and animatedly defend different opinions at different times, depending on the context, in an ever-shifting system of alliances. The requests for help from the rest of Italy and the world accompanied hostility toward those who dared set foot in the city and even take pictures. Volunteers, as well as occasional visitors, tended to be portrayed as "vultures" and "disaster tourists." Fearing she was a likely candidate for inclusion in one of those categories, Sara felt uneasy and tried to keep a low profile.

She found it hard to follow the pinwheel of people and entities with pompous sounding names, like the Extraordinary Commissary, the Technical Structure of the Mission, the Emergency Management, and the Experts Committee. The animated discussions in Concetta's small kitchen didn't always clarify things. The conversation became particularly heated every time that Aldo, Concetta's oldest son, took part in it, happy to stress his role in the reconstruction process. Aldo used some recurring phrases to counter all criticism against the government. He downplayed the delays and presented himself as the only one around the table who actually knew how things worked. His favorite slogans were "It's not that simple," "That's easier said than done," and "I would like to see you in that capacity." Any initiative that came directly from the people, like clearing the streets and the piazzas of the debris, was, in Aldo's eyes, futile, ridiculous, a total waste of time. He mocked expressions that were dear to Alessandro and his friends, like "rebuilding from the bottom up" and "participation," by repeating them in a high-pitched voice, as if to suggest that those slogans belonged to children and women, who luckily were not expected to make important decisions. To make matters worse, Concetta seemed to idolize her older son, and tended to amplify his argument in a way that, Sara noticed, drove Alessandro crazy. She sensed that the ideological differences between the brothers exacerbated old tensions that dated back to their childhood, or maybe even before their births, when their roles in the family puzzle had been assigned. Aldo, the first born, had quelled the ever-present fear of infertility and worthlessness, of going down in history as the sterile branch of the family tree. Then Alessandro came, so that Aldo would not grow up as an only child. Sara noticed some patterns of her difficult relationship with Richard in the way the brothers communicated. While she instinctively sided with Alessandro—she found Aldo's legalistic obtuseness regarding Nonna Ali's last wishes unfor-

givable—she detected in Alessandro's arguments a radical-
ness, a stubbornness, a wish to exacerbate conflicts that was
not completely foreign to her.

Sara's progress was as slow as the rebuilding of the city,
and just as frustrating. She felt the time wasn't right, but she
couldn't explain her hesitations in rational terms. Concetta
seemed to have adjusted very well to Sara's presence but the
apartment, plasma TV and champagne bucket notwithstand-
ing, was quite small, and there wasn't even a café nearby
where she could go spend some time and read. People stared
blankly at her when she mentioned public libraries.

One evening Alessandro, exasperated by Aldo's sarcastic
retorts, stormed out of the apartment, slamming the door on
his way out, and Sara instinctively got up and followed him.
The scene she had just witnessed reminded her of her many
arguments with Richard. Her older brother never lost his cool,
while she always ended up raising her voice and cursing, with
the result of being wrong even if she could have been right, as
Jane loved to say. That was why, when Concetta began to talk
about Alessandro's inability to hold a civil conversation with
his brother, Sara felt she couldn't take it any longer and left.
She followed Alessandro as he angrily made his way through
the puddles, mud, and drowned saplings. She stopped only
when he got into his car, but Alessandro must have noticed
her, because he opened the door on the passenger's side.

"Hop in, come on."

"Where are we going?"

"I wasn't planning on going anywhere. There's no place
to go. I just got in to avoid freezing outside, but if you have
something in mind, sure, let's go."

Sara shook her head. She thought of Rome, just seventy
miles away. It would have been so easy to go, she and Una
had driven twice that distance once, to take pictures of the
bighorn sheep in Canyonlands. She struggled to chase away
her feelings of nostalgia. People seemed to have a different

perception of distance in L'Aquila. She knew that Rome seemed far away to Alessandro. Even suggesting such a trip at that hour would seem extravagant, "American." Alessandro smoked angrily and cursed his destiny, his place in the family constellation... the Red Dwarf!

"They consider you a red... dwarf? You are a dwarf, and... red?!" Sara asked, surprised that somebody would try to insult Alessandro on the basis of his height that was absolutely adequate, at least according to local standards. "Red" kind of made sense, it could be an allusion to his political leanings.

"No!" he bursted out laughing despite his anger. "A red dwarf is a low-mass star. It shines so faintly that it is difficult to observe. This according to an American stellar classification, I thought you'd be familiar with it."

Sara felt herself blush in the dark. Here's another entry for my notebook, she thought.

"We are such a mess, I am sorry, it must be hard for you to follow," he said after a pause.

"Well, no, not really. You're just very passionate about the future of your city, that's all. And I feel I understand you a little better every day. I may miss a reference or misunderstand things sometimes, as I just did with the red dwarf, but overall I can follow quite well now. I don't speak very much because you mostly talk about people I don't know, and you rarely talk about something other than L'Aquila."

"You're so right! We rarely talk about the rest of the world. And yet, that would do us some good. For instance, I am doing better since you arrived. I no longer feel like I can't breathe."

"You can't breathe?"

"Yes, that's right. This city takes you by the throat, and not because of what happened two years ago. The earthquake was a tragedy, for sure. And yet, to be honest, some of us felt it could also be an opportunity. We hoped that the pettiness, the prejudice, the conservatism that imprisoned us had crumbled with the buildings. That night, when I fled, like the others, in my pajamas, through the dust, the screams, and the smell of gas, I ran into a friend in Piazza Duomo. After realizing that his house right outside the city wall was miraculously intact, his first instinct was to go looking for his friends. He headed downtown while everyone was fleeing in the opposite direction, found us as we walked around dazed and scared, and brought us all to his house. Between the aftershocks, the news cycle, the sheer joy and guilt of finding ourselves alive and together, we almost never slept, all we did was talk and talk about how we should rebuild the city. The dreams we had! We thought of turning the river banks into a state park, building a real university campus, bike lanes, community gardens, and installing free WiFi everywhere. We spent days and nights discussing and drafting our connected, accessible, progressive, sustainable city."

He looked straight in front of him, as if he could still see that invisible city.

"And then?" Sara spurred him on.

"And then, and then…They quickly got to it, the builders, the lawyers, the politicians, the few bigshots who have always run everything in this city. We spoke of better ways of living together; they were only interested in squeezing every penny out of this tragedy. They claimed damages they hadn't sustained, were assigned contracts worth millions of euros to rebuild larger and uglier. They were even caught on tape the night of the earthquake, laughing in anticipation of the good deals ahead. They hit the ground running, following their usual motto: if we want everything to stay the same, everything must change."

Sara had problems following Alessandro's fast and emotional speech, but the last sentence sounded strangely familiar. She remembered hearing something similar from Nonna Ali. She nodded encouragingly, but Alessandro seemed tired of venting and abruptly changed the topic.

"What do you study in college?"

It was so rare for someone to show interest in her that Sara weighed her words, as if afraid to ruin the opportunity.

"Actually, I haven't started yet. A lot has happened recently, and I'm taking some time off between high school and college. I'm not in a rush, I haven't decided my major yet. In the U.S. for the first couple of years we study a bit of everything anyway, so I have time. I think I'd like to do something concerning human rights, sustainable development, that sort of thing. But so much has happened in the past few months... I need to reflect, and I don't even know where to begin."

It was too complicated, in any language, to try to summarize the events of the last few months.

"Your grandma loved literature, right? She's the only woman the Professor seems to respect... almost revere, actually."

"Yes, he seems to be the only one who remembers her, and what vivid memories he has! Do you remember the day I arrived? He was able to describe his trip to Rome with my grandmother as if it had happened the day before, not half a century ago..."

Alessandro smiled in the darkness. Sara waited for him to say something. When the silence went on for too long, she decided to inquire.

"Why are you smiling?"

"No particular reason..."

"What do you know about her? About my grandma?"

"Why? I only know what my mom told me. Very little, to tell you the truth."

"And what's this very little that your mother told you?"

"She told me that she was engaged to the Professor, and they were going to be married. Then one day she gave a ride to an American, and soon after she left for the States. You know the rest."

"I don't know much either. I know the bare facts, that's all. Yes, I figured there was something between her and the Professor, a strong friendship at the very least, but you are saying that they were actually engaged…?"

"That's what my mother told me. As you might have noticed, though, she is a bit conservative. Perhaps they were only going out, and to her it looked like an engagement. Or she wanted to make her friend, your grandma, look respectable, and the only proper way to go out with a guy back then was to be engaged. But she's convinced it was something very serious because she claims the Professor never got over it. That's why, still according to my mom, he never married. He kept waiting for Alice to come back."

That explained a few things, Sara thought. What an old-fashioned, romantic story. It was hard to imagine Nonna Ali and the Professor as young people, even harder than picturing Nonna Ali and Nonno Eric, at least they left behind a photo. And yet, something was missing.

"And what about Alberto?"

"Who?"

"Alberto Arienti," Sara explained. "You were right, you know? My grandmother's last name is the same as one of the nine martyrs, Arienti. And you were also right about the first name, it started with an 'A,' Alberto."

"Alberto! Yes, that's it. Maybe he and your grandmother were related… which would mean that you were also related to Alberto Arienti!"

He looked at Sara fondly, almost with admiration.

"But still," he continued "I can't see a link between Alberto's death and your grandma's decision to leave. A good fifteen years went by between his murder and her departure."

True, thought Sara. And yet, she had the impression that the two events were somehow connected. Some people live their longest life after they die.

"Do you want my advice?" Alessandro smiled bitterly. "Consider majoring in anthropology. You have conducted quite a bit of fieldwork in the last few weeks, and you sure have a talent for asking the right questions. Consider this trip to L'Aquila your internship."

Sara looked thoughtful.

"Listen, I don't know if this is one of the right questions, but there's something I don't quite understand. If you don't like it here, if you felt suffocated even before the earthquake, why don't you leave?"

Alessandro gave her a surprised look.

"Leave? But I was born here!"

"Well, sure, everyone must be born somewhere, but that's purely by chance, isn't it? You were born here, but you could have been born anywhere else. It's not like we choose where we're born, and we often don't even choose where we die. Where we live, though, that's something we get to decide, or at least we can try."

"Do you really feel that way?"

They sat in silence for a moment. When he started talking again, there was a strange determination in his voice.

"No, that's not true, it's not by chance that I was born here. I was born here because my father was born here, and so was my mother, and my grandparents. I've been drinking this water and breathing this air since way before I was born. It's been centuries. Anyway, if I really had wanted to leave, I should have done it a long time ago. Now, it would be a betrayal. Listen to you! You considered Celestine a 'quitter' and now you'd have me abandon everything and go, I don't know, to Australia…"

Sara smiled. Alessandro had clearly taken the time to check the meaning of "quitter" in a dictionary, it was funny that he couldn't come up with an Italian equivalent.

"Now that you mention it, I wanted to apologize for the other day. I was a little harsh on poor Celestine."

"No way! You can't take it back now, you made me reflect on the consequences of having someone like him as our local hero. We should fire him and get someone tougher. We need a warrior like Saint George, or Saint Michael the Archangel, someone like that. I've learned my lesson, now I know that it's important to rise to the occasion. Celestine quits; Alessandro puts up a fight."

He laughed, and Sara noticed how handsome he looked when he laughed, with his curls bouncing, his white teeth under his barely parted lips. She laughed too, but he soon became serious again.

"You on the other hand..."

"Me?" asked Sara.

"Yes, you. You were born in America just by chance. That only happened because your grandma, for some strange reason, ended up there. And that's why you don't feel like you belong there. But you know what?"

He hesitated for a moment.

"What?" Sara asked, encouragingly.

"This is your opportunity to steer your life in the right direction, and correct your family's history at the same time. I've been thinking about that a lot over the past few days. It's so weird that your grandma, a woman that almost no one remembers, who left on a whim and never came back, not even for a visit, asked that her ashes be scattered here. And it's even more weird that you, who had never crossed the ocean, decided to honor her wish. And then you find out that you're related to, maybe you are even the niece of, Alberto Arienti, who gave his life so that we'd have the luxury of living in peace and having this talk tonight. Add the fact that you got here in a moment like this, right after the earthquake, when everything is in flux, when we are all struggling to define ourselves. I told you, since you arrived it feels easier to breathe, but it's not just me... This city needs you. This is what I have been thinking about. Your grandma didn't simply send her ashes. With all due respect, what help are her ashes to us? I know we were a bit harsh the day you arrived, when you told us why you came here, and we reacted the way we did. I am

sorry if we hurt your feelings, but I think that you can understand our point of view a little better now. No, your grandmother didn't send her ashes; she sent you. You are here to
correct the mistake she made when she left, you are here to
satisfy her deepest wish. You can resume her story and stay in
L'Aquila, as she should have done. This was her destiny, and
you can make it yours."

Alessandro's interpretation was as irrational as it was
intriguing. Sara was afraid that she had once again missed
something, or that she hadn't fully understood all the impli-
cations of his theory. She chose her words carefully.

"It's all very complicated, I need to think about it..."

Why did Alessandro say she didn't fit in in the U.S.? And
where in the U.S.? She was tempted to tell him about Moab.
There were times when she felt that she belonged there. She
wasn't sure she'd be able to explain herself well enough for
him to follow. She decided instead to tell him what she had
been pondering during those discussions around the table.

"I'd hold on to Celestine if I were you, but maybe it would
be good to put a fighter next to him, like you said. Even better,
you can do without patron saints altogether. You and your
friends are already wary of power like Celestine and determined like Michael the Archangel. I like your stubbornness,
your resistance. You know what you want, and I'm honored
that you'd like me to join in. I don't understand all the legal
nuances, the practical obstacles and all the rest, but I admire
your unwillingness to give up, your will to save yourselves
from the future that awaits you if you give up. It's a scary future, it looks a bit like this."

She pointed at the scenery. Before them, beyond the windshield, the large apartment complex lay somberly on its anti-seismic plates. The illuminated windows showed the pro-
files of people washing dishes, talking, getting ready for bed.
A few, in spite of the cold, leaned out the windows to smoke.
The image reminded Sara of a sports bar, with its wall of television screens broadcasting different channels.

Alessandro took in the scene with a dismayed look as though he were seeing it for the first time. Then, suddenly, he started screaming, his hands gripping the steering wheel so hard that his knuckles turned white. Sara was startled. She wondered if she should try to stop him, and worried that someone might hear him. She decided that it was good for him to cry and good for other people to hear him. Perhaps that would wake everybody up. She remembered herself screaming along the Colorado River, the day she found out about Nonna Ali's death; the coyotes responding in a chorus; her headlong race towards the small campsite, her safe haven; Una waiting by the fire. But the desolation of the canyon was nothing compared to what she saw around her now. The apartment windows continued to broadcast their evening shows. She could even see a television set in some of the units, a frame within a frame. Alessandro yelled out in rage and nostalgia, then he collapsed exhausted onto the steering wheel. Sara repressed the urge to take his hand.

Several long minutes passed. Sara, who in her hurry to follow Alessandro hadn't put her coat on, was shivering. He opened his eyes.

"You should go home now," he said.

"Aren't you coming back up?"

"I'd rather not. My mother will say that I'm stressed because I study too much, and Aldo will complain that it's impossible to hold a civilized conversation with me. Please reassure them. I'm fine and I wish everyone a good night."

He tried to smile. Sara moved closer to give him a friendly hug, but she soon realized that was a misstep, like putting a foot on a slippery rock and losing your balance while going downhill on a steep mountain. She felt dizzy, and had the strange impression that the car had suddenly shrunk. As if in slow motion, she saw Alessandro stretch an arm out around her shoulders, bringing her closer to him and preventing her from returning to her seat. She put a hand on his chest in a move that could be interpreted as a repulse or a caress. She felt Alessandro's heart. Its rhythm travelled up her arm and seemed to echo in her own chest. All of sudden she wasn't shivering anymore, as the radiating heat of their combined breath fogged up the windows and protected them from the world outside. Alessandro held her hand to his chest, moved his fingers slowly along her forearm, her elbow. Sara felt a shiver of pleasure and fear. Having another warm body so close to hers melted the loneliness of the past week, filled her with anticipation. Then, unexpectedly, Una's serious expression flashed in front of her eyes. They hadn't spoken about the possibility of meeting someone else. Their relationship was so complex that talking about fidelity seemed out of place. And Una was far away. If Sara didn't tell her, she would never find out about Alessandro. Everything that happened in L'Aquila was so difficult to translate back into English, Sara doubted she would manage to say much once she got back home. But if that was the case, then perhaps the attraction that was slowly pulling her toward Alessandro could also remain in a crack of her memory, lost in translation. Everything he had told her made their closeness seem natural and inevitable, a way to set the record straight. This was her opportunity to resume Nonna Ali's story from the point she had left it. Is this what she wanted? Something didn't feel right. She was being offered another role she wasn't ready to play. She had to be faithful to herself, more than to Una. She pushed her palm more forcefully against Alessandro's chest and retreated to her seat.

Alessandro looked at her like a beaten dog.

"It's late, I guess. We better go to sleep."

"Really, you don't want to come in?" Sara asked, trying to go back to the conversation that their awkward contact had interrupted.

"Certainly not."

Sara opened the car door, gaining a few more precious inches. She turned around before getting out.

"We'll talk soon, okay?"

"Sure," he answered, his breathing almost back to normal. "Goodnight, and… thanks for the support. Remember: cultural anthropology, that's your future!"

Sara smiled and got out. She returned to the apartment almost at a run, pierced by the cold. She stopped before ringing the doorbell to catch her breath and compose herself. She thought about Alessandro's advice, even though she wasn't sure she knew exactly what cultural anthropology meant. If it was something that had to do with observation, though, she felt like she'd done nothing but take notes since her arrival in that foreign country. So foreign. Much more foreign than she'd thought. And yet this trip to Italy, this comparison, or clash, between her American and Italian selves, were also a unique opportunity for her to learn something about herself. Could anthropology possibly merge with psychology? And didn't literature encompass them both?

"Of course! Literature encompasses everything," Nonna Ali confirmed. There she was, Nonna Ali, in her apron, with her finger raised, in one of her peremptory statements that drove Jane mad. But why did she look so tall? Sara struggled to bring her memory into focus. She was looking at her grandmother from below. In order to answer, Nonna Ali stopped doing the dishes and turned around, and now that she had her back to the window and sink, a strange glow outlined her shape. Despite her efforts, Sara couldn't remember what had caused Nonna Ali to start talking about literature, though she needed little prompting for that. She remembered, however, that those words had reached her while she was sticking her finger into a blueberry that boldly and invitingly stuck out of a muffin. Its skin had broken immediately, a dense blue liquid wet her fingertip, seeping under her nail and overflowing onto the golden top of the muffin. It evoked an unpleasant memory, that of the inkwell that she had overturned onto Nonna Ali's wooden desk, staining it indelibly. Who knows who that powerful Lady Literature was. Sara was afraid she'd get into trouble again. She quickly put her finger in her mouth to hide her misdeed.

"Does Lady Literature encompass blueberries too?" she asked, a bit unsure as to the meaning of "encompass" but proud of having said it right, even with a finger in her mouth.

Nonna Ali laughed, lifting her up effortlessly to the countertop and cleaning her fingers with a paper towel. She must have still been relatively young then, still healthy and strong.

"Of course it does," she said, "whole bushels of them!"

Sara waited for the memory to fade away before ringing the doorbell.

The television was blaring an update on a scandal concerning prime minister Silvio Berlusconi and his alleged affair with an underage prostitute known as Ruby Rubacuori, Ruby the Heartstealer. The latest development concerned Berlusconi's pressure on the Milan police to have the woman released. What a tacky soap opera, Sara thought. She had decided to keep on watching just to stay with the others, and by the end she couldn't help being taken in by the whole story.

"Why didn't Alessandro come in?" Concetta asked her once the program ended.

"He had to go to sleep, he has to wake up early tomorrow morning."

"I worry about him, he's always so nervous… He studies too much."

"That for sure, but it is a shame that it has become impossible to have a civilized conversation with him," Aldo added. "The last thing we need is all this resentment. This is the time to stick together and try to make something good come out of this tragedy."

He seemed keen on getting Sara's approval.

"I think I'm going to bed now, I am very tired," Sara said. "Alessandro told me to wish you all a good night, he'll call tomorrow," she added as she disappeared into her room.

L'AQUILA, ITALY
JANUARY 19, 2011

When Sara got up, Concetta was already busy in the kitchen.

"Good morning, there was something for you in the mail."

"For me?" Sara asked, stumbling in her slippers. The cold from the night before, together with the cigarette smoke lingering in the apartment, made her throat dry and sore. A small FedEx package lay on the table.

"It arrived this morning," continued Concetta, always grateful for the slightest variation in her routine and for a topic of conversation with Sara. "I was going to wake you in ten minutes, like you asked."

Sara looked at her watch. It was ten o'clock! How could her sleep schedule still be this irregular? She struggled to fall asleep and then didn't wake up until late in the morning. The FedEx box contained a package wrapped in brown paper and an envelope with a note in Jane's hurried handwriting:

"From what you said, I thought this might be important. Let me know when you get it. Have a good trip and try to go to Florence at least."

There was also a P.S., "buy yourself something nice," which must have referred to the 300 euros that accompanied the letter and that Sara quickly put back into the envelope before looking at the package. It had been wrapped very carefully, and Sara had to work hard to open it. It was a big worn out volume. *The Flower of Russian Poetry*. Sara delicately leafed through its pages and found the dedication: *A Nadia, per sempre. Osia*. Nadia? Osia? Forever? There was also a place and a date. *Rome, February 12, 1958*.

Sara welcomed the volume as if it were an old friend. She would have liked to spend the rest of the day reading it, but she needed a way to do so without offending Concetta. She suspected that her host disapproved of her staying in her room to read instead of joining her in front of the television. She had the impression too that Concetta didn't trust her enough to leave her alone in the house. Maybe the garbage disposal incident justified her apprehension. Her hospitality was generous, but it also entailed lots of unwritten rules that Sara was just beginning to learn.

Sara was still looking for a way to solve her dilemma when the phone rang. Alessandro wanted to talk to her, but first he had to undergo Concetta's questioning, discuss the events of the previous night, and promise a visit. When Concetta finally decided to hand Sara the phone, Alessandro was exasperated.

"Listen, I need a favor. We want to post information about the situation in L'Aquila on social media and some international blogs. We need to be straight and to the point, which is not always our forte, especially in English. We could use some help with the translation."

"Sure, when?"

"Today, now. We also need to print some flyers about the experts who came here after months of tremors to tell us not to worry, and this only a few days before the big one. They are lobbying to get support from the international scientific community by circulating false information. They claim that they are on trial because they failed to predict the earthquake, while they did the exact opposite, they reassured us that an earthquake would *not* occur. It's infuriating, you should see how many times they invoke the name of Galileo to pretend that they are being persecuted for their commitment to science. This weekend there will be an important international astrophysics conference in L'Aquila. It's a good opportunity to distribute some flyers and reach at least a few scientists."

"Do you have a printer?"

"Yes, we do. If it's alright with you, I'll come pick you up and bring you to our office, you can work there, there's also a guy who can help with the formatting. Then, when you're done, I'll find someone to take you home. I would normally take care of this myself, but I'm also busy with organizing this conference."

"No problem, there's no rush to get me back here. Do you think I could stay there to read once I'm done with the translation and the flyer?"

"Of course, you can stay as long as you like. I can pick you up in an hour. Is that OK?"

Sara was in a very good mood as she dunked her cookies in her cappuccino. Every morning she said to herself she should try to have something healthier for breakfast, but she had grown quite fond of the Atene cookies, so named because of the Greek frieze that decorated them. She made a mental note to tell Valerie about them, perhaps she could even tease her by suggesting that she distribute the cookies during her school visits to get kids interested in the ancient world. The day started to look very promising all of a sudden, and she couldn't wait to have a few hours to herself. She realized that she might have to skip lunch, which gave her the perfect excuse to dunk another couple of Atenes into her cappuccino. She had discovered very early on that they tasted better when eaten two at a time. She drank the rest of her cappuccino. When it was all gone, it took her a second to recognize her own face on the shiny bottom of the mug. For a fleeting moment, the woman in the reflection looked like Nonna Ali, smiling and winking at her.

***

"You know, at the beginning I was afraid you were in a mad rush to complete your grand tour and you were going to leave before getting to know us at all. But now I'm worried about the opposite. It would be a shame if you went back home without visiting at least Rome, Florence and Venice."

The professor stopped talking to clean his fogged-up glasses. A waiter came over with two cups of hot chocolate.

"Which is to say, the past," Sara said after the waiter left.

"What do you mean, the past?"

"Well, you're suggesting I visit monuments that are crumbling little by little—the ruins of Pompeii, Venice sinking... But I am beginning to believe that L'Aquila, with its historic center overtaken by rats, its ugly suburbs, its plasma TVs in every home, its shopping malls, is very revealing of the true state of Italy, and perhaps the world."

The Professor gave her a disapproving look.

"The prophets of doom are almost invariably wrong. You've been spending too much time with Alessandro. He's a smart kid, but he is also extreme in his views, a bit of a radical. He worries me."

Sara smiled, wondering what the Professor would think of Alessandro's screams the night before.

She had spent the whole day in a small building that Alessandro and his friends had illegally occupied and turned into the headquarters for their association. As they drove, Alessandro explained with a smile that the place was actually part of the city's old psychiatric hospital, near the church of Santa Maria di Collemaggio where that other crazy guy, Celestine, had been made pope. The reference to Celestine took her back to their conversation of the night before and to what had almost happened between them. Everything seemed very distant now, and the car no longer felt uncomfortably small. In the daylight, things that happen at night often take on a dreamlike quality. It was nice to feel relaxed and safe again next to Alessandro. Her gaze fell on the rose window on the facade of Santa Maria di Collemaggio. Nonna Ali's last wishes, and Jane's impulsiveness in donating the necklace, were two more episodes to add to the list of events loosely tied to that church. It truly was an extraordinary place.

It did not take long for her to translate the information that Alessandro and his friends wanted to circulate on social media. The man in charge of formatting the flyer turned out to be a skilled editor, and the final result looked sleek and professional. After he left, Sara had the whole place to herself. She brought a chair next to the window, wrapped her scarf around her shoulders—the small radiator in the corner struggled to warm up the room—and took the book from her bag.

Alice had loved *The Flower of Russian Poetry*, you could tell by the sorry condition of the volume. She must have snuggled with it and carried it around like a child with a teddy bear. Sara caressed the coffee stains on some of the pages. It was a large volume, she would never be able to finish it in an afternoon, but some well-loved books are like tracks in the snow, you find yourself following the path traced by those who preceded you. You hesitate at the same crossroads, stumble where they fell, regain your balance, and move on. Alice had underlined some passages and taken notes in the margins. Sara simply had to follow her guidance to find a direction. She found herself lingering where Alice had lingered, reading through her eyes. Some passages came to Sara as if amplified by the echo of Alice's thoughts that had been distilled into quick annotations, sometimes accompanied by a date.

> *And I don't know whether fate*
> *Is going to lead me astray*
> *Whether further away I'll come across*
> *Happiness or dismay.*

Alice had marked Alexander Blok's verses with a question mark and a note: "Rome-New York, February 12, 1958." She had begun to read the collection while crossing the Atlantic for the first—and, as it would turn out, the last—time. As she was leaving Italy, she must have felt that Blok's poem resonated with her same fears, doubts, and hopes.

Maybe Sara was thinking of Alice's notes as a path in the snow because big and heavy flakes had begun to fall early in the afternoon, making everything fresher and brighter. Sara alternated reading poetry and observing the changes in the scenery outside her window. She felt, for the first time in years, absolutely, perfectly happy. This must be what I came here for, she thought, though the idea didn't make much sense. Jane had mailed her the book from the States, there was no need for her to take such a long journey to read it. And yet everything—the poetry, the snow, the rose window of the basilica that she could see from her chair—seemed to come together beautifully. And now, sitting with the Professor in their usual café in Piazza Duomo, she found herself thinking the same thing. This is what I came here for.

"Professor, why did my grandmother leave?"

The Professor was busy with his hot chocolate. They made it especially for him at the café, knowing he would send back anything made from a mix. It was so thick that you could almost eat it with a spoon rather than drink it. The Professor coughed at the question that interfered with his culinary pleasure.

"What do you mean?"

"The other day you said she ran away. That's the word you used. But why? From whom or what was she fleeing?

"Don't you know the story already? She met Gérard Phili... No, wait, we decided it was James Dean on his white horse. He said 'Hop on, blondie,' and how could she possibly resist..."

Sara laughed at the tangle of images that sprung from the

Professor's love and jealousy. It was incredible that those feelings had survived intact for half a century. You only needed
to half-open the lid and they jumped right out at you, like a
jack-in-the-box.

"As you told me once, that doesn't mean much. That's
merely the sequence of events. What I'd like to know are her
real motivations. She dropped everything to follow a guy she
barely knew. That doesn't fit with the image I have of Nonna Ali. Was she that impulsive when she was young? Or was
there something else that made her leave?"

The Professor seemed embarrassed. Sara realized she was
on the right track.

"You are the only one who knew her well. She never told
you why she decided to abandon everything?"

Just a few people ventured out on such a cold, snowy day.
Sara and the Professor had claimed their favorite table, in the
corner, and the café was quiet enough for Sara to hear the
man's spoon scraping the sides of his cup. He seemed to have
lost all interest in his hot chocolate.

"A few days ago, you asked me if we had written to each
other, and my answer was a bit evasive. The truth is that I
wrote to her a few times, when I found out that her husband,
or whoever he was, had died. I didn't hear from her for a few
years but then, finally, I got this letter."

He pulled a plastic bag from his pocket. He took an envelope from the bag and then a piece of paper from the envelope
which he carefully unfolded before placing it in Sara's hands.

Unforgettable Osia,
I thank you for your letters and your concern for me. I am writ-
ing first of all to let you know that I am doing well and that, after a
rather brutal first impact, I have gotten used to the American way of
life. I don't want to bore you with the bureaucratic details related to
my immigration status. Suffice it to say that the family of the man
who should have been my husband became very worried at the idea

that I would take Jane away. They did everything in their power to find the right channels to allow me to stay in the U.S. Do you remember Carlo Altoviti, the guy who was born Venetian and died Italian? I am beginning to feel a bit like him. I was born Italian, and I will likely live the rest of my life, and die, as an American.

The other important news is that I'm not a cashier anymore! I had to accept that job when I first arrived to feed Jane. You wouldn't believe how different American English is from our "life's but a walking shadow." I didn't have a chance to get a good job without learning the language well first. But for the last two months I've been working... in a library! I know you will understand my joy. Public libraries here are so very different from ours. People are allowed to peruse the shelves on their own. Some read sitting on the floor, others at the tables that we have scattered here and there (we don't have enough space for a proper reading room.) There are people taking notes, others discussing, and the occasional homeless person who uses the library as a day shelter. Nothing against our Tommasiana, of course, but that is a library for scholars, this one is for everybody. The Italian section is almost nonexistent and so I organized a fund-raiser event with the Italian community. They are incredible people, they built skyscrapers while eating bread and onions. I had to come to the States to discover how hard-working Italians can be. But I digress, I am sorry. Anyway, the Italian-American community gave generously for the creation of an Italian section, provided that we also offered language classes. Guess who is going to be the teach-er...?! Yes, that's right, I am going to go back to teaching after all.

One of the advantages of working in a library is that, of course, I am surrounded by books! I have developed a passion for languages, and I spend my free time reading foreign language grammar books. The ways language shapes people's minds never cease to fascinate me. A thought that can't be expressed doesn't remain a thought for long. It vanishes, it evaporates. In the past few years I have often felt crippled because of my shaky command of English. All the things I couldn't put into words slipped into a sort of murky abstraction. I've tried to recover them by talking to you, Osia. If you've heard voices, it was me. After a day when my conversation revolved around the items on sale and the arrangement of underwear on the shelves—around nothing, that is—I would summon you to talk about our poets, about that war that seemed to go on forever and then one day finally ended, and about the smell of the pine trees at Madonna Fore. Now, incredibly, I've started speaking Italian with Jane. It's normal, I guess, but to me it feels like a miracle. It's also a bit absurd that this girl who was born here and is her father's splitting image, is the one that allows me to stay in touch with everything that is dear to me. Because I read her our poetry, I speak to her in Italian, and she answers to me. Language is our umbilical cord, between the two of us and between us and Italy. If we hold on to it, we will never lose sight of what we are.

Forgive me if I struggle to keep on track. The fact is that I'm still an apprentice at the library and so, to make ends meet, I work two nights a week as a waitress. The pay is awful but the tips are generous, and so I hope that within a couple of years I will be able to buy a little house here in Bethesda. I am sorry, I've lost my thread yet again! I was telling you that in my free time I read books on the grammar of various languages, and a couple of days ago I made an important discovery that made me think of you, of us. It seems that some languages don't have the subjunctive, and thus don't have the hypothetical clause. You can't say things like: If I had bet on red, I would have won a thousand dollars. Once a possibility has not materialized, it disappears forever and can no longer be resurrected, not even as a hypothesis. Isn't that fascinating? I wonder about the consequences of this feature on the psyche of the speakers. Perhaps they have more trouble than we do in abandoning reality to create scenarios that never existed and never will. But that, right now, seems like a blessing to me. There is no need to torment ourselves with the way things could/should/might have been. And so, listen, Osia: I, for my part, declare war on the hypothetical clause. It is pointless to say "if I hadn't opened that drawer, I wouldn't have left that way," or "if I hadn't stopped to give that guy a ride, we would've gotten married." The fact is: I opened it, I stopped, the die was cast. *We have to be strong and accept the world we contributed to create when we behaved in a certain way and not in another. 'Il faut s'assumer,' as the French say. We must take responsibility for what we are and what we have done. We have no right, no need, and no time to indulge in regrets.*

Also, Osia, I have been meaning to thank you for the generosity and the open mindedness that you demonstrate by inviting me to come back to you with Jane. I can't even begin to tell you how much I appreciate that. Deep down, though, I am sure you know as well as I do that this could never work out. We would be on two different levels. You would be a saint and I would be the beneficiary of your miracles. Love can only exist among equals. Therefore, thanks but no thanks. As for the contents of your drawer, I don't really understand if you're offering an apology or if you're simply upholding notions that are foreign to me, such as loyalty to family ties, the need to forget the past, and the importance of not scrutinizing this marvelous Italian Republic of ours too closely. You find that the consequences of that event are disproportionate to its importance, and you may even be right. But that episode gave me tangible proof that fascism is not over. It is within us, we drank it with our mothers' milk, we sons and daughters of the she-wolf. It is an insidious disease. It crept under our skins, it seems to be dozing off but it's always ready to bite. The signs are everywhere, and everybody should be able to read them by now: the massacre of Portella della Ginestra, the enduring power of Gaetano Azzariti and the like, the priests still dictating our code of conduct, the many articles of the Rocco Code that are still in force. With all due respect, it is now clear that fascism wasn't a disease in a healthy body, but a revelation of Italy's true nature. And if this is the case, there's no hope. Now you will object that it's absurd to find refuge from fascism in the country of Joseph McCarthy, but here I feel it's easier to restart, an immigrant like everybody else, without anybody or anything that reminds me of my past. I am digging my lair, filling it with books and memories, and I feel at peace with myself. And the Italy that I love, so different from the one we grew up in and also from the one of this uncertain,

feeble peace, I will always carry that Italy with me. It is a country of
paper, eternal and fragile. I am its honorary citizen, along with all
the exiles who built it. There, I will continue to meet you, Osia, at
every verse, at every hesitation, at every hour that melts a sailor's
heart with longing.

You ask me if your letters bother me. How could they? But it is
too much to request a response, and a prompt one at that. It is one
of those obligations that my departure and my bitter freedom have
given me the right and the luxury to disregard.

Nadia
P.S. Thanks for the book. How did you manage to slip it into my
purse without my noticing?

It took Sara a while to read the letter. Alice's handwriting was
very neat, but she was obviously referring to episodes that
Sara wasn't familiar with. It was apparent at this point that
she and Eric hadn't had the time to get married—now that
Sara thought about it, that explained why she had never seen
a picture from their wedding. She made mental notes about
Portella della Ginestra, Azzariti, the Rocco Code, all things
that she could google later on. But the rest? A drawer? And
again, Nadia and Osia. When she raised her eyes, she met the
Professor's gaze.

"So?"

"So…"

She didn't know how to even begin.

"I don't know… there's a lot."

"For example…?" asked the Professor, without being able
to avoid the tone that terrified his students during an exam.

"For example, what she says about language is very true.
Nonna Ali always insisted on speaking Italian with my mother and me. For some reason, that annoyed my mother and
delighted me, but the point is that Italian really became a code
that bound us. We went through highs and lows in our rela-

tionships, but when we resurfaced after a crisis our language was always there, waiting for us. I guess this is what having a "mother tongue" means. I believe Nonna Ali exaggerated her problems with English. After all, she learned five languages, she was the director of a library, she couldn't have been as inept as she liked to paint herself. She pretended not to be able to speak English just to maintain that connection with her daughter, and later with me, and with Italy, as she says."

"And then her daughter, what's her name, Jane, in turn passed this gift down to you. Your Italian is excellent."

Sara felt herself blush. It was no small compliment.

"Thank you. It wasn't my mother, though, who taught me Italian. Between law school first and her law firm later, she never had the time. My Italian goes back to Nonna Ali, who was basically my primary caregiver when I was little. My mother had put her career on hold to raise her first two children, and just when she was about to go back to school she got pregnant again. She wasn't exactly ecstatic. In fact, she told me that she would have terminated the pregnancy if it hadn't been for Nonna Ali, who promised to help her and practically forced her to play her part well, as she was fond of repeating."

Sara was surprised to be able to summarize the history and prehistory of her relationship with Jane in such a detached, objective manner. Not bad for a failed abortion. Was this really the expression she had used when fighting with her Mom? Failed abortion? That was awful, poor Jane. Even the Professor, who must not be the most progressive guy around, wasn't horrified by Jane's doubts.

"…But Nonna Ali also worked, so she often took me to the library with her. To lull me to sleep, she used to read me the Italian classics. That way I learned Italian like you learned English. I learned an old language, I too lived in a country of paper, as she says, and ever since I arrived in L'Aquila I feel I'm going through a refresher course… a bit brutal, as a refresher course, to tell you the truth, but I feel I'm learning quite a bit."

"Forget about the refresher course, please! Or else you'll end up speaking like Alessandro and his friends, with swear words and Anglicisms in every sentence to show that they are so very cool and international. You have heard about Venice sinking, Pompei crumbling, but let me tell you, people who lose their language are bound to become slaves. That's something Alice understood very well. What did she use to read to you?"

Sara had barely followed the Professor's tirade and had lost hope that the conversation would ever pick up again where it had left off. The final question caught her by surprise, and the Professor was forced to repeat it.

"Yes, you told me that Alice read the Italian classics to you. Which ones in particular?"

"Ah, well, you know…Dante, Ariosto, chivalric poems in general. She thought they would be easier for me to follow, since there were adventures on every page."

"Which ones?"

"Well, a bit of everything, but her favorite was Torquato Tasso, especially *Jerusalem Delivered*."

"Which is really an epic poem, not a chivalric one, I don't know if you've read Tasso's *Discourses on the Art of Poetry and on the Heroic Poem…*"

Sara shifted uncomfortably in her seat.

"Yes, well, of course, I imagine… epic, yes. But no, that other book you said no, the *Discourses on the Art of Poetry…* no, I don't recall her mentioning it."

"That's unfortunate. But what about *Jerusalem Delivered*? Did you like it? Do you still remember it?"

"I loved it! And yes, of course I still remember it. Not all of it but some passages here and there, yes, sure."

"Not all of it!'" the Professor repeated. "There aren't too many people left who know all of it these days, in any country. But what do you remember? Is there a passage you, or Alice, particularly liked?"

Sara tried to concentrate and cleared her throat. At first she was afraid she'd botch the pronunciation, but she gradually became more and more sure of herself, as if Nonna Ali were sitting next to her, cheering her on.

While the faithful and the pagan
in this manner fiercely fought
the proud sultan climbed the tower,
and from the distant balcony looked below.

She paused and looked at the Professor. His eyes had moistened, and he seemed to be trembling.

"Continue," he said in a faint voice.

He watched (as in a theater or an arena)
The bitter tragedy of the human state;

"What's wrong, aren't you feeling well?"

The Professor had covered his face with his hands. With a faint voice, but perfectly audible, Sara heard him complete the lines:

the various assaults, the cruel horror of death,
and the great games of fate and chance.

The Professor didn't move, he seemed smaller and older in his seat. The bartender looked at them with some concern and Sara made a quick gesture to indicate that everything was fine.

"You're not feeling well?" she asked again in a whisper.

The Professor nodded. After a minute or so, he put his glasses on the table, took out a large handkerchief from his pocket and noisily blew his nose.

"We studied *Jerusalem Delivered* together for Alice's Italian literature exam in college," he explained.

Then, with an expression that struck Sara as both out of character and at the same time reassuring, he added: "What magnificent verses! But tell me, did she really refer to the *Jerusalem Delivered* as a chivalric poem? Because, Tasso, among other things, was an attentive reader of Aristotle's *Poetics*, and he set out to write a modern epic poem, the new *Aeneid*, not an Ariosto-style chivalric tale…"

Sara thought the conversation was taking an unexpected and unproductive turn. The Professor risked going off on some critical and philological tangent that she couldn't possibly follow.

"I don't really remember. You know, I was only a kid, she probably tried to make things easy for me."

"Ah well, of course," he said, comforted. Then, as if interrogating himself:

"The nineteenth of *Jerusalem Delivered* …?" he asked.

"What?"

"No, it must be the twentieth, the last canto, the end. And then? What else did she read to you?"

"Well, a little bit of everything, French and Russian authors, but mostly in Italian translation, so we could work on my Italian at the same time."

The Professor looked as if waiting for something. Sara mustered the courage, cleared her throat.

My dear friend, we'll meet again
as I always carry you in my heart.
The time that forces us to part,
one day is bound to reunite us.
Farewell, my friend, with no words,
no smiles or tears. To die
is nothing new under the sun
but living is nothing newer.

As soon as Sara finished reciting the last verse she regretted having chosen that poem, because it wasn't true that Nonna Ali had read it to her. She had just learned it that afternoon as she read by the window while the snow was falling. The book had easily opened on that page, as if Nonna Ali had gone over those lines many times. But it was the note in the margins that had struck Sara the most. It was written in a trembling cursive, the handwriting of Nonna Ali's illness: "October 9, 2010. Time to go."

It was the only note written in ink, and it must have been the last she ever wrote, since October 9, 2010 was the date of her death. She could picture her flipping through the pages, too tired to look for a pencil, jotting that thought down, closing the book and heading towards the Capital Crescent Trail. Time to go, indeed. Was the Professor the "dear friend" she was thinking about? Sara was afraid she had caused him more pain by quoting those lines, but her fear of not delivering what might have been Nonna Ali's last message for him had been stronger. The Professor looked at her intently.

"Yesenin. *Goodbye my friend, goodbye.*"

Sara nodded. She waited for a comment that never came, then searched for the right words to continue the conversation.

"The letter that you had me read… Was it the only one she sent you during all these years?" she asked.

"Yes, the only one. Then, after the earthquake, she actually called on the phone, but I wasn't there. She left a message on the answering machine. It made me happy, but I was afraid she had called out of pity. I thought of a way to reassure her, and in the end I sent her one of those necklaces… you know, the ones with the rose window of Santa Maria di Collemaggio. Who knows if she ever received it. I didn't know she was that ill."

Sara's heart skipped a beat.

"Yes, she got it," she said quickly, hoping the Professor wouldn't ask for further details.

Sara went over the letter again.

"Why did you call each other 'Osia' and 'Nadia'?"

The Professor looked at her surprised, a shadow of disappointment in his eyes.

"It was one of our little secrets. Those were our code names. We signed our letters as Osia Mandelstam, the Russian poet who died in a gulag, and his wife Nadia, the woman who saved Mandelstam's poems by memorizing them. Even if I must say that Nadia was much more devoted and understanding to Osia than Alice was to me."

Sara smiled. There was something else that escaped her, though.

"Professor, all of these references to fascism, to an incident... I don't really understand."

"Well, you know, Benedetto Croce maintained that fascism was an illness..."

"I understand Nonna Ali's take on fascism," Sara lied, trying to dodge a lecture, "But the incident, the incident with the drawer, the episode that made Nonna Ali think that fascism wasn't dead..."

"Ah, that... If I may say so, Alice was a touch too fond of radical solutions and dramatic plot twists. I hope you didn't inherit her tendency."

Maybe a bit, Sara admitted to herself, but this certainly was no time to indulge in self-analysis.

"Yes, but what was she referring to exactly?"

It was difficult to decipher the expressions of the Professor's shriveled up face in the dim light of the café, but Sara had the impression he was blushing.

"These aren't easy things to talk about, even after all these years..."

Sara continued to look at him questioningly.

"Professor, please, I'm about to go back home. This may

be the last chance we have to talk about it, don't you think? Perhaps Nonna Ali sent me here just to hear your story."

He continued to attentively examine what was left of his hot chocolate, helping himself with the spoon.

"Let's go, come on, it's too hot in here."

They went out into the fresh air, enchanted by the snow that had placed a white hat on the elegant male nude of the fountains in Piazza Duomo. Dense flakes eased down lazily on the luminous strips projected by the streetlamps, soaking up the light before they disappeared.

The Professor walked to the entrance of an alleyway. He stood in front of the fence and the sign that blocked access. He grabbed the wire with his bare hands, staring inside the alleyway's black tunnel. Sara tried to do the same but couldn't see anything. The yellow light of the streetlamps, already softened by the snow, died out about five yards beyond the fence. Yet the Professor kept staring.

"We have to go inside."

He looked around, then pushed the cinderblock to create an opening just big enough for the two of them to sneak in, as Alessandro had done a few days before.

"Where are we going?"

The Professor didn't respond, he disappeared into the darkness of the alleyway. After a few seconds Sara saw a light shine.

"What do you have, a flashlight?!"

"Of course. In L'Aquila, a flashlight is a primary necessity, I recommend you get one too. Apart from the fact that the night of the earthquake I wouldn't have survived without a flashlight, as you can see the city authorities are a bit, shall we say, parsimonious when it comes to public lighting."

"Well, maybe they don't expect people to go into restricted zones..."

"Nonsense, we don't need anybody's permission to enter our own home."

Sara smiled as she recognized Alessandro's reasoning in the Professor's words.

"You know," she told him as she reached him, "Alessandro also tried to enter the Red Zone the other day, from an alley on the Corso, but a soldier stopped him and threatened to put him in jail."

"Alessandro is way too impulsive, I told you. How can you possibly enter the Red Zone in broad daylight, from the Corso? Of course they'd stop you, they have nothing better to do. But if you wait until dark and take little alleys you can go anywhere you want, especially on nights like this, with such bad weather and nobody around. Watch out for the rubble though."

The alleyway led to a square. A screen of falling snow enhanced the brightness of the full moon that allowed Sara to make out a fountain surrounded by empty flower beds. Wooden beams braced the window frames of the buildings, chains and locks kept their doors closed. The Professor moved swiftly across the square, at a safe distance from the shaky houses, until he stopped and directed the beam of his flashlight on the wall in front of him.

Piazza Nove Martiri Aquilani.

Sara recognized the sign she had seen on the Internet. This was the monument to the nine partisans, the nine martyrs. Three small plaques carried three names each, in alphabetical order. The first was Alberto Arienti.

"Are they buried here?" Sara asked.

"No, they are buried in the cemetery, but there's rubble there too, you can't even get to their grave. But even before, I didn't go there much. I felt Alberto's presence much more in this square, he loved it so much... He loved it so much, in fact, that he refused to call it Piazza XXVIII October."

Sara looked at him.

"Piazza XXVIII October?"

"Yes. The fascists, in their urge to leave their mark every-where, had a passion for nomenclature. Not even this little corner of the world escaped their attention. It became Piazza XXVIII October, to commemorate the day Mussolini seized power in 1922. But after the war, it was renamed Piazza Nine Martyrs. If you ask around, I bet very few people will remember its previous name. Yet there is a connection, don't you think, between Mussolini's rise to power and the death of Alberto and his friends? I would even say there is a cause-and-effect relationship between October 28th, 1922 and September 23, 1943, when the Nine Martyrs were murdered. It is important to keep that link in mind, don't you think? I even wrote a petition to keep the old name alongside the new — Piazza Nine Martyrs, formerly known as Piazza XXVIII October. But I was outvoted, most people wanted to bury the past and move on. They insisted that the fascist name never really caught on, and they were right about that. Alberto and I, we always referred to this place as the little piazza, the *piazzetta*. When we said 'I'll see you in the *piazzetta*', this is what we meant."

He looked around as if he expected to see Alberto emerge from an alley to meet him there, in the *piazzetta*.

"Where are you planning on going?"

"To Colle Brincioni first, then to Bosco Martese. We're not the only ones, you know! The colonel said there are thousands of us, all over Italy, rising up, to show that we are not a bunch of cowards."

"But is it worth it…?"

"What kind of question is that?"

"My father says that the war is over, we must hang on just a few more weeks, everything is going to be alright…"

"Your father says that because he hopes we'll forget what a fascist he is. But when we win we'll give him the castor oil treatment, as he did to so many people. It's nice to be a bully with the wind

*at your back, huh? Your father doesn't show his face around much
these days, does he?"*

"Stop that, you know these are old stories!"

*"Of course, these stories are old. The new story is that we have
the Germans in town saying we need to register with them, and once
we register who knows what will happen... Will we have to work in
their labor camps? Fight for the Third Reich? Torture, maim, and
kill, as they have done all over Europe, as they are doing all over
Italy?"*

*"But not us, right? The public notice was very clear. Only those
born between 1910 and 1925 need to go to the police headquarters.
We aren't eighteen yet, this doesn't apply to us!"*

*"Listen to you! Did your father tell you this too? So, tell me,
what does he suggest we do, in his great wisdom, just stay put until
they come after us? Don't you realize it could be too late by then?
It's now or never, understand? Now or never!"*

Alberto seemed suddenly worried.

*"Listen, this story about me not being eighteen yet... don't men-
tion it, okay? Because the others didn't want me to go either. They
say I'm too young, so I swore I just turned eighteen. Luckily I'm so
tall that they believed me. And now I have to go..."*

The Professor looked at one of the dark alleys.

"So he went away, and I followed."

"Went... where?"

"Towards the Square of Santa Maria Paganica. He was
right, there were many of them, right in front of the church..."

"Alberto!

*Carmine enthusiastically hugged his friend. Everyone was
speaking loudly as if they had been drinking. Some were armed, others talked about places where they hoped to find weapons. Someone started to sing the International but was overpowered by those
singing the Italian national anthem. The time for action had come.
Between the Nazis' arrival in town and their raid on the Gran Sasso*

to free Mussolini, the war had suddenly come very close. General Kesselring's order that all the young men in L'Aquila register at the police station showed that the Germans were not planning a retreat any time soon. Amidst all the uncertainty, the group gathering in front of Santa Maria Paganica knew one thing for sure: enough with receiving orders from a bunch of criminals, enough of keeping a low profile and waiting, just waiting for the nightmare to be over. And so there they were, those who were leaving and the others, many more, who had come to say goodbye. There was no time to linger, though, a gathering of that sort would inevitably attract attention. If a German patrol arrived, they'd have to fight them right there and then, in front of the statue of the Madonna who clutched her child and watched over the streets with trepidation, from her perch on the main door of the church.

Fulvio had struggled to keep up with Alberto, especially because his untied shoelace forced him to drag his foot.

"What about him?" Carmine asked, pointing at him, a hint of annoyance in his voice.

"He followed me," replied Alberto, "but he is not coming, he's only a kid."

Fulvio felt that Alberto had somehow gotten away from him, as if he had jumped over a fence. He belonged to them, to his new comrades set on making history, while he stayed back to tie his shoelaces and worry about an excuse to explain why he hadn't gone home for lunch. The discussion went back to their firearms, which were few and in bad shape. Alberto proudly described his father's hunting rifle, though Fulvio had never heard him mention hunting before and was not sure he'd know how to use it. Then one of the boys opened his jacket and took out a sausage from his breast pocket, and everybody laughed. As if on cue, the others also showed pieces of cheese, frittata sandwiches, wine in cloth sacks. No risk of running out of water, they would quench their thirst in the mountain springs.

Suddenly Alberto looked uncomfortable, as if remembering something he needed to do before leaving. He looked around and saw Fulvio staring at him. He reached him in a few anxious strides.

"Listen, it's ridiculous how much stuff I have on me..."

He pulled off a scarf from his neck and gave it to him.

"Ahh! That feels better already. Two scarves in September! Mom really went overboard."

He furtively took out of his pocket a bundle of papers tied together by a purple ribbon and gave them to Fulvio.

"These are my poems. Keep them until I come back, they'd only be a nuisance to me now."

"Let's move, come on. Jamo, quatrà!" yelled Carmine, and others did the same.

They left almost at a run. Fulvio had hoped for one last look, a wave, but Alberto was too eager to be part of the group, too determined to make everybody believe he was already a man, ready for the call. Fulvio felt abandoned as he watched them head towards the Fountain of Lights.

The only people left on the street were the carpenter who had watched the whole scene from the door to his store, with his little boy clinging to his leg. Fulvio sensed their eyes on him, he crouched down and carefully began to tie his shoe. Finally! It had been bothering him all day.

"Hey, Fulvio..."

His father reached him out of breath.

"What are you doing here? Why didn't you come home for lunch?"

"Nothing." He lied instinctively.

"What do you mean nothing? I heard rumors. It seems that there are some boys heading for the mountains."

"No way."

"Tell me the truth, your friend is going with them, isn't he? That Alberto..."

Fulvio shrugged.

"I bet they'll be back soon," his father continued, "I bet that as soon as night falls, they'll miss their mommies and come running home."

He looked at his son and decided to change strategy.

"What, you wanted to go too? Look, if you care so much about it I'll take you, we'll catch up with them."

Fulvio looked at him surprised.

"Really, why not? They're smart boys, and they're organized, right? There's even an army captain who's planning to meet with them."

"A colonel."

"What?"

"A colonel, not a captain."

"Yes, you're right. But regardless of the rank, they are facing quite a challenge. The road to the Sirente mountains is long."

"They're not going to Sirente right away. They're only going to Colle Brincioni and they'll wait there for instructions..."

As soon as the words left his mouth, he realized he had made a huge mistake. Looking at the triumphant smile that spread across his father's thin lips, Fulvio realized with certainty that he had never really thought of accompanying him, not even for a minute.

"Thank you. Go straight home now, alright? Your mother saved you some lunch. I'll take care of this."

"Wait. What are you going to do?"

"It doesn't concern you; you've already done enough for today."

His father's tone didn't allow for a reply.

"Let's try to stop these foolhardy initiatives. You go straight home, don't make me repeat it. Straight home and let's not speak of this ever again. "

He disappeared into one of the alleys. The carpenter looked at Fulvio for a moment before turning around and going back inside his shop, with his little boy in tow.

Fulvio was left alone in the street.

Alone as he now felt under Sara's gaze.

"And then?" Sara encouraged him.

"Then, then... You know the rest, don't you? They were captured right away. Those who were unarmed were released right away. But Alberto, Carmine, and the others who had weapons on them were beaten, forced to dig their own graves, shot..."

"But are you sure it was your father..."

"Sure? Do you think I could have asked him? And even if I had, do you think he would have answered me? This is a city where you can never be sure of anything, the truth is as shaky as the ground..."

"And Alice?"

"Alice! You knew her, of course you remember that she couldn't stand hypocrisy and half-truths. She had seen Alberto leave that morning, euphoric, ecstatic, with the hunting rifle. She had watched him as he stuffed his jacket with poems. They had laughed together when their mom put a prayer card in his pocket and two scarves around his neck. 'Don't worry, I'll free Italy and come back!' It was straight out of a fairytale, or an epic poem if you wish, this image of the hero who leaves everything behind, who sacrifices himself. Nothing could be further from the closed, cautious, conservative mentality of this town."

Sara thought of Alessandro with his restlessness, his anger.

"Not all the Aquilani are like that, you know..."

"No, of course not, and not all Italians are like that either. But maybe years of servitude turned us into opportunists, more inclined to wait at the window than take to the streets."

Sara noticed that the snow was settling on the Professor's hat, she felt her own wet and cold feet inside her boots. She was afraid of the philosophizing turn that the conversation was taking. The Italians' real or presumed national traits were not her main concern, at least not right now.

"Let's assume that your father was indeed the one who turned them in. I understand it must have been awful for you to live with that suspicion. But still, what has that got to do with Nonna Ali's departure?"

What a daring decision it was, to spend the night with Fulvio. The rest of his family was busy working in their olive grove, but he had an essay to write, so he convinced them to let him stay behind. Alice told her mother she would be out of town, subbing in a school in Avezzano. The job actually existed, but it started in two days. Her parents didn't ask any questions, they did not pay much attention to her. They had not been the same since they discovered that Alberto had not been interned in Germany or Poland, but he had never left L'Aquila. All those evenings his mother set the table for him too, all those nights his father took a last look at the street before locking the door, Alberto was right around the corner, a few inches below the ground. They just couldn't get over it. They kept wondering who, among the people they saw in town every day, knew what happened but didn't tell them, never dropped a hint, didn't even send an anonymous letter. Time had gone by without healing their wounds. All other events and concerns had become somewhat distant, a bit dull. Then again, Alice had been subbing all over the province, in distant villages perched on vertiginous cliffs, travelling treacherous roads. Her parents didn't expect her to come home every night, especially during the winter months. Alice prepared her books and notes, accepted some provisions, wrapped a small gift for the widow who would host her in Avezzano, and said goodbye to her folks. But as soon as it got out of the Southern Gate, her Fiat 1100 turned onto a small unpaved road and hid in Fulvio's garage. Fulvio's hands were trembling as he closed the doors behind her. They had devised their plan carefully. As the road only led to his home, it was unlikely that somebody would spot Alice's car. There was no reason for them to go out at all for the next couple of days. She would then leave before dawn and get to Avezzano just in time to teach. And so, Alice was there, now, between the sheets, while Fulvio worked on brewing coffee in the cold kitchen, finally feeling like an adult, almost married. Even Alice's voice from the bedroom sounded different.

"Hurry up, come on, it's freezing in here..."

"I'm coming, take one of my sweaters from the chest, if you want. They are in the top drawer."

Fulvio was trying to move as fast as he could but everything was a bit foreign to him in that house, his mother took care of everything. He had to open every cabinet to gather together a sugar bowl, spoons, plates, and a couple of cookies. And once he did that he realized that in order to save time he should have started the coffee first. The whole operation took longer than he thought, but he finally returned to the bedroom rather proud of himself, with two steaming cups and a full tray.

Alice was fully dressed, though, and was even wearing her coat. Fulvio suddenly felt ridiculous in his wool boxers.

"Sugar?"

"One, thank you."

"Are you really this cold? Didn't you find a sweater?"

She shook her head, she barely wet her lips with coffee and stared at him. Fulvio wondered if she was ashamed, or disappointed.

"Listen, those stories that are going around..."

"Which stories?"

Alice was sitting on the only chair in the room. Fulvio had no choice but to sit on the bed, in front of her. He watched the little whirlpool that his spoon created in the coffee.

"The stories about the tip-off that led to the capture of Alberto and his friends."

"Again, with this story? After all these years?"

"Always like this...Even when the war had just ended, the refrain was always the same. 'Again, with this story?' Yes, again. You are never done talking about a story that you never talk about."

"Fine, let's talk then. But we don't know anything new about it, do we? Those were very confusing days, perhaps you don't remember them..."

"Oh, I remember them alright! Don't act all mature, you're only two years older than me. I remember many things, I remember Alberto taking dad's rifle, mom stuffing him with clothes and chocolate as if he were a child..."

Her eyes traveled to the wall behind Fulvio, as if following Alberto's rushed preparation that day. Fulvio forced himself not to turn around.

"I too loved Alberto, and I understand this story is important to you, to your entire family..."

"But...?"

"But it doesn't do any good to dwell on it. If he died for something, it was to allow us to live in peace. For older people maybe it's too late, but for you, for us..."

"I won't be able to live in peace until I find out what happened to him."

Fulvio was taken aback by the determination in her voice.

"I'm sorry, but how can you find out anything more than what we already know? The people who could have told us more died with him."

"This is only true to a certain point. First of all, who knows why some were shot and others were spared."

"Well, we know this much. Those who carried weapons looked dangerous, the others must have just seemed like harmless fools."

"And then," she continued as if she hadn't heard him, "how come the colonel who had orchestrated everything didn't show up to meet them, though his son was part of the group?"

"He turned out to be unreliable, I guess."

"Forget about him, he's not the one who interests me now. Finally, how come the Germans, who were still fairly new to the area, went straight to Colle Brincioni and were able to capture them so easily?"

Fulvio lifted some coffee with his spoon, but his hand was shaking. When it started spilling he faked nonchalance by letting it all fall back into the cup.

"Put the two things together," Alice continued. "The colonel didn't show up because he knew it was useless and dangerous, he knew they would be captured right away..."

Fulvio managed to bring a spoonful of coffee to his lips. It was already getting cold.

"...Because they had been betrayed."

Alice's assertion didn't allow a reply.

"Now, what I'd like to know," she resumed, suddenly calm, care-

*fully articulating her words, "what I would like to know from you—
from you, mind you, not from his friends who can no longer talk,
not from the fascist collaborators who can't be bothered to remember
this episode because we have turned the page and we can't be stuck
in the past..."*

*She got up and stood no more than two feet from him. He didn't
dare look up.*

*"What I would like to know, from you, is whether it is true what
Pietro keeps saying...*

"Who?"

*"Pietro, you know, the carpenter's son, the one with a shop near
Santa Maria Paganica."*

*"Pietro Pea-Brain? Come on now, you can't be serious! He was
a child at the time, he started to say those things to make himself
seem more important and he never stopped. He's mentally ill!"*

*"Only you were grown up and lucid at that time, huh? I was too
young, Pietro was and still is an idiot..."*

*"But maybe we need people like us," continued Alice without
giving him the time to retort. "Perhaps we need a little girl who
doesn't stop asking questions and a mentally ill boy who doesn't
stop answering them and telling the truth..."*

"But what truth..."

*"That you accompanied Alberto to Santa Maria Paganica, but
you preferred to tie your shoelaces while he left... Celestine!"*

*"Alice, please! Alberto was young and inexperienced and, frank-
ly, chances are he would've been more of a burden than anything
else if his group had really gotten into a fight. But what about me? I
was fifteen years old! And because, in fact, I was fifteen and I didn't
listen to Radio London like the colonel and his buddies, and because
school hadn't started yet, I didn't have any reason to be in L'Aquila.
I was in the countryside for the grape harvest, like I've told you I
don't know how many times!"*

*"You have told me many times, that's true. What's strange,
however, is that Pietro remembers you very well. He remembers Alberto talking to you and giving you his poems so that he could travel
lighter."*

"Please, Alice..."

"He remembers your father arriving just a few minutes later."

"Oh, come on..."

"And the funny thing is that he never stopped saying the same things, over and over again, despite his father's smacks and everyone mocking him..."

"Can't you see that he keeps saying the same things over and over again precisely because this way, at least, he gets his father to smack him and other people to mock him? He is dying to get some attention! If he didn't act that way, nobody would bother with him. Alice, for the last time..."

Fulvio looked up, and regretted it immediately. Because, as if she had been waiting to read the confirmation she was looking for in his eyes, Alice took a bundle of papers tied together with a purple ribbon from her coat pocket.

"Thank you for keeping them safe all these years."

"Alice! Where did you find them?"

"In the drawer, under your sweaters, and under Alberto's scarf. I didn't mean to root through your things, I promise you. Let's just say this was meant to happen."

"I can explain..."

"That's not necessary. Thank you for not throwing Alberto's poems away, as it would have been safer to do. I take it as a sign that you really did love him, or that maybe in some way you wanted the truth to come to light. Either way, I'm sorry, these things belong to me now."

The Professor had gotten increasingly agitated as he drew closer to the end of the story, shifting his gaze between the ground and a point in front of him. He knew everything he was saying was true but at the same time the story, as he recounted it, struck him as invented, like the plot of a novel. It already felt unreal back then, on the day Alice made the discovery that changed their lives. His father never mentioned their conversation in front of Santa Maria Paganica, and when

Fulvio timidly referred to it he pretended not to understand what he was talking about. As there was no one else he could talk to, he pushed the events of that day to a remote corner of his mind, the same way he had stuffed Alberto's scarf and poems in the corner of his drawer. He almost convinced himself that he had imagined it all. His dreams throughout the years replayed and amplified the events, with Alberto standing tall and proud and Fulvio always forced to chase him while encumbered by something like his shoes, his bulky Latin dictionary, or a crutch. In the most embarrassing version of the same dream he was pedaling after him and falling further and further behind, until he realized that his bicycle had training wheels, like a little child's. As the years went by, his memory of the real farewell merged with those surreal, tormenting dreams. His surprise at seeing Alberto's poems resurface from the drawer was sincere, although he could not expect Alice to understand that. From then on, Alberto wouldn't be the only one to leave, in the hazy dawns of Fulvio's dreams. Alice intruded into the sequence, grabbing the poems out of his hand, staring at him in a way that humiliated him. Then she disappeared behind her brother, with the bold stride of the disheveled female partisans who have something more than just the enemy to shake off their backs.

The Professor took a deep breath, waited for the darkness to swallow Alice's quivering steps and indignant profile.

"That's all," he said. "She up and left. She couldn't go home, because then her parents would realize she had lied to them, so she figured she'd go to Avezzano, find an excuse to explain to her landlady why she got there a day earlier. Or perhaps she didn't really have a plan, she just needed to get out of my place, get away from me. She must have still been distraught when she stopped to give a ride to a young American hitchhiking his way through Europe. A chance encounter... I'm not surprised it didn't turn out to be the most solid foundation for a life together. You can't build your future on chance."

This conclusion left Sara puzzled. She thought about Nonna Ali's letter. It was destiny, she thought. But even that interpretation was not completely satisfying. It was destiny disguised as chance, she ventured. The great games of fate and chance, perhaps. She stood behind the Professor who furiously retraced his steps, not bothering to replace the fence at the entrance of the alley. He walked briskly, leaving fresh footprints in the snow on which Sara instinctively tried to put her boots in order not to get quite so wet. She was surprised by the Professor's fast pace, as if the confession had awakened the strength and the confusion of the boy he was back in 1943. He didn't even stop when they reached Piazza Duomo. He kept walking the length of the square, then turned left, alongside the Cathedral of San Massimo, passed in front of the Church of the Blessed Souls, and finally reached the café. Sara thought the Professor wanted to restore his strength with another hot chocolate or maybe a glass of Montepulciano, but the café was closing down because of the weather.

"I'll take you home."

With the heat turned all the way up, the Professor's car resembled a tropical greenhouse. Sara felt the moisture evaporate from her soaked boots and coat the windows with condensation. Large snowflakes continued to fall. Brushed away by the wipers, they hung on the sides of the windshield while the Professor drove in a low gear, careful to avoid sudden braking and acceleration. He looked very focused, his face close to the glass. A strenuous splashing accompanied the turning of the wheels.

"Here we are. I'll see you later."

These were his first words since they'd gotten into the car. Sara felt that she couldn't let the moment slip away.

"What time are we meeting tomorrow?" she asked.

"Tomorrow?"

"Yes, tomorrow. Listen, you know why I'm here. I'm sure you know a place, you can think of a place, where it would be right to do what Nonna Ali... what your Alice, your Nadia wanted us to do. When do you want to meet?"

"Tomorrow!?" repeated the Professor.

"Yes, tomorrow, unless you think that there are other things I should learn and understand. Listen, in case you don't want to call Concetta's house, I'll leave you my phone number here. It's an intercontinental call, I know, but we don't have to stay on the line and chit chat, just tell me when and where you want to meet, and I'll be there. Can I use that pen and notepad?"

She took off her gloves and scrawled down her number with her numb fingers. She turned on the car light to make sure it was legible and handed it to Fulvio, who glanced at it and put it in his pocket.

There was one more thing to do. Sara took an envelope out of her backpack.

"Here, I think you should have this."

"What is it?"

The Flower of Russian Poetry seemed to leap from the envelope into the Professor's hands, as if by magic. He took off his glasses, astonished.

"But... How did you...?"

"It's a long story. It's my grandmother's gift to you. Goodnight, Osia."

L'AQUILA, ITALY
JANUARY 20, 2011

Time to go home.

Standing in front of the open window early in the morning, the urn with Nonna Ali's remains in her arms, Sara went over everything she had learned the day before: *The Flower of Russian Poetry* in the mail, the Professor's flashlight leading her down the alley, Alberto leaving everything behind to liberate Italy, Alice's distraught escape, an American hitchhiker in an indigo shirt picking up his bag and running toward a car stopped on the side of the road. And snow, snow, all that snow that fell and bridged the gap between the before and the after, the places and the people, the dead and the living. What a long day it had been. The incubation period had been slow, yet the blossoming so sudden, like springtime in some Scandinavian country.

Footsteps outside the door announced Concetta's return. Sara hurried back into her room and put the urn back.

"Sara... what are you doing, aren't you cold?"

"I just wanted to air out the room a bit, sorry..."

Sara returned to the kitchen, quickly closed the window, and asked about the neighbors.

"All is well, apart from the fact that the lady on the ground floor has been admitted to the hospital, her ulcer is acting up again. Would you like to come with me to visit her? Alessandro can drive us."

"No! I mean, I don't even know her…"

"The hospital is very close to L'Aquilone, we can drop you off there and pick you up on the way back."

Sara wasn't sure whether the offer derived from Concetta's tendency to consider solitude the saddest condition, to be avoided at all costs, or simply from her reluctance to leave her alone in the house. She decided to ignore her hint and tried to come up with a good excuse.

"You know, yesterday's walk in the snow has left me with a bit of a sore throat. I wouldn't want to make it worse at the mall or, worse yet, spread it among the patients at the hospital."

The sentence was unnecessarily complex, too correct and cautious not to arouse suspicion. Concetta looked at her, perplexed, but didn't dare argue. She began a long list of recommendations on what to do if something happened while she was out.

Sara was relieved when Alessandro walked in.

"The translations were great, thanks, and the flyer looks so professional! We need to keep the pressure on now. We also need to explain why we have occupied another building downtown. It's an old daycare center that was completely abandoned on the night of the earthquake and was empty for about twenty-one months, despite it being barely damaged. Can you believe that?"

Sara nodded, unsure as to whether her answer was needed.

"But we're taking some big risks, some people have asked the police to intervene immediately. The situation is getting worse every day, we are being sued right and left, the police even seized some of our wheelbarrows. The city center is still in ruins, and the police act as if it's the wheelbarrows that are creating problems! We have to let everyone know about the real condition of the town. You won't believe the number of people out there who still believe in 'L'Aquila's miracle.'"

"Why must you always go looking for trouble?" shouted Concetta from her room. "You are always playing the rabble rouser, instead of minding your own business. Good thing your brother is here to look after the family, otherwise we wouldn't even have been assigned this apartment."

"Since you mention it, I didn't want this apartment, and as you might have noticed I haven't spent a single night here. I'd rather sleep in a tent than be complicit in Berlusconi's shady deals and jerry-building!"

"'Shady deals!' 'Jerry-building!'" rebutted Concetta. "Listen to you! What did you want us to do, live in a trailer for twenty years, like those poor people in Irpinia? Haven't you heard Bruno Vespa on TV?"

"Bruno Vespa is such a disaster, between him and the earthquake no wonder this city is in trouble!"

"Can you believe it?" Alessandro said under his breath, partly to Sara, partly to himself. "They believe everything they hear on TV. They only care about themselves, about their petty interests. How can we possibly rebuild a city with these people?"

Something in that exchange struck Sara.

"But where do you live, then?" she asked, surprised that she hadn't wondered about that before. She had been content with seeing him appear every time she needed him, as if he was always waiting behind the door.

"I've built myself a little house in the mountains, though my mother calls it a hut. I didn't want to take one red cent from these vultures. The moment you start accepting money and help from them you become complicit and lose legitimacy, credibility, everything. Then you no longer think about the city you want to rebuild, you only try to snag an extra square meter, or a bigger check. You understand?"

"I... more or less... Yes, I think so."

"That's why I've gone off into the mountains, like the partisans, like your great-uncle," Alessandro smiled. "Every

once in a while you need to start over, and that's a good place
to do just that. Sure, it's not comfortable, but I feel at home
there. The earth and its tremors no longer scare me ever since
I moved."

He lowered his voice.

"I'd like to show it to you someday."

Concetta walked into the dining room, saving Sara from
having to come up with a reply.

"You can count on me if you need more translations or
editing," said Sara, as if she hadn't heard Alessandro's last
sentence. "You know I'm on your side."

"Really?"

"Of course!"

"Thank you. Mom, let's go now, I have a lot of things to
do today."

"A busy man indeed!" Concetta exclaimed. "He has a lot
of things to do, like shouting into a megaphone, begging pass-
ers-by to sign the latest petition, breaking into the red zone,
insulting the authorities…"

"The authorities!!!" Alessandro retorted, exasperated.
"We'd better just go."

"Yes, let's go. Sara, if you're staying at home for another
hour, can I run the dishwasher?" asked Concetta.

"I… am not planning on going out at all."

She sensed Concetta's hesitation.

"My sore throat…" she quickly reminded her.

They finally left after Concetta's last-minute recommendations. Relieved, Sara logged onto the computer, waited
patiently for the slow connection to download her messages,
the ads, the friend requests on Facebook, and the like. In the
midst of all that junk, Valerie's response.

"I'm sorry it took me so long to get back to you, but you
put me in a bit of a quandary with your question. Antaeus
had to rest on his mother, the earth, to gather his energy, but
why does your grandmother need strength? Why did she ask

you to scatter her ashes in L'Aquila? After much thought, I came up with a hypothesis that may strike you as completely irrational, but that I must share with you anyway. She needs to lay down on her mother earth to die. There, I told you that it didn't make any sense. Much love and best of luck."

There was also a P.S.: "Do you see how my brain works? How could I possibly get along with your brother in the long run?"

Sara read over the message a few times. That Valerie was something else, Richard was no match for her.

She went through the list of new messages, sifted through junk and trash, then scanned the news. The U.S. offered its daily litany of murders, thoughts and prayers. She turned to the Italian sites for some international news. Tunisia, Algeria, Jordan, Oman: protests were spreading through the Arab world. There was also mention of some link between Berlusconi's sweetheart, Ruby Rubacuori—Sara realized she'd never manage to forget her nickname—and Egyptian president Hosni Mubarak; she couldn't quite figure out whether the connection was real or fictional and decided not to investigate further. The outside world was screaming, and there she was in the protective bubble of Concetta's apartment, trying to put her grandmother's story together, to preserve that historical past that Alice had defended until the end in her mind and in her speech. An overpowering feeling of unreality washed over her, she pinched her thigh to make sure she wasn't dreaming, like in a cartoon. She closed all the windows and was about to turn the computer off when a familiar buzz announced an incoming message. She shuddered when she saw it was from Una. When she realized a picture was downloading, she made herself close her eyes. Ten, nine, eight... no, she was counting too fast. One-Mississippi, two-Mississippi, three-Mississippi... Certain things cannot be rushed. They mature on their own, at the right time. What had these weeks in L'Aquila been, if not an exercise in patience? The picture had slowly taken shape before her eyes. The narrow strokes of color, insignificant if seen separately, now formed a coherent landscape as they lay one next to the other. Ten-Mississippi. She opened her eyes.

The full moon appeared inside the stone arch, suspended in mid-air. The photo must have been taken at sunset. The striations of the arch, created by millennia of patient erosion, were perfectly visible, brick-colored shades alternated with lighter ones. The scars of time—the irregularities, the crevices, the hollows—conveyed resoluteness more than fragility. The stocky foundations of the arch resembled the legs of the dinosaurs that for millions of years had roamed the land. Sun and moon must have faced each other for a moment, in perfect equilibrium. The planet's soft light accentuated the ochre hues that seemed to bleed over the low and sparse clouds and the pale moon.

It truly was a beautiful picture, and Sara tried to figure out the exact spot from which it had been taken. Una, despite having her back to the setting sun, had managed to keep the shadow of the surrounding mountains and that of her own body outside of the frame, helping the viewer focus on the essential details. Sara sensed, behind the apparent simplicity of the composition, Una's care, her patient attention.

"Great pic," she wrote. She looked at the screen, dissatisfied. She erased the sentence and wrote again.

"I love you."

She pressed 'send' quickly to avoid any second thoughts, shut down the computer, and went to hide between the covers, closing her eyes and trying to recreate the image of the moon under Delicate Arch in her mind. She stayed in this half-sleeping state until the image faded, then she shook herself awake. She needed to start packing, check the bus schedule, and find a way to get to the station.

The buzz of her cell phone made her jump.

"Professor..."

"No, no, it's me!" laughed Jane.

"Mom, what are you doing, do you keep dialing my number all day long? How is it possible that every time I turn my phone on, I get a call from you?"

"How sweet, I'm also so thrilled to hear your voice!" Jane said ironically.

"Of course I'm happy, but we decided that you wouldn't call, remember? Roaming charges are high on my phone plan!"

"Listen, let's not go overboard with the tales of woe. For this month I'll pay your bill, OK? That way you can relax."

What a disaster, Sara thought, with this excuse she'll call me every day now.

"And don't worry, I won't take advantage of my offer to call you every day!" Jane added, laughing, confident that she had once again guessed her daughter's thoughts. Sara smiled despite herself.

"Where are you, in Florence?"

"No, I'm still in L'Aquila!"

"Ah, thank goodness… so you've received the Fedex package then, right?"

"Ah yes, thank you."

Sara hoped that her mom would not ask about the book.

"And did you also find the three hundred euros?"

"Yes, you didn't need to. I mean, you didn't need to but I sure appreciate the gift, thank you."

"You're still in L'Aquila," repeated Jane, pensively. "Then you must really like it! What are people like over there?"

"Well… interesting."

"Interesting? What is that supposed to mean?"

Sara thought of the right way to put it.

"Complicated… No, maybe it's more accurate to say complex. Complex, but also a little complicated… They're at the same time very fond of their past and eager to forget it, it's strange."

Jane tried to figure out what her daughter meant.

"Did something happen?"

"So many things have happened, I'll tell you all about it when I get home."

"Are you OK? Did you do what you were supposed to do?"

"Not yet, but don't worry, everything is fine."

Jane remembered the therapist's advice: avoid vague questions, like "how are you" or "are you having fun." She redirected her energy, rephrased her queries.

"What are your plans for this morning? Have you already had breakfast? It's still morning over there, right?"

"Nothing in particular… yeah, it's still morning."

I'm thinking about the full moon, is what she would have liked to say. But Jane's comment made her notice the time difference.

"But it's not even 5:00 a.m. in Bethesda!" she exclaimed. "What are you doing awake at this hour?

"Something incredible has happened, I just had to tell you, but I waited until I thought I wouldn't wake you up… Are you listening?" continued Jane, tired of waiting for her daughter's strained contributions to the conversation, abandoning her good resolutions and the therapist's suggestions. "Listen to this. Jeff and I went back to Hyattsville to take care of another eviction. You know, there are some neighborhoods where most of the houses belong to the banks by now. It's kind of sad, actually. You say we don't have a heart, but I can assure you that we're not as insensitive as you think."

Sara repressed a sarcastic comment.

"So," Jane resumed, after waiting in vain for a sign of encouragement, "when they built this block of houses, they tried to transform it into a real neighborhood. They opened a hairdresser, and there are a few shops. Jeff and I were early for our appointment, so we went looking for a cup of coffee. But almost everything has closed down, and the only place that showed any signs of life was a pawn shop. We ended up walking up and down the street out of boredom. It was a gloomy day, this winter has really been depressing. So, I just happened to look at the pawn shop window. You won't believe this! Guess what I saw?"

"What?" blurted Sara, captured by her mother's story in spite of herself.

"Nonna Ali's necklace! Yes, the very one I gave to that poor woman, the veteran's wife. Do you remember how upset Jeff was? And you were not particularly supportive either, I must say. But never mind. I always thought that, if the necklace wanted to come back to me, it would find a way."

Sara didn't dare interrupt, eager as she was to get to the end of the story.

"Even Jeff was stunned," Jane continued. "We rushed in. You see, the house where that couple lived is only a few blocks away, so it's not much of a surprise that the necklace ended up in the pawn shop."

"But are you really sure it's the same one?"

"Well, it's pretty unique, isn't it? The guy in the shop told me about a woman who walked into the shop with a baby in her arms and left the necklace as collateral, a few months ago. She had gotten the necklace as a gift, she said, and she was really sorry that she had to part with it, but she and her husband didn't even have enough money to fill the tank and get back to her mother's place. Sometimes people make up stories like that just to get a few extra bucks, the guy said, but she sounded sincere, and he remembered seeing the foreclosure sign on their house. He actually thought he had offered her more than the necklace was worth, a bit out of pity and a bit out of fear of the big guy in camouflage who walked in while they were talking and kept staring at him. It must have been them! I kept asking questions, so after a while the guy realized that the necklace was important to me for some reason, and asked for an exorbitant price. Good thing Jeff jumped in. He made it clear that the necklace had been stolen, and told the guy he could get into some serious trouble if he didn't cooperate…"

"But it hadn't been stolen!" Sara objected.

"Well, it kind of had… Anyway, the most important thing is that we got it back, don't you think?"

"Wait a minute! Didn't you say that your gift to that woman was part of some arcane plan?"

"Well, sure, and finding the necklace again could very well be part of the same plan."

"Ok, fine. Now go lock it up in your jewelry box and let it rest, it's been running around enough as it is. And maybe take this opportunity to rest a bit yourself."

"Yes, I'll keep it for now, but as soon as I had it back in my hands, I remembered what I was supposed to do with it."

"Did you?! Are you planning on donating it to the Society for the Preservation of the Monk Seal? To then spend its weight in gold when you decide you want it back two months from now? Or did you finally decide to convert to Buddhism and sacrifice this worthless Christian symbol for the restoration of the great Stupa of Dhamarkaya?"

"Oh, stop it, silly!" laughed Jane. "Don't you remember the will? This necklace is Nonna Ali's bequest to you! And even if it wasn't, you've definitely earned it at this point."

"No kidding… Well, fair enough, I'll do my best to be worthy of it."

"You already are, sweetie, you already are."

An embarrassed silence ensued. What was up with all these compliments? "You've earned it," "Sweetie"… really?

"Um, you're doing alright, mom, aren't you?" Sara asked hesitantly.

"Of course, I'm doing just fine."

"Nothing unusual in your test results or anything of that sort, right?"

"Nothing at all. I am super healthy, I haven't even been drinking much lately. And how about you? It sounds like you like it over there. If you want to stay a little longer, don't worry, go ahead."

"No, I'm ready to get back now, I'm getting a bit homesick. I'll see you in a few days. Can you take me back to that Lebanese restaurant? The one where we had lunch the day I left. I'm getting tired of pasta and pizza, pizza and pasta."

"When exactly is your flight?"

"In a couple of days, I emailed you all the information when I bought the ticket."

Sara suddenly got suspicious.

"But you knew that... Why are you asking? What's going on?"

"Listen, I'm so sorry... I would love to see you too, but Jeff just surprised me with a trip to Las Vegas. Besides, I thought perhaps you'd change your return trip, since you haven't had the time to do any sightseeing yet. You can still do that, you know. Just tell me your new return date and I'll take care of everything."

Always the same, thought Sara. Unreliable, volatile, always in need of somebody to lean on.

"Alright, don't worry about it," she said coldly.

"Don't you want to know what we'll be doing in Vegas?"

This was another one of the therapist's tips: instead of complaining about the lack of interest in your interlocutors, suggest the questions you want to hear from them.

"Oh, I can imagine it alright. A little ride in a gondola on the fake Venetian lagoon, then a walk with a yard-long glass of mimosa, fireworks over the replica of the Eiffel tower, and a little gambling to top it off and lose an average person's yearly salary in two hours. Or rather, as Jeff would have it, the yearly salary of one of those sleazy, unambitious, irresponsible people..."

If only you could suggest not only the questions, but also the answers, Jane thought, the conversations would certainly be more gratifying.

"No… Well sort of, but that's not really the main goal. That's the other thing I meant to announce at Thanksgiving. Jeff asked me to marry him!"

"What?!"

"Yes! Listen, don't you think it's ridiculous at our age to be playing boyfriend and girlfriend? Now that you've all gone your own way, that Nonna Ali is no longer here…"

Sara noticed a crack in Jane's voice. She pictured her nervously pacing across the dining room. She felt her anxious loneliness. But still…

"What's the big rush? You always told us to wait, to take our time…"

"It's one thing to take your time when you are young, quite another to do it when you're in your fifties. I've made him wait long enough, between the divorce from your father, Nonna Ali's illness, my own health scare… But I'm sorry now not to be here the one time you say you're homesick, I don't know whether I should feel touched or worried…"

Sara cut her off.

"Let me help you with that. When I said I was homesick, I meant to say that I missed Moab, where I intend to resume my studies in non-verbal communication."

"Impertinent, cheeky…!" protested Jane, feigning indignation. God, what she wouldn't give to fall in love again!

The words Sara had said just to hurt her mother suddenly struck her as truthful. She did want to go home, back to Moab.

It took a lot of insisting to convince Alessandro that it was OK to leave her at the entrance of the Red Zone. She didn't need his company and didn't want him to wait to take her home. He was puzzled and a bit offended. A young woman alone, at night, in a devastated city, doing who knows what. Sara regretted accepting his ride, the most convenient solutions often end up being the worst. She would have liked to part from him in a different way, add something to the short, sour sentences of their last exchange. She couldn't come up with the right words. She quickly thanked him, without even the polite lie of a "see you." She would have liked to explain that the epilogue he had suggested was not wrong, in and of itself. The idea that Sara could stay in L'Aquila and pick up where her grandmother had left off had a certain logic to it, an enticing coherence. Nonna Ali's chance could translate into Sara's destiny. It was a possible conclusion. But for a different story.

She began her ghostly descent down Via XX September, the long street that led from the center to the outskirts of the city. It was along that street that the earthquake had claimed the highest number of victims. Alessandro and his friend had even drafted a petition to change its name into Via 6 Aprile, the date of the disaster. The devastation was still apparent. She stopped in front of what was left of the student dorms, where a makeshift sign honored the victims. Luca. Marco. Luciana. Davide. Angela. Francesco. Michelone. Alessio. The roll call reminded her of the plaque of the Nine Martyrs that she'd read the night before. It seemed to her that the city had once again been incapable of protecting its youth, its future. The dreams of the dead seemed to hang from the fence that blocked access to the site and that friends and relatives had decorated with pictures, flowers, t-shirts, and loving notes. Other objects, like a hat or an umbrella, were more mysterious, coded messages for their invisible recipients.

"Here is your city, Nonna Ali," whispered Sara to the backpack on her shoulders. Alice thought she detected a hint of reproach in Sara's voice. She had not anticipated that her last wish would force her granddaughter to trek through a disaster zone. How could she? Not even the war had reduced L'Aquila to such a state. How could something like that have happened, where did everybody go? Enough, enough with the ruins, the justifications, the excuses. It's time to leave.

Sara lingered in front of the student dorms, searching for a prayer, a tribute to add to those already scattered amid the rubble. Then, dissatisfied, she continued her descent. She left the main street and turned left, down a steep hill, towards the meeting place.

When she arrived, the Professor was already there. He had shaved and combed his hair with care, maybe he had even been to the barber. His best pants stuck out from underneath his coat, with the front pleat neatly ironed. Despite his hiking boots, which the snow had forced him to wear and which slightly ruined the overall effect, he had dressed up as if for a date, Sara thought. And after all, this was indeed his last date with Alice. He walked toward Sara with a spring in his step.

"Professor... Have you been waiting long?"

"No, no, only fifteen minutes. Is everything alright?"

He looked at her with anxious eyes.

"My apologies, you know," he continued, without waiting for a response, "My apologies for suggesting that we meet at night. I didn't want to run into anybody. I hope this hasn't created problems for you."

They stood in front of a church so completely covered in scaffolding that it was hardly recognizable.

"The convent of Santa Chiara, or what's left of it. A wound as painful as the one in the center of town, at least for me. This is perhaps the oldest part of the town, where the Church of Santa Maria d'Acquili used to be."

"D'Acquili?" asked Sara.

"Yes, because of the water, *l'acqua*. This area is rich in springs, and it is possible that the first nucleus of L'Aquila formed here. Water allowed the town to come into being, and gave it its name.

"What do you mean, its name? I always thought that the name 'L'Aquila' came from the bird of prey, the eagle."

She roughly mimed the flapping of wings with her arms to explain herself better.

"That's also possible. But the idea that the city derives its name from the eagle is only a theory, and not the most convincing one, if you ask me. This is via Borgo Rivera, like the French word *rivière*, you see? The nearby river, the springs, the importance of water, especially back then, for health and survival… These are all signs that lead me to believe the name Aquila could very well derive from the Latin word for water, *aqua*."

"The eagle is pretty impressive on a coat of arms, though, isn't it?"

"Of course, how could it not be, birds of prey have a tight grip on people's imagination. Please forgive the pun."

They stood silent, lulled by the sounds of the night. The fallen snow gave the scenery a peculiar brightness.

"But this statue didn't collapse," said the Professor, approaching a column. "It is intact, with its reassuring message to weary travelers."

Sara realized that the man was taking his own personal pilgrimage. She didn't dare interrupt.

"We had planned to marry here," he continued, almost in a sigh. "Yes, I know, two atheists like us, getting married in a church… But our parents would have been devastated if we had just gone to the town hall, very few people dared do that back then. And even for us marriage was something sacred, I can't quite explain it… And then this place was very dear to us because of its peace, because of its sound. Can you hear it?"

Sara listened carefully. Something similar to a whisper rose out of the darkness.

"Yes, I do. What is it?

"The water, the voice of the water… It hasn't changed, this is the same voice that we used to hear when we came here secretly, at night."

They continued to go down the hill. The earthquake had done tremendous damage, they skirted eviscerated buildings and closed courtyards. Abandon reigned supreme.

They reached a small, poorly lit square. The Professor pointed to a church on their right, covered in scaffolding.

"This is another place that was important to us. The Church of San Vito, with its exquisite sundials."

"Sundials?

"Yes, on the facade, one on each side of the rose window. The earthquake cut their lines in half, disturbing the normal flow of time."

The whisper in the background was growing louder.

The Professor headed towards a dark railing on his right, entered a sloping path, and turned to look at her.

"Be careful, it's very slippery."

Sara followed him down the path, which was paved with smooth, white stones. The Professor took her by the hand and led her to the center of a small square. At first glance, Sara felt as though she was surrounded by church facades. She had already seen this hypnotic alternating pattern of white and pink stones.

"Just like Collemaggio!" she exclaimed.

"Yes… well, no. Similar, though. This fountain was built in the same period and was inspired by the same idea."

"What about those?"

Water streamed from a succession of openings on the three sides of the wall framing the square. Sara got closer and realized that the holes corresponded to the mouths of strange creatures sculpted in the stone. Some looked almost human, while others resembled cats or fish. The water that poured from their mouths filled the upper basin of the fountain and gently spilled into the lower level.

"The Fountain of the Ninety-Nine Spouts," explained the Professor. "Ninety-nine, one for each of the mythical founders of the city. But, for a long time, it was more commonly known as the Fontana della Rivera. Women came here to do their laundry, then hung it out in this square, so that it would dry in the sun."

They listened to the splashing of the water.

"Do you know what I used to do at night, when I couldn't

sleep? I'd go out and make sure the water was still flowing in the fountains, in the city's veins. I thought that if the flow ever stopped, L'Aquila would die."

Sara looked at him.

"But it hasn't stopped, has it? The water hasn't stopped flowing, L'Aquila isn't dead!"

The Professor sadly slumped his shoulders, but Sara continued.

"L'Aquila isn't dead, it can't die! Listen, earlier on, I spoke a bit... well, hastily. Maybe the eagle looks better on a coat of arms, but it's only because it can be captured, pictured, carved, whereas the water is unstoppable, it's always here and there..."

"*Utile et humile et pretiosa et casta*, as Saint Francis would have it... Useful and humble and precious and pure."

"Yes, certainly... But then, if L'Aquila is water... it's obvious, isn't it? It can't die! You and I, we'll both die, like Nonna Ali, like Alberto. What is it then, to die...? Aren't we also made of water?"

There, that's it. We are made of water, of water and dreams. Such stuff as dreams are made on. Let me go.

The Professor was quivering, his eyes fixed on her. Sara put down her backpack, waiting for a signal.

"Here?"

Here, thanks.

Needles of freezing air fell from the icy stars. The moon proudly detached itself from the silver edges of a cloud. Time to go home, just in time for the new moon.

"It's starting to wane," she said.

The Professor didn't understand at first, then followed her gaze.

"Yes. Just barely, though..."

Now.

"I... think this is the right time, the right place."

Sara opened the backpack, her fingers numb from the cold, and took out the urn.

The Professor's face paled under the moon's rays.

"Alice... Alice is in there?"

Here I am, Fulvio, farewell.

The Professor removed his gloves and delicately placed his hands on the urn. They were burly farmer's hands, despite never having worked a day in the fields. Sara looked at their outline on the black container.

Thank you for everything, but let me go now.

The Professor pulled his hands back. Sara opened the urn.

Alice leapt into the air, weightless. The wind was barely perceptible and yet strong enough to lift her up and make her flutter into the sky. She felt Sara and Fulvio's eyes following her as she drifted away, and she wished she had arms to wave at them, to tell them not to worry, to assure them that everything was absolutely fine, the way it was meant to be. The boundaries that limited her perspective crumbled and she embraced space and time without fear. She flew over the ravaged center of the city, the statue of Sallustius, the silent bell tower, the gutted transept of Collemaggio. She saw young men gathering in front of the Church of Santa Maria Paganica and then disappear into the mountains, while the earth began to shake and the roof of the church suddenly caved in. Above the darkness of the abandoned city the stars shone low and bright, as they did in the gleaming summer nights of her youth, before raining down in a stream of incandescent meteorites. Overlapping voices accompanied her flight, contrasting notes combining to form the magnificent concert of her life: Alberto Arienti joyfully announces the birth of his little sister Alice... I've worn out seven pairs of shoes trying to find you... wake up or you'll be late for school... He was my North, my South, my East and West...

Then, out of the darkness, a raspy voice.

One of these mornings, you are gonna rise, rise up singing...

Alice smiled, clinging to the song that carried her higher still.

You're gonna spread your wings and take to the sky.

Just like her, finally, with ever bigger wings of ever finer dust.

Nothing is gonna harm you now...

Then the light started flashing, the music grew louder, the wind picked up. Janis threw her head back, laughed her boisterous laughter, and Alice realized it was time for her to die. Once and for all.

AFTERWORD

Many of the details surrounding the murder of L'Aquila's Nine Martyrs remain mysterious to this day. Some information can be found in Walter Cavalieri, *L'Aquila: dall'armistizio alla Repubblica, 1943-1946. La seconda guerra mondiale all'Aquila e provincia* (Studio 7, 1994) and Corrado Colacito, *I martiri aquilani del 23 settembre 1943* (Textus, 1996). Alberto Arienti, an imaginary figure, combines some of the characteristics of these partisans, such as their young age and their love of poetry.

The epigraph comes from Italo Calvino, *The Path to the Spiders' Nest*, trans. Archibald Colquhoun, rev. Martin McLaughlin (Ecco Press, 1998)

Osip Mandelstam's poem *Leningrad* is taken from *The Selected Poems of Osip Mandelstam*, trans. Clarence Brown and C.S. Merwin (Atheneum, 1973). The poem *Francis Turner* is from Edgar Lee Masters, *Spoon River Anthology* (The Macmillan Company, 1915). The translations from Renato Poggioli's *Il fiore del verso russo* and Torquato Tasso's *Gerusalemme liberata* are mine.

The description of the Professor's night strolls is inspired by Sandro Cordeschi's essay "L'Aquila—I luoghi della poesia," in *Un popolo di visionari e poeti. Segni di viaggiatori anomali dall'Abruzzo e dal mondo*, edited by David Maria Adacher, Antonio Porto, and Sandro Cordeschi (2009).

This novel was first published in Italian as *Un paese di carta*, thanks to the wonderful team of Pacini Editore and in particular Francesca Pacini, Giacomo Bertagni, Lisa Lorusso, and Francesca Petrucci. I would never have attempted to rewrite it into English if it weren't for Donatella Melucci (Georgetown University), who in 2019 chose it as the focus of her translation course. I would like to thank her and her students—Martina Benedetti Marshall, Arthur Canonica-Babcock, Ishanee Chanda, Alex Giorgioni, Erin LeGoff, Anna-Sofia Neil, Kayleigh O'Connor, Harry Rose, Luke Ross, and Julia Tagliabue—for providing a complete English translation of the book. Their version formed the basis for my rewriting. The extent of my additions, deletions, and editing was such that *A Country of Paper* can be considered a new novel, rather than the English translation of *Un paese di carta*. I would like to thank Amara Lakhous, a master in the art of intercultural crossings, for his example and encouragement; Emily Langer and Brad Marshall, for many precious suggestions; and Louise Hipwell, for her unfailing editing skills and her patience.

This novel is dedicated to L'Aquila, my town of paper.

www.ingramcontent.com/pod-product-compliance
Lightning Source LLC
Chambersburg PA
CBHW030033030726
47500CB00001B/86